prince
of
power

ELISABETH STAAB

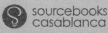

sourcebooks
casablanca

Published by Sourcebooks Casablanca, an imprint of Sourcebooks, Inc.
P.O. Box 4410, Naperville, Illinois 60567-4410
(630) 961-3900
FAX: (630) 961-2168
www.sourcebooks.com

Printed and bound in Canada
WC 10 9 8 7 6 5 4 3 2 1

Dedicated to all the vampire lovers. Thank you for spending time with mine.

Chapter 1

TYRA LET OUT A WARNING GROWL. SOMEONE WAS touching her.

She pried her eyes open but couldn't see a thing. A whole lot of bright and blurry invaded her senses. She was lying down, while someone stood over her. Calloused fingers brushed her face. A fellow vampire would have spoken up and identified themselves right then. This was a bad sign.

A very bad sign.

Fueled by adrenaline and fear and strength she wasn't sure she had in her, Tyra launched herself, fangs bared, at the threat. She may have been half human, but she let the royal, feral blood of her vampire ancestors take the lead. Lying down with someone over her meant she was in enemy hands. No way was anybody cutting her chest open to take out her heart. Clawing and scraping against a tile floor, she pulled a heavy body beneath her.

"Tyra."

A soft, flannel shirt tangled in her grasp. Stubble scraped under her hand. A male gasped when her fangs sank cleanly into the warm skin of his throat.

"Tyra."

Thick, smoky blood hit her tongue.

"Tyra, are you okay?"

That voice. Things were so fuzzy, but she could swear she knew it from somewhere. Her first instinct had been to drain the man, enough to immobilize him at least. She realized he wasn't fighting back. His body had gone still beneath her, save for the tentative tap of fingertips on her shoulder.

Something familiar in the taste on her tongue and the touch on her skin gave her pause. Why was he asking if she was all right? Confusion warred with the hum of fresh plasma hitting her system.

Unbelievably, his head tipped back to give her easier access. "If you need to feed, Tyra, go ahead."

Please, Tyra… Please feed from me.

"Oh my God. Oh my *God*." Her head snapped up so fast she almost—almost—forgot to lick closed his wound. "Anton."

The voice. The smoky, almost piney taste of blood. She remembered now. Tyra clapped her hands over her face. *No.*

Please feed from me.

"It's me, yeah. Is something wrong with your eyes? Can I call someone? What can I do to help?" Those warm fingers of his were brushing her face again.

For one infinitely dangerous moment she forgot everything. Allowed his hand to linger as his fingers slid comfortably into the grooves between hers. *No.*

She shook her head, and pulled back, rubbing the collected grit from her puffy eyes. "I'll be fine." Her vision was already clearing. Thanks to his blood. Like the blood she'd drunk from him right before she'd passed out.

Please feed from me.

Another rub of her eyes and a few hard blinks, and finally she could match a real face with the memory: His strong, square jaw had a heavy dusting of stubble that would be a beard soon if he didn't shave. Short, soft-looking hair and a strong nose with a slight bump like maybe he'd broken it before. Wow. Those eyes. Sharp and steel gray, but amazingly kind, considering...

Holy crap, she was still on top of him... and he was aroused.

Instantly Tyra shot into the air. First to the bed she'd been lying on and then up to standing, so fast it was like she was in one of those pinball machines she'd seen once in a pizza parlor. Anton ejected himself in the opposite direction like he, too, had realized their awkward physical situation. Metal scraped on linoleum when he pulled out the desk chair to sit down.

He stared at her in the way she imagined a hungry, stray dog would: leery but hopeful. "You're sure you're okay?" His knees bounced nervously. One hand dabbed at the bite on his neck, checking for residual blood or something.

Heat crept up the back of Tyra's neck, and she swiped a hand across her lips. It came away with a trace of crimson. "Fine," she said. "Confused..." She took in the metal desk and the dingy, chipped linoleum floor. "This is your room." Anton had been a resident at the shelter in Ash Falls, Virginia, where Tyra volunteered. Just another homeless human with amnesia, they'd thought at first. Not even close.

He swallowed hard. His eyelids drooped for a moment, but he took a deep breath and repositioned in his seat. Trying to make himself look taller? "You passed out. The chances of someone finding you were way lower here than in your office." He blinked and lifted one shoulder awkwardly. "More comfortable, too, maybe."

Sweaty, shoulder-length curls clung to her face and neck. She pushed them away with an impatient hand. Her heart pounded wildly, almost painfully. To hope that his intentions were truly good was so dangerous. "You're a wizard. I remember you telling me that before I—" The abhorrent realization hit that she'd drunk blood from a wizard not once but twice now…

Only it hadn't been the least bit disgusting. That unique woodsy flavor had actually been sort of… nice. "Your species and mine have been at war for centuries. I'm the vampire king's sister. This can't be happening."

Anton blew out a breath. "I'm not evil. I promise you. The wizard clan sent me to kidnap you because they want to study your unique powers. I refused, though, Tyra. I couldn't do that to you. I was tortured and cast out for my trouble. You remember that part, right? I've kept you safe this whole time while you were unconscious."

Not evil. Promise. That alone was enough to make her brain do the whole pop-bang-fizz business. The idea of a wizard promising safety to a vampire was like a drug dealer promising his profits would go to cancer research.

Without warning, he jumped up from his chair. "We should get you out of here now that you're awake. It isn't safe. We need to get you back to your kind. You can teleport, right? That's one of your powers? Or I can help you sneak out the back—"

"Wait a second." *This whole time?* Fingers combed through her damp hair. Elevated body temperature was a sign of suspended animation.

Dark shadows lingered underneath Anton's gray eyes, and he needed a great deal of effort to hold himself up. He was worn out. Keyed up. She would bet he was running on fumes.

"I've been in torpor," she said. "How long?"

On the desk lay a stack of those little two-packs of saltine crackers. The kind that came from the salad bars of restaurants. Or in this case, probably the shelter dining hall. He scratched his head, then picked each one up and counted as he slapped them back onto the desk. "One… two… three… four… five… six… seven… eight… nine… Ten days."

Tyra squeezed her eyes shut.

He pointed to the crackers. "I brought some back for you every day from the dining hall at dinner. Stupid, but it made me feel like I was doing something for you. Other than that—and taking a piss—I didn't go anywhere. Didn't want to leave you alone."

Holy cow. He'd watched over her all that time. She didn't know quite what to say to that. An odd warmth bloomed in her chest.

His body snapped to attention again. "Seriously, though. We should get you out of here."

Something about that rubbed her the wrong way. She didn't take orders well even when she was *supposed* to, and the utter confusion of this whole situation made her feel vulnerable.

"Look, I appreciate you keeping an eye out, but I can take care of myself." She straightened and sighed quietly. "I'm not really sure what I should even do about you. I should kill you, you know. Just because of what you are. At the very least, I should erase your memory." Even as she said that, the words tasted sour on her tongue.

Tyra had to hand it to him; he didn't back down. In fact, he took a step closer. "You could go that way," he said. His lips pressed together. "I was hoping maybe I could help your side out. Help you put my father out of business."

She nearly swallowed her own tongue. Anton wasn't just born of an enemy race to the vampires; he was the son of their leader. *That's right, Tyra. He might as well be the son of Satan.*

Was he suggesting what it sounded like? Tyra wondered at the way his jaw squared. The clench of his fingers and the glint of fire in his steely, narrowed eyes. "You'd really do that? You'd help kill your own father?"

With another step forward, Anton pulled aside the collar of his shirt. He stretched it wide to reveal an angry scar across his collarbone that had only recently healed over. "Tortured and cast out. Remember, Tyra?" His voice was a rough whisper. "My father did this."

Holy hell. She reached to brush her finger over the long ridge of puckered skin that disappeared under the bunched fabric of his shirt. A subtle buzz in her blood told her that her powers were coming back online. No time like the present to flex her ability to read emotions.

Just then Anton opened his mouth to speak, but she didn't get the chance to hear what he was about to say. The air stirred around them, followed by the quiet open and close of the door. Anton, incredibly, sidled in front of her. Guarding her, even though what had just entered could have easily taken him down.

—◁∙▷—

"Dammit to Hell, Siddoh!" Thad brushed a hand over his hair. "You need to work with me here, or I am going to set *fire* to your ass. Don't think I won't."

He almost welcomed the opportunity. His blood and adrenaline had been on a hard boil for over a week now since his half sister and best friend had gone missing. He was exhausted; his teeth and body ached; and his nerves were so far beyond frayed they would've blown away in a stiff breeze.

Across the room, Siddoh sagged against one of the built-in bookshelves that lined Thad's office walls. His second in command sniffed and looked around like just being in the king's study offended him. And maybe it did. In the wake of Thad's parents' death, everything was getting overhauled. The creamy beige carpet Thad's father put in had been replaced so recently with something plush and navy blue that the smell of factory chemicals from the padding still hung in the air. Furniture from Pottery Barn had taken the place of the late king's more elegant furnishings.

For his own sanity, Thad had needed to make this room his own.

"Thad, look—"

"No. I'm not gonna look. You don't fucking tell me to look. *You* need to tap someone to take over for the next forty-eight hours right fucking now, or I will do it for you." Blood rushed in Thad's ears. He envisioned the heat rolling off of his body in a wave. Lee, his best friend and first in command, had disappeared before he could help Thad learn to get a handle on his fire ability. Still, Thad had found this mental exercise helped keep things at bay when his emotions were spiraling out of control. Right now, he was really on the verge.

"I'm still in charge of the fighters while Lee is out, Thad," Siddoh snarled.

Thad let out the world's longest breath and then crossed his arms over his chest. Even in battle, Siddoh was known to be pretty damn easygoing. But Siddoh and Tyra had been in an awkward on-again, off-again relationship for a number of years, and Thad didn't know how much of this was fueled by old ties. The older male's hair was disheveled, and there were lines around his eyes.

"Last I checked, I'm still king, which makes me in charge of everything. Including you."

Siddoh shifted uncomfortably and grunted.

"Siddoh, you look like shit," Thad murmured. "I know this is about getting Tyra back home, but if there's still a snowball's chance of that, everybody's gotta be strong. The troops see you fraying around the edges, morale is gonna drop. You know that."

"You can't talk like she's already dead, Thad." Siddoh's typically jovial voice was quiet.

"Siddoh." Thad softened his tone as well. He had to tread carefully here. "You've gotta know I want them to come home more than anyone. Ty's my sister, for fuck's sake." Thad lowered himself into an overstuffed micro-suede chair, leaning forward onto his legs and pounding his balled-up hands against his forehead. "I'm all about the power of positive thinking, but we're coming up on two weeks."

Siddoh shook his head hard enough that, even from where Thad sat, he heard stuff crack in Siddoh's neck.

"She isn't gone. She is not gone. I would know. I would feel it."

Thad was afraid to hope. An unexpected sting pressed behind his eyes at the thought of losing two more that he loved. *This* shit was the big downside to getting a handle on his rage. Thad had fought hard to jump into his role as king, to be taken seriously despite being so young. And it wasn't like he and Siddoh had ever been buddies. Ragged nerves, hot vampire blood, and awkward emotions made for a bad combo any day of the week.

He inspected the new egg-and-dart molding on the ceiling, waiting for the sensation to pass. "We have to be prepared, Siddoh."

"I would know, Thad. Just because we never mated doesn't mean she wasn't important to me, and we drank from each other plenty in the last twenty-five years. Just like when your parents—"

Hell no. Thad pushed to his feet. "My parents were mated for a century before my father died. You cannot make a comparison there."

A loud sound of someone clearing their throat broke into the room. Isabel, Thad's queen, stood in the doorway next to an albino half-vampire. Agnessa. His missing guard's former mate. The cloying scent of Agnessa's gardenia perfume clogged Thad's nostrils.

"Hey, Agnessa. Hey, Isabel."

Agnessa blinked, eyelids shuttering over her crimson eyes in a way that gave Thad the urge to twitch a little. He couldn't believe he'd once let that female lure him into bed.

Isabel shot Thad the look. "I found her wandering the halls, so I offered to escort her."

Propriety had never been Agnessa's strong suit. Thad sighed again and stifled a yawn. Siddoh's narrowed eyes and low growl weren't lost on him. Sure, Thad was tired too, but he wasn't the one out combing the streets. "Thanks, Izzy. I've got it from here."

Isabel smiled tightly and left as Agnessa nudged the door closed with one of those pricey-looking stilettos she always wore. What were the odds he was going to get an earful about this later? He was fairly certain that if it were up to Isabel, Agnessa would no longer be allowed inside the estate.

"How's tricks, Agnessa?" Siddoh all but growled the thinly veiled jab, but Agnessa seemed to ignore it.

"I thought you could use my help, Thad."

The real kick in the balls was that maybe they could. Agnessa was one of the few remaining Oracles who knew the craft of their kind, and Lee and Agnessa had been mated for a long time. But she'd been across the estate this whole time, and just now she was showing up? He hadn't really gotten a handle on how she operated, and it hadn't been at the top of his to-do list.

"I've been in meditation," she said as if she could read his thoughts. She couldn't, could she? And who in the hell meditated for over a week straight? Long, pale fingers tipped with red polish flipped a swath of platinum hair over one shoulder. She smiled faintly, revealing a pearly white fang. "Lee's alive. They both are. I thought you would want to know. I was only just able to feel either of them a short while ago."

"Where?" This time Thad growled and the question came out as a command. He crossed the room and was nose to forehead with Agnessa in a few paces. The display did little to affect the lithe female's demeanor.

"I don't know. My blood ties with Lee are not what they once were. I can't feel him very strongly right now. But he's powerful and proficient. He'll be fine. And Tyra…" Agnessa leveled her gaze at Siddoh. "She's stuck somehow. I know that much. But I've seen that she's going to get free of whatever is holding her. You don't need to wear yourself out like this."

Thad took a step back. His body burned and his heart stuttered. Part hope, part fear. He attempted to breathe evenly as he weighed her words. Wait. Just *wait*. It couldn't possibly be that simple.

A long, low growl came from Siddoh across the way. He stared hard at Agnessa as new understanding dawned on his tired face. Perhaps now he guessed one of the reasons why Thad had allowed her to stick around after she had nearly turned Thad and Lee against each other.

And probably even why Lee thought all Oracles were "wackos."

"No way. No *fucking* way. Agnessa's your new Oracle? Can't trust her to predict the damn weather, Thad."

Chapter 2

TYRA'S SENSES SHARPENED QUICKLY, AND THE SULFUR smell of beef and cabbage from down the hall told her that it was roughly seven o'clock. Dinnertime at the shelter. The scent of cooking food wasn't nearly as strong as the sudden and palpable tension right there in Anton's little residential room.

Lee Goram, Tyra's friend and the king's royal guard, crowded the small doorway he'd just come through with his massive body. He looked like he had been to hell and back, and for Lee that was really saying something. Tyra had done battle beside him on more than one occasion over the past century. Lee didn't get hurt easily.

While Tyra was unique in having multiple powers, most vampires had a single powerful ability. Lee's was the capacity to produce energy shields that blocked almost any attack. If that didn't keep him unscathed, the centuries of fighting experience under his belt usually did. To see him spattered in blood and sporting a black eye was out of place.

"Lee, you look like shit."

He leaned his considerable weight against the door behind him that led from Anton's room out into the men's wing of the residential hall.

Tyra cringed. With hope that blood on Lee's clothing was dry, or it was going to leave a smear.

"I feel like it, so that's appropriate."

"What happened to you? What are you doing here?" Tyra leaned herself against the small metal desk by the bed and hoped nobody noticed that she needed a little extra support. Looked like Lee was too busy wiping blood from an oozing elbow wound.

Anton was too busy staring at Lee. He stood close to Tyra now, radiating heat and tension. His head moved up and down like he was sizing up Lee, who had a good few inches on Anton's six feet of height and a little more bulky muscle.

Lee's gaze flicked to Anton.

He doesn't know. He can't tell that Anton's a wizard. Tyra pegged Lee with a glare, warning him not to do anything threatening.

"It's a long story. Let's say I got into a fight and it went badly. We need to get back. We've both been gone too long. Thad's gotta be out of his mind."

"You haven't been in touch with him?"

Lee shrugged his massive shoulders, giving the tattered leather jacket hanging off them a run for its money. "Ran into a problem. Got separated from my phone."

She lifted an eyebrow. "Must have been some problem."

"Yeah, well." Lee shrugged again. Never was much of a talker, that one. At last he acknowledged Anton, who still sat against the wall looking at Lee like the force of nature that he was.

"Thanks for keeping an eye on her, pal." Lee made a subtle motion toward Anton but locked his blue-green eyes on Tyra. "This isn't really the place for discussion. We need to clean things up and get out of here."

The "cleanup" he was referring to, of course, was Anton. Tyra wasn't ready yet to mess with Anton's head. Not without getting more information. She moved alongside Anton and placed a hand on the back of the metal desk chair. For support, but hopefully she managed to do it casually. She nodded to Lee. "Go ahead back home. Let Thad know I'm okay. I'll be right behind you."

He crossed his arms over his chest. "No way, Ty. I can't show up to see Thad after being gone for over a week and not bring his sister. He'll shit bricks."

Tyra closed her eyes and did a slow backward count from ten. "Fine. Please get the hell out of here for a minute at least. I don't want to risk that someone here at the shelter catches a glimpse of you and loses their sanity." She squinted. Something clung to his elbow that looked very much like a chunk of scalp. "Or their dinner."

Lee didn't move.

"Lee. Let me handle this and I will meet you out back. Two minutes. *Please*."

He stared her down with his nastiest set-you-on-fire-with-his-eyes glare, before a blur of motion took him out the door as fast as he had come in. Luckily for Tyra, she'd had more than a century to get used to that stare, and it didn't make her tremble so much anymore. A lot of shit was going to hit the fan if Lee figured out who Anton was. Getting Lee out of that room had been crucial.

She stared hard at Anton. He'd turned to face her, somewhat relaxed in the wake of Lee's departure, and his eyelids had drifted to half-mast. "You really haven't slept, have you?" she said quietly.

It was amazing, right then, how easily she could forget who he was. Wizards killed vampires and used blood sacrifice to steal their supernatural powers. They wore stupid-looking out-of-date hooded robes that would have been laughable but for the damage and death they represented. This guy seemed like a regular guy. Jeans. Flannel shirt. Sneakers. Almost human. *Careful, Tyra.*

He dipped his head and cleared his throat quietly. "Tried not to. I wanted to be sure you were safe. I left at mealtimes because I didn't want to give anybody reason to check up on me." He pressed his lips together for a beat. "I'm glad you're okay. I wasn't sure what to do if you didn't wake up soon."

Something in his words and in his fatigued expression squeezed at Tyra's heart, and she hated the feeling for how very, very complicated it made things. Duty dictated that she kill him because of what he was. But he had stayed with her; protected her when he had every opportunity to slice her open and take the beating heart right out of her body. So why hadn't he, and where did she go from here?

"I don't know what to do about you." She examined a chipped spot in the dingy tile floor.

"That's understandable." He cocked his head to the side, as if unwilling to let her avoid eye contact. Even though he was tired, the heat of his steel-gray eyes was intense.

She pressed her hands to her face. Still woozy from her long, long nap, she wouldn't be wise to try and read him right now, no matter how much she wanted to. And the curiosity was making her itch all over. What little energy she had now from his blood would be necessary for teleporting out of this room and getting home.

An important fact stuck in Tyra's mind: *Lee hadn't*

known. Tyra herself had never had strong abilities for detecting the evil aura that surrounded their wizard foes, but Lee's radar was historically very good. He'd acted as if Anton were a human who needed to be dealt with, not a wizard enemy.

Anton was the wizard leader's son. What if he was legit and he meant what he said about helping them kill his father? No question he could prove useful. With her powers, she might be able to ensure that he would be. It was risky, but it was a chance to ensure the safety of her race if she succeeded. If she could do that, it would mean everything.

She inhaled sharply and pulled back her shoulders. Stepping forward into his space, she caught another whiff of his blood. It smelled as good as it had tasted. Like the forest at night.

Never mind, Tyra. She forced herself to make eye contact. That she remember who and what they both were to each other was extremely important. He hadn't killed her in her sleep, and damned if that watching-over-her thing didn't make her heart melt a little, but there was an awful lot of "what the fuck" going on here still. Too much for blind faith, especially given the circumstances.

"I want you to stay here. You and I have an awful lot to talk about, and now is not the time. If I don't get out there, Lee's gonna come back and heaven help us both if he figures out who you are. But I swear to you, Anton, if you give me any reason to be sorry I left this room with your body and your brain intact, I will take you down myself." After Thad was finished raking her over the coals.

He nodded. "I promise, Tyra."

Promise. There it was again. She held her hand up. "No offense, but it's going to take a lot more than just promises. I want to believe you mean to do the right thing, but just accepting the word of a wizard would go against everything I've been raised to believe." Deep in the core of her was a terror so cold it almost burned. She had been so weak in front of him. He had seen a vulnerability in her that nobody ever had and that he might have been able to use against her. He still *could* use it against her.

He lifted a hand that hovered, stopping just short of touching her face. "It wasn't just about doing the right thing, Tyra. I didn't deliver you to my father because I love—"

"I have to go." She couldn't hear that. She just couldn't. Before he could say anything more, she summoned her power to teleport. Lee was waiting for her outside, and she didn't want to be spotted leaving the building. She kept sight of those hands of his until they faded away. The warmth of them still lingered on her skin.

Anton braced his hands on the metal desk chair in the tiny, dingy, uncomfortable room where he had spent so many hours watching Tyra like she was a modern-day Sleeping Beauty. The room he was presently being kicked out of.

"I'm sorry, Mr. Smith."

The petite, senior African American lady wore a kind expression behind her wire-rimmed glasses, but the take-no-shit attitude she wielded might as well have been a baseball bat in her hands.

"I don't understand, ma'am." Something in his wrist popped from squeezing the chair so hard. As a young wizard he'd been raised to wear his rage like a cloak and to swing it like a club. Out here in the human world, he had to keep it under wraps. Times like these, it was such a challenge.

The back of his head throbbed—a reminder of the injury from his father's recent attempt to kill him. Anton rubbed at it carefully. The woman had sidelined him that morning coming back from breakfast in the dining hall, and he didn't entirely understand what was going on.

He squinted against the bright overhead light in the room. "I thought I had more time to stay."

"It may have been a computer glitch. The shelter's been taken over by private ownership. There have been changes in policy, changes in computer systems…" She shifted with her clipboard and shook her head. "Look, Mr. Smith, I hate to be the bearer of bad news. It's a difficult time of year. The weather is cold. We're always overbooked. They're adding beds to the common areas so we'll have more capacity. But you're a healthy man in your thirties. Others need to be here more than you do."

"I'm twenty-seven," he said. *Nice one, Anton.* As if letting them know that he was *younger* than they'd thought when they'd first checked him in would help his case here. "I don't have anywhere else to stay." An equally smart thing to blurt out. As if the others did. At least he'd gotten a night's sleep before they dropped the bomb.

"I can leave you with a list of other shelters and soup kitchens in the area. You've got until tomorrow. That's the best I can offer you."

He mumbled a string of obscenities under his breath as the door closed behind her.

In his hands were two black trash bags with red drawstring ties. For his belongings. For *what* belongings? He'd been wearing the same secondhand clothing for longer than he cared to think. Ever since he was released from the hospital.

Now what?

Tyra hadn't returned. Given her insistence that she'd be back, he'd foolishly made the assumption that it would be *soon*. He'd been too tired to think clearly. And frankly, nervous. What fighting skills he had were probably no match for hers. Certainly not unarmed. Definitely not once her friend had shown up. And did he really want to fight Tyra? Of course not.

He didn't especially want to die, either.

There was no question of how it was going to look if he was gone when she returned. And he wasn't certain where else he would go. But he did know one thing: "I don't have any clothes to pack," he said to himself.

Sure, his father had more wealth than Croesus, and theoretically Anton was in line to get some of that money... Or he might be if only the old man hadn't been busy trying to wipe Anton off the face of the planet. He did a slow circle in the empty room, and the garbage bags hit the desk with a soft crinkle.

For a minute he stood there in the center of the room, jiggling his leg like a kid who had to go to the bathroom. And then it hit him: his wizard ring. He reached into his back pocket and pulled out the small, heart-embossed signet ring that all the members of his wizard clan had worn. It was the key to finding his way back to his father.

Take him to the woods and finish him…

Those words were the last Anton could remember his father saying. The Master had decided to punish him for failing to deliver Tyra Morgan as ordered. Thankfully, most of the torture was only a vague impression in his memory, but those words rang out loud and clear in his head.

He flipped his hand palm up and shoved up his shirtsleeve. The cheap watch around his wrist didn't work. He'd traded a small box of Whitman's chocolates that one of the shelter volunteers had given him for it right after Christmas. The small razor blade it hid so nicely was the real reason he wore it. He slid the blade out now and used it to score his palm again. The cut from yesterday was already healed.

Focusing intently, Anton summoned his healing power. Warm tingles pulsed at the tips of his fingers and spread through his hand, bathing the extremity in an amber glow. Itchy sensations prickled up and down his palm as the skin knit back together. In no time at all, the bleeding had stopped. He rose up onto the balls of his feet and smiled at his small accomplishment. He'd tried to practice on Tyra and on his larger injuries, but small things like cuts and scrapes were better for helping him to learn control.

"And I'm getting faster," he said to the small empty room. As if the dented metal desk cared at all.

The ritual that wizards used to claim a vampire's power was hideously disgusting, and Anton had been forced to participate twice. The first time, he'd gotten too sick from it for the power to even take hold. The second time he'd acquired this power to heal. He would never do it again.

He closed his eyes. Saw Tyra in his mind's eye, from all those weeks he'd watched her under his father's orders. Her kind face with that smooth golden skin, expressive brown eyes, and generous smile. Never in a million years would he forget the day it had hit home that his kind wasn't just killing a competing species of creature; they were killing *her* species. He'd vowed then to put an end to it, and he would. Shelter or not, whether Tyra was able to come back before he had to leave or not.

No question, he didn't have the level of supremacy his father had. But he'd learned to fight. He could use a weapon. And for all he knew, the Master presumed him dead. Perhaps he could employ the element of surprise. He'd have a shot to rid the world of his father's destruction and redeem himself for the damage he'd done.

But he'd only have one.

Chapter 3

"VITALS ARE EXCELLENT. CAN YOU MAKE A FIREBALL for me?"

Thad's doctor, Greg Brayden, stepped back from Tyra's seat on the edge of her bed and gave her that detached but expectant look all medical professionals seemed to have practiced to perfection.

Thad still didn't trust her worth a damn, but they had managed to broker an agreement: if Brayden cleared it, she could go back on active duty. More importantly, back to the shelter. She had some serious unfinished business there.

"Brayden, my powers are fine." Well, that was the biggest, fattest, baldest lie she had ever told. Truth was, the initial burst of energy she'd gotten from that gulp of Anton's blood had been blown on her teleporting from the homeless shelter to her bedroom at her brother's royal estate. Since then, her body had resisted her with every move. If she flexed her powers again, she would sap what little get-up-and-go she had left. Instead of heading straight back to the shelter once she was finally free of prying eyes, she'd be forced to rest up first.

"It never hurts to check."

She batted her eyelashes a little. "You don't want me to overtire myself, do you, Doctor?" When all else failed, a little flirting and levity rolled into one should work, right?

"A small one will be fine."

Or not.

Brayden rested an elbow on her tall chest of drawers and gave a friendly smile. His thumb clicked the switch on the pen light he'd been flashing in her eyes. On. Off. On. Off. Waiting. It was clear that he didn't intend to take no for an answer.

Tyra grabbed a fistful of her rose-colored comforter. This whole business was getting old. "Jeez, Brayden. Even you don't trust me now?"

"No, that's still me."

Tyra's head and neck made a slow swivel. Everything was a little stiff from that week-plus-long nap. Thad stood stock-still in her bedroom doorway with his forehead creased down the center and his shoulders jacked up to his ears. His hands were jammed into the pockets of his fatigues.

She didn't need her supercharged abilities to know that Thad was still pissed off about her disappearance. He used to stand that way when he was mad that she wouldn't play with him as a child.

"Thad, come on."

"Make a fireball for the nice man, and then you can go back to your regularly scheduled habits of neglecting yourself until you collapse. Maybe the *next* time you'll be lucky and not wind up in torpor for days while our entire military is out combing the streets for you."

Don't hold back, Thad. Tell me how you really feel.

"Thad, I have apologized. I was saving lives."

"Any of our other fighters could have carried those unconscious vampires, Ty."

"I thought I could handle it."

Thad's nostrils flared. The anger melted off his face, but what was left behind had her feeling like an even bigger shit-heel than she already did. Deep lines traversed his face, and in the early morning gray of her bedroom, the shadows accentuated dark hollows in his cheeks and under his eyes. It brought home what a strain her disappearance had put on everyone, and it also reminded her of the way that Anton had looked when she'd woken up.

It still seemed impossible that he had kept a vigil by her side the whole time. That was the stuff of fairy tales. Or the stuff of newspaper headlines that started "Dead Body Found…" So much depended on Anton's true intentions.

It still seemed impossible that she could trust him.

"Look, Ty. You are strong, stronger than most of us. I think it's easy for us all to forget that the flip side is how easily your fuse blows. This isn't the first time you've pushed your limits too far. It's only the first time you've gotten into real trouble for it. If you want to keep fighting, I need to know you can be trusted to tag out before you become a liability."

Tyra opened her mouth and then closed it. Open. Close. Like a gasping, gaping fish. There was no way on earth that she could explain the reality: yes, she had pushed the envelope, but she hadn't gone over the edge until one of their sworn enemies had confessed to a recent stint of wizard stalking and then professed his love for her. Cuh-razy.

Her eyelids were at half-mast, but she held Thad's intent look. "I promise, Thad."

The icy blue of her brother's stare was immutable. No, she was talking to Thad the king now. Her baby brother had grown up while she was away on her un-scheduled vacation. And in part, she had forced that on him.

So, okay. She would play nicely for right now. Tyra focused her mind and a tiny flame flickered in her palm, nothing more than a tea-light votive could power. But lo, there was fire.

"Is that all you can do?"

She narrowed her eyes at Brayden. "You said a small one was fine."

He smiled evenly. "I'm just trying to assess your energy levels."

Tyra made a point of sitting straighter. She held out her hand again. A moment of intense concentration and the heat of her palm built, gathered, and fanned out until her palm and all five fingers were engulfed in flame. She blew it out with a puff of air, shaking her hand to clear the smoke trail.

Let's see how he likes them apples.

"Don't need to be a show-off, Ty." Thad came for-ward. His few inches of height advantage and scornful glare were sufficiently intimidating when he stood over her like that. He turned to Brayden. "Got everything you need, Doc?"

Brayden's head bobbed. He backed out quietly. Ever the polite gentleman, the young doctor made a point of turning the knob on his way out so the door closed with little more than a subtle tap of wood against the frame.

Tyra's hand dropped to the bed. Damn, she needed to lie down now. She was going to regret that little display she had made. Originally her hope had been to head straight back to the shelter once she was free from prying eyes. She rolled her head around on her shoulders, pretending to unkink tired neck muscles, while she surreptitiously checked the clock on her bedside table. She'd already been gone from the shelter overnight. Maybe she could make it a power nap.

Thad's shadow fell over her. He sat next to her and hooked an arm around her shoulder, pulling her sideways for a too-tight squeeze. Perhaps her baby brother was still around after all.

"I was so worried about you. I'm glad you're back, Ty." Another quick squeeze around her shoulders and he jumped to his feet, heading for the door. "I can see that you're exhausted. Get some rest."

She gave her best effort at returning his smile. "I'm glad to be back, Thad."

Lying to him like this made her ill.

Alexia raced through the forested grounds surrounding the estate, feet pounding the ground beneath her. She sped as fast as her legs could manage, her chest burning and her breath gasping in shallow pants that echoed in her own ears like a chugging locomotive. Her nose and lungs burned with the effort of drawing breath, and her heart burned like it might explode out of her.

Dawn broke overhead in a wash of pinks and grays. She was human, so the sun's rays wouldn't hurt her, but the royal estate was eerily dead for miles during the day. Creepy and lonely, especially outdoors. As the only person living in a community full of vampires, she was all stocked up on creepy and lonely as it was. These vamps might not be the kind of pasty undead creatures you saw in horror movies, but she was constantly reminded of her outsider status.

The back of the mansion loomed up ahead, and the double doors of the rear entrance beckoned to her. Almost. Almost. *Almost…*

Alexia's hand smacked the keypad and punched in the now-familiar security code automatically. By the time the little indicator light had changed from red to green, her other arm had reached to wrench open the door. She slipped in and pulled it shut behind her as quietly as she could. The heavy drapes that covered the windowed doors were down for the day to keep the sun out, and it was a struggle not to feel suffocated when they hit her in the face.

"Oh, God," she whispered to herself.

Hands braced on her knees, she needed all of her willpower not to collapse right there in the back hall. It was a good thing the household was all in bed asleep by now.

Alexia straightened and tugged the hem of her shirt up to wipe the sweat from her face. Her lungs burned, but she could breathe.

"Shouldn't be out by yourself past dawn, Alexia."

"Holy shit, Lee."

She jerked her top down to find the source of the voice, even though she recognized it right away. The few times she had heard him speak were enough to burn it into her memory. Her haste caused her to lose her footing, and she fell with an extremely unladylike thud against the pristine white wall.

"Jesus Christ. You scared the crap out of me."

Thad's bodyguard was very much as she remembered

him: tall, broad, and extremely unnerving. He stood against the opposite wall with his arms crossed over his chest. His normally tan skin was sort of ashy, and he looked quite tired but otherwise as gorgeous as before. Damn him. The hall chandelier cast a dim yellow glow, and a sheen of water dotted the top of his marine-style haircut like he had showered recently. Instead of what she thought of as his badass street-fighting clothes, jeans stretched across his muscular thighs and a soft, gray waffle henley shirt almost gave him the appearance of casual.

Almost.

He used his chin to gesture toward the door. "What were you doing out there?"

Like it was any business of his. "Jogging. Where the hell have you even been?"

His brow creased and his blue-green eyes narrowed at her. "That wasn't jogging. Jogging is what folks do at the park with their dogs and their headphones and their velour tracksuits and shit. The way you barreled into the back hall was a scene in a horror movie where the big-chested airhead runs to escape the masked man with the chainsaw."

Alexia sucked down some more oxygen and pushed away from the wall, stepping toward him with all the bravado she could muster despite over a foot in height difference between them. Her pulse gave an extra hard kick when she got close to him.

"Seriously, Lee. You have been gone for like a week. You left without any word to anyone, and Thad has been going out of his mind. Everybody has. Does he know you're back yet?"

His head dipped. "Not that it's any business of yours, but Tyra and I got back to the estate last night. We decided it was best to get cleaned up and rested before we announced our presence. I just came over from her place."

"Tyra's back too? And you stayed with her last night?" There was no reason in the world for that to bother her. None. At all.

"That she is." Lee pushed off and started to turn from her. His boot steps left subtle impressions in the flowered carpet. "Listen," he continued. "I mean it, Alexia. You shouldn't be out by yourself during daylight hours."

Nnng. You could have played music with her tightly strung neck muscles. No freaking way was he telling her what she could and couldn't do, or when she could or couldn't do it. She took a step and planted her feet wide, making a grab for his arm. Her fingers barely snagged his shirt, but that was enough to irritate him, judging from the flash in his eyes. Score one for the short girl.

"What the hell are you talking about? I'm on a two-hundred-acre estate that is protected by both a human security system and vampire hoodoo. What could possibly happen?"

Truthfully, thanks to a growing problem with insomnia, Alexia's sleep cycles were wacky these days. Typically she was back inside the mansion before it was fully light outside. She'd poke a fork in her own eye, though, before she defended herself to Lee.

He shrugged. "Can't be too careful." He reached out and chucked her under the chin. Like a kid, for fuck's sake. "Already had to use my blood to save your ass once. Don't go wasting it by being stupid." And with that, he turned again and headed down the hallway.

Alexia was speechless. God *damn* him. She snorted quietly. What an unbelievable asshole. So Lee had saved her life and ever since then she'd had some sort of stupid little crush thing going for the big bastard. But he was an arrogant jerk and she was *so* over it. She threw her shoulders back and straightened her spine to begin the long march down the hall to her room.

The confident display felt important even if he wasn't there to witness it.

Chapter 4

WHEN DR. BRAYDEN HAD COME UP THROUGH THE tunnels that morning to assist with Theresa's birth, he'd given word that the search for the king's sister and Lee was resolved. Good news, but Xander was disappointed to have missed all the action. It was his own fault, though. Besides, he'd been witnessing life-or-death drama of a different nature entirely.

So much blood.

And the screams.

Xander had never been party to anything so horrific. All the times he'd done battle against the wizards, and yet he hadn't even had the stomach to watch the outcome of the terror in that room.

He bowed his head quietly and prayed to a God he wasn't sure he believed in anymore. He was perched uncomfortably in a rust-colored leather chair that was not his own, murmuring words that were equally rusty and foreign, when Theresa's bedroom door off to his left clicked open.

"Alexander."

He lifted his head. Greg Brayden took a seat across from him. The normally neat doctor looked as if someone had tossed him into a clothes dryer for a few cycles. "Brayden. How is everything?"

"The midwife is stitching her up." The doctor lowered his head. "I know. It always looks like a great deal of blood loss, but I think she's going to be fine."

Xander cleared his throat, willing away the lump he couldn't swallow around. "Thank goodness."

Brayden closed his eyes for a moment. "Yeah. Lucky she made it. She's been through an awful lot."

Xander cleared his throat again. That lump wouldn't go away. He toed at the dark brown carpet with his boot. "Absolutely." Though he never would have admitted it to a soul, his body shook a little. Theresa had recently lost her mate in battle. The sight of all that blood and the midwife's grim facial expressions, along with quietly whispered words like "tearing" and "breech" had been enough to push Xander from the room.

All that screaming…

During every day of his guard duty in this house, the cozy living room with its rust-colored leather furniture and flat-screen television had reminded Xander that his friend and fellow soldier, who had clearly picked out the furnishings, would never be coming back. Theresa's mate would never be coming back. That child's father… would never know him.

The idea of leaving that newborn without any parents was more than Xander could handle. He himself had grown up without a family. He'd had someone to raise him, sure. But to not have someone who truly claimed you as their own? A child deserved love.

He sighed and rubbed his forehead. Brayden must have stood while he wasn't looking, because then a hand landed on his shoulder and a voice spoke low in his ear. "She's going to need to feed, my friend."

The temperature in the room dropped. Funny how somebody you barely knew was suddenly your friend when they needed to deliver bad news. "And why are you telling me?" As if he needed to ask.

Brayden had always seemed like a mild-mannered gentleman. Quiet. Professional. But his stare was hard at that moment. "You recently lost a mate yourself. You know how difficult this is going to be for her. Doubly so because she just went through the pain and exhaustion of bringing life into the world. She needs to heal from that, Alexander."

Xander opened and closed his fists. The doctor's insistence on referring to him by his full name was grating. "Then you understand why I don't want to be the one to do it, *Gregory*. Can you not get somebody else? Blood Service?"

His head fell back in the chair. If only Brayden would leave and he could get some rest. Admittedly, he tired easily these days, even while on guard duty. He ought to feed. He knew he ought to. But he couldn't. It meant betraying Tam. He wasn't ready.

Brayden's hand tightened its grip on his shoulder. "Think how Theresa must feel. Her mate's death was only a couple of weeks ago. She gave birth a few hours ago. To a baby she'll have to raise alone."

Something invisible punched Xander in the chest. He was wrong here, and he was being selfish. Still, he wasn't sure he could handle another female drinking from him. The very thought of it made him want to jump out of his skin.

The universe or perhaps even God himself decided that Xander's uncertainty needed a nudge. Once again the bedroom door opened, and out walked the midwife. Her dark clothes were wet and disheveled, her braid askew, but she was carrying the most perfect baby boy Xander had ever laid eyes upon. Okay, its face was a little splotchy, but whatever. Perfect all the same.

"My assistant is performing a cleansing ritual, and then mom needs to rest. So someone has to hold him for a bit." The tall female smiled broadly and leaned down to hand the child to Xander as if the matter had already been decided.

The baby was swaddled in a muslin blanket with its head covered in a blue cap and was sleeping soundly with his lips formed into a tiny pout. Xander couldn't believe how something that would someday be as large as he was fit into the whole of his two palms side by side.

"Support his head," she murmured.

The miniscule body was surprisingly warm but feather-light. Xander's giant hands and leather-jacket-clad arms weren't at all worthy to be holding this soft bundle.

"He's been nursed, so he should sleep awhile. If he starts to wake, though, you can take him back to her for more milk," said the midwife.

Xander chewed his lip. "Not blood?" How stupid that he didn't even know what babies ate or drank.

The corners of her eyes crinkled. She smiled broadly. "He'll begin teething sometime between two and nine months of age. Front teeth first, like humans. When his milk fangs come in, then he can start weaning to blood and solid foods like a big boy." The female bustled with blankets and bags as she not so quietly made her exit. *I thought that Theresa needed to sleep?*

That stuff with the baby teeth sounded complicated.

Xander was glad not to have things like that to worry about. He was barely aware of Brayden's hand squeezing his shoulder again but he looked up, and their stares bored into each other again.

He would never, from this moment on, think of Brayden as mild-mannered.

The doctor glanced pointedly down at the baby, over to the closed bedroom door, and then back at Xander. "I'm not going to call Blood Service," he hissed. "It should be somebody she knows. She deserves that much." Brayden pulled his hand away, reaching for his coat and his bag. "You've been here on guard duty. You've kept her company since Eamon's death. Better than anyone else, you can relate to what she's feeling. I think it would be best if you were the one to give her blood. If you can't manage it, I'll do it."

The bundle in Xander's hands twitched and made a cranky whine in its sleep. *So much upheaval from such a little thing*. He shook his head, even as he tucked the child closer to his body. He placed one too-large hand on the baby's chest, and it rose and fell with each breath the infant took. "I'll do it," he said.

"Going somewhere?"

When Tyra teleported into Anton's room at the shelter, his back was turned. He froze mid-action, like a kid caught with porn. He released the red handles of the black garbage bag into which he'd been tossing a few meager items and turned around.

"Nice luggage," Tyra said. Hell, she was as incensed that he was packing to leave as she was surprised that he wasn't gone yet. Her intended short power nap? Turned out her body had needed some serious refueling, even after the long hibernation there in Anton's room. She'd wound up sleeping an entire day and night. Tyra was stronger than most vampires, but the flip side of her strength and her multiple powers was that she burned through her energy more easily as well.

She studied his face. The time and distance she'd been gone had allowed uncertainty to creep in. Mistrust. A debriefing from Lee revealed that during her extended power nap he'd been hunting down Anton's father himself. Some sort of tip that he'd been cagey about going into the details of. As they'd always suspected, there had been traps, tricks, and decoys once Lee had finally found what he'd thought was the actual wizard hidey-hole. The news had been a heavy splash of cold water for Tyra—another reminder that she couldn't afford to take Anton at face value. She'd shown up here wondering if the next time they crossed paths she might be forced to erase his memory or kill him.

Anton shrugged. "You know how it is. They don't exactly bust out the good stuff for you around here. Some older lady—Beverly, I think her name was—felt bad about kicking me out and rustled up some spare clothes."

Wait. *"What?"* She cringed. That had come out much louder than intended. Tyra checked the door lock. Dropping her voice, she said, "What do you mean they're kicking you out? I was the volunteer who checked you in. You should have more time."

He shrugged again. Males and their noncommittal gestures. "That Beverly woman came and said someone else was scheduled to move into this room today. In fact..." The flannel sleeve of his shirt slid down when he pointed up to the wire-covered clock on the wall. Why was he wearing a watch with a smashed face?

"She said I had until eight a.m. to pack, so I'm running short on time to make myself scarce. Computer mix-up or policy change or something. She wasn't clear. I didn't think it mattered. Wasn't much option about it either way. You look so much better." He managed a smile, but it seemed forced. Those eyes of his were always so intense and serious. Then again, this encounter was incredibly awkward for both of them.

Despite the awkwardness and the weird... whatever it was between them, the corner of her mouth gave a little twitch in reply. "Well, given that you last saw me coming off a week and a half in torpor, the bar wasn't set very high."

He, on the other hand, still looked weary and wrung out. At the same time, his body was on high alert. His muscles were strung tight, his shoulders tense, fingers twitchy. Was he waiting for her to attack him or something?

If he was, it was a legitimate expectation. So why did that bother her? She stepped forward and then stopped short. Her hand lifted to brush a stray curl from her face, but she stopped in the middle of the nervous gesture and dropped her hand to her side. Instead she clasped her fingers behind her back.

There were a lot of questions to ask. She certainly hadn't counted on the shelter kicking him out, and it wasn't like she could go and make a big stink about it. As far as anybody else at the shelter knew, she'd left to go on vacation the night she disappeared. "Sit with me," she said.

"Sure." Anton sat with an unceremonious crinkle on the plastic bag that he'd been given to use as a make-shift suitcase.

"Why didn't you kill me when you had the chance?"

He shook his head. "I told you—oh." His eyes widened in understanding when the tips of Tyra's fingers rested lightly on his forearm. His gray eyes were sharp when they focused on hers. "You can read my mind or something when you touch me, can't you?"

Her skin heated. "Not your thoughts, exactly. I mean, if you started to recite a cooking recipe in your head I wouldn't suddenly know how to make your granny's famous clam chowder. Mostly vague impressions. Emotions. Things like that." It was one of those random, offhand comments, but it brought forward a rush of unanticipated sadness from Anton.

Tyra nearly smacked herself on the head. They didn't know much about the wizard race, but it would stand to reason that he probably hadn't been raised by what she thought of as a family. No grandmother. No home-cooked clam chowder. "I'm sorry," Tyra said.

"It's… don't apologize to me. It's fine." His arm twitched under her fingers. "Well, don't apologize, anyway."

K. Time to change the subject. "Look, I know you already told me, but please. Explain to me again what's going on here. The whole situation with your father and why you were following me. I need to hear it now, when I'm healthy and lucid." Comparatively, at least. She paused to study his face. There was a lot going on behind those eyes of his, despite the weariness in them. "And yes, I need to feel it. It's the only way we'll both be able to trust here."

"I won't be able to read your emotions," he said.

She wasn't the one with the evil lineage, thank you very much. The back of her neck tightened. "I will be straight with you as long as you're straight with me. Can we agree on that much?"

"Huh. Sure." A grimace spread over his face and his hands rubbed his thighs like they were sweaty or something. "I kept an eye on you while you were in a coma. Torpor. Whatever it was you called it. When you woke up, you threatened to kill me and then disappeared without another word.

"Now you're telling me I should hand you my blind faith? Unlike you, I've barely slept in a week and I'm not the one who's armed." He glanced pointedly at her ankle holster. "I've already told you I'm willing to offer my help to you, Tyra, but you have to admit that I'm at a disadvantage in the trust department."

Though delivered in calm, even tones, his words might as well have been a slap across the face. Forgetting herself completely, Tyra pulled her hand away. Neither of them spoke, and heat built in her chest as anger bubbled up. It wasn't like he didn't have a point, but—

But what? He was exactly, completely, one hundred percent right. Nevertheless, wow, did it piss her off. *Brush it off, Ty. You're here for information.*

"Okay. Let's just do this." With a deep breath, Tyra flexed her fingers and rubbed her hands together to get a little energy going. She was about to touch him again when a knock sounded at the door.

"Mr. Smith?"

Shit. Without even thinking, her fingers closed around his. They were out of time.

Chapter 5

THAD THREW A FIREBALL FROM ONE END OF HIS PRACTICE gym to the other. Considering that he hadn't slept well since his parents' death a few months before—and sure as hell not in the time while Lee and Tyra were missing—the fireball was a decent one. The orange-sized orb hit Lee's protective shield and fizzled out on impact.

"That the best you got?" Lee adjusted his stance, sinking into a semi-squat. "Come on, hit me again."

Thad snarled, as much at Lee as at his own reflection visible in the mirrored wall over his best friend's shoulder. "Lee, it's been a long night, for fuck's sake." But Thad focused his power and threw again. This time the fireball was easily as big as one of the heavy balls they had down the hall in the mansion's underground bowling alley.

Lee rocked back on his heels, thrown for a moment by the force of impact against his shield. "Not bad," he said approvingly. "Shit, Thad. You didn't need my help to learn control of your power after all." He looked much older than his seven hundred years when he straightened and reached for a towel and some water. "And for all he's shown himself to be an irresponsible asshole in the past, Siddoh's stepped up and taken command of the fighters. Don't really need me around anymore."

For fuck's sake. "What's this about, Lee?" Thad stripped off his sweaty T-shirt and finished toweling down.

He grabbed a bottle of water from beside the padded blue floor mat and stared hard at his friend and bodyguard.

Only weeks ago their roles had been reversed. Before the death of Thad's parents, Lee had been in service to Thad's father. Thad had been one of dozens of fighters in the royal military wing. He'd been the one to answer to the seven-hundred-year-old guard, not the other way around. Having their roles reversed like this still smacked of wrong to Thad.

Lee ran a hand over his military buzz cut and toyed with the little plastic ring around the neck of his water while he stared intently at the floor. "Thad, I fucked up. There's no excuse for it. I'm fully prepared to step down. Leave the estate, even. My being here is an embarrassment, and there's no reason for me to stay on."

Thad's fangs ripped through his gums. He shot across to Lee's bench and knocked the older male to the floor before he could do more than drop his water bottle. This time, Lee was too surprised to fight back.

"Don't be stupid," Thad growled.

Lee's head bounced off the floor mat. "Thad."

Thad tackled, and this time it wasn't good-natured sparring. A choking, gurgling sound came out of Lee's throat, and Thad pulled his knee off the older vampire's neck. Slowly, Thad stood and backed to the other bench. His entire body was practically on fire.

Lee was right. Disappearing that way without backup? Without as much as a cell phone? Leaving Tyra in the hands of a human? They were such unforgiveable, boneheaded moves that Thad didn't see how anybody could have made them, let alone someone with Lee's experience.

Truth was, he loved Lee like a brother. Thad had recently lost his parents, and Isabel had come awfully damn close to being killed by wizards before they'd even had a chance to get to know each other. Hell, he could have lost his half sister in the past week. And feeling his way through this new gig as king? He didn't have a clue half the time. He couldn't handle losing Lee, too.

Not that he knew how to say that out loud. So he paced. "I don't want you to step down, Lee."

"You haven't put me back on active duty."

That made him stop again. "You haven't been back very long. Wasn't sure you were ready. I still don't have a clear picture of what happened."

Lee rubbed his chest and throat, struggled up from the floor, and sat again with his hands braced on the bench. "That night I left, Agnessa had shown up in my room. I admit I didn't handle it well."

Thad dropped to the bench. "Siddoh figured out that she'd been there. We thought that might've had something to do with it."

Lee shook his head sadly. "You think you're over something… Anyway, I went down to your father's office to clean it out like you asked me to. I wound up letting my anger run away with me and busted up a desk. Sorry about that, by the way."

Well, that explained how that had happened. Thad's gums ached as his anger cooled and his fangs started to recede. "I was going to replace the furniture anyway."

Lee's jaw worked side to side. "Thad, I found some important information hidden in your father's desk. About Ty."

Thad's pulse picked up its tempo. "What kind of information?"

Lee took a drink of water and wiped his mouth. Hard, almost like he was slapping himself in the face. "Our suspicions were correct that they were gunning for her specifically. Your father went out that night to try and put a stop to it." He pulled an envelope from his pocket and handed it to Thad.

The cream-colored note inside was wrinkled and stained. The late king's words were perfectly legible, though. And their meaning was clear. Thad pegged Lee with a hard stare. "You haven't told her about this, have you?"

"No way." Lee held up a hand. "No question, she's going to shoot the messenger. And I haven't shared the info with anybody else, either. Nobody knows about it right now except you, me, and all of these barbells."

Thad nodded. His head was full of noise all of a sudden. "How am I going to tell Tyra that her mother wasn't human?" Tyra, older than Thad by a quarter century, had been conceived before Thad's parents were mated. The big, scandalous story was that their father had fallen in love with a human. It had ended badly, as those things tended to, and months later Tyra's mother had dropped off a baby. Nobody had ever heard from her again. Nobody had questioned Tyra's half-human lineage. Why would they have?

Before Lee could answer, the double doors to the gym pushed open with a creak. Isabel stepped in, clad in a tank top and fuzzy pajama pants covered with glow-stick-wielding bunnies. Thad had found his queen at a rave in Florida, of all places. You could take the vampire out of the party, but not the party out of the vampire. In her hands was a skinny mutt of a dog. Something called a whippet mix, whatever that meant.

Damn, but he was glad to see them both right now.

"Thad, I hate to ask, but I'm having trouble sleeping. It's already after eight. Do you think you could come upstairs when you and Lee are done here?"

Really glad. "I'll come now."

He clapped Lee on the shoulder. "Thank you." He crumpled the note in his hand and pointed a commanding finger at his friend on his way out of the room. "No more talk of you leaving."

"This is a terrible idea."

Tyra fought the good fight, but in the end she rolled her eyes at Anton anyway. "It's a perfectly good idea."

"You can't possibly believe that." Anton dropped his plastic garbage bag on her bed. He all but sneered at her walnut Ethan Allen dresser and sleigh bed like they were beneath him. "We are in your home. On your brother's estate. *On the vampire king's estate*. This is the most hideous idea in the history of bad ideas. Trust me, I've been party to plenty."

The eggshell-painted wall was comfortingly cool against Tyra's skin when she leaned against it for support. What was *wrong* with her? She'd slept far longer than any vampire had a right to, and yet that teleport had left her a little woozy. Anton seemed to have handled it fine for a first-timer, bad attitude aside. Folks didn't always.

She could blame the light-headedness on extreme

frustration. Maybe also stress and anxiety. Bringing him to the estate had been a nerve-wracking decision. No plan was perfect in situations like these. There wasn't exactly a *Planning a Secret Takedown with the Scion of All Evil* rule book.

She rubbed her eyes. "They were kicking you out of the shelter. We had to move you in a hurry, right? I don't recall you coming up with a better idea."

His long fingers curled into a fist. "I suggested a hotel. Even one of the abandoned buildings downtown would have been better than this."

"Look." Tyra pressed her palms against her closed eyes for a moment. Neon-looking lines appeared in her field of vision from the pressure. This entire experience was as surreal as those lines. Talk about conversations she never expected to have. "Okay, first of all, sit down. You're standing there like you expect my bathrobe to jump out of the closet and attack you."

Instead of sitting, he stepped forward. "You've put me behind enemy lines here, you know."

Tyra pushed away from the wall and crossed her arms over her chest. "Of course. I know what I'm doing, Anton."

For a while they stared at each other, both with narrowed eyes and flared nostrils. Anton swallowed, rubbed the back of his neck, and looked around some more before finally—slowly—his butt landed on her rose-colored silk duvet. He perched on the end of her bed, as ill at ease as before.

"Anton, it's the middle of winter. We'd have both frozen our asses off in an abandoned building. The key problem," she said as she crossed to sit on the damask settee opposite Anton's position on the bed, "is that right now pretty much *anywhere* is behind enemy lines for you. You couldn't stay at the shelter, and I couldn't have protected you very easily anyplace other than here."

Anton looked a little like she had just struck him across the mouth, but she kept going. "You're as safe as you can be here. It's daylight, and I've told everyone I need to rest, so nobody's going to bother me for a while. This place is like Fort Knox inside Fort Knox. We'll get you situated by nightfall, get some rest, and then work on a plan. It'll be fine."

He kept staring. His tongue made a slow, thoughtful sweep over his lips. Her body heated a little, remembering that he'd been touching her face when she woke from torpor. That he'd been leaning so close to her face that he practically could have kissed her.

Was it really possible that he *loved* her? It couldn't be. She almost snorted at the thought. The idea that he believed what the wizards were doing was wrong and wanted to help her kind—she could almost buy into that. She was banking hard on his good intentions, in fact. But the notion that he was doing this because he had fallen for her while watching her from afar? Well that was naked-with-a-megaphone-on-the-street-corner crazy. No way could it possibly be true.

"You know…" Anton leaned forward, and despite the prior weeks of strain, his chest and biceps bulged under the worn flannel he wore. Goodness. Not all wizards were so well put together. "I don't appreciate the idea that you think *you* need to be the one protecting *me*."

It took only her a few short paces to cross the room. She ignored the breath he drew when she knelt in front of him. Her sanity took leave as she tugged at his shirt's neckline and ran her finger over the scar that was visible just above the opening. His skin was warm. Surprisingly so. "Your own crew tortured you and left you for dead in the woods. You're still healing from a head injury. Do you really think you could defend against them on your own if they found you right now?"

Tyra realized that her thumb had been rubbing the same strip of scarred skin under his collarbone for longer than was strictly necessary to prove her point. A little zing of sensation made her pulse speed up. They were nearly nose to nose.

Anton's short hair was askew from the teleport. His breath came hot and fast against her mouth. "My own father stripped the skin off my body and bashed my head against a wall. And I'm willing to bet that's nothing compared to what will happen to me here if anyone finds out who I am. What I am."

If she'd leaned in a fraction, his lips would have brushed against her skin. The realization sent a jolt through Tyra's system. She stood quickly. "That's not going to happen," she said. "Lee couldn't tell, and he's been fighting your kind longer than anyone else around here."

Anton's body language closed up. She hadn't been feeling for his emotions right then, but his expression was cloudy. He tapped his feet. Dropped his hands back to his knees. The whole shuffle-tap-fidget routine went on until Tyra thought she might very well lose her mind.

Her nails dug into her palms. Possessed though she was by a case of the squirmies herself, she thought one of them ought to be able to stay still. She'd perched in treetops waiting for wizards late at night before, dammit. She was on the verge of losing her cool when Anton flopped unceremoniously onto the bed.

His arms landed above his head, and the move shifted his clothing enough to expose a strip of hard, dark skin on his abdomen. Without warning, he jumped to standing and stomped forward. His entire body was rigid and his stance was combative.

Tyra's blood rushed and her adrenaline spiked. If the rubber met the road, she could most likely beat him in a fight. She had power that he didn't, but shit. She hadn't honestly believed that he would attack her. Stupid, *stupid*.

"You can't guarantee anything," he ground out. "Now, I'm good with that. When I said I'd help you get to my father, I wasn't signing up for a paradise vacation. But let's not kid ourselves here." Gray eyes stared her down, pupils dilated. His nostrils flared.

"Fine," she said quietly. Her long exhale failed to relax her. "Let's just get some rest. We both need it." She pointed to the bed. The soft flannel of his sleeve brushed her bare arm when she pulled away. "You can sleep there. I'll take the couch. Once we're both rested, we can start planning how we're going to, you know, lay siege to your father's evil lair." She didn't wait for him to say anything before she walked out of the room.

She rested her head against the door after she pulled it shut. Her heart hammered harder in her chest than it ever had when facing an enemy. *Was* he an enemy? Boy, she hoped to hell she was playing this thing right. Not a chance she was going to get any sleep, but she grabbed a blanket from the linen closet anyway, ready to hit the sofa.

A familiar rush lit up Tyra's veins. Only someone whose blood she'd drunk more of than Anton's would do that. She was aware of that vampire's approach only seconds before a thuddy rap came at the door. Siddoh, her old lover.

Chapter 6

ANTON HAD ALWAYS TAKEN PRIDE IN THE FACT THAT he was nothing—*nothing*—like his father. Yet here he stood in such a blind rage that he shook from it. Dying to rip a vampire's heart out and eat it whole. He could almost taste the fibrous muscle between his teeth.

But it wasn't an indiscriminate desire. Not just any vampire, but the one uttering the low murmurs on the other side of Tyra's bedroom door. That vampire had shown up a few minutes earlier, and he knew her real fucking well. *Knew her* in "that way." Anton would have bet his life on it.

The intense desire to slice the bastard from stem to stern might have been more alarming, but it clashed with Anton's effort to keep his feet glued to the floor, under penalty of the painful death Tyra had promised him. He cared far more about pleasing her than he did about the potential dangers of facing down the enemy on the other side of the door.

"Siddoh, I'm fine. Really."

"You look exhausted, Ty. Listen, if you're having trouble sleeping again I could—"

Anton's fists tightened. The rest of the sentence was muffled, but Anton could only imagine what the vampire would be willing to do to help Tyra sleep. *Over my dead fucking body, you son of a bitch.*

"I'm okay, really. In fact, I just got back from the

shelter and I was about to turn in. You're right, I am tired. You should go get some rest too, right? It's awfully early in the afternoon for you to be awake."

"Hey, listen. I'm not trying to tell you what to do here, but don't you think you need to take a break from everything? The fighting and the volunteer work. You're spreading yourself too thin. Get your head on straight. Make sure you're a hundred percent and all that."

"You're absolutely right. I'm going to, I swear. I needed to go over there and check on things, you know? I mean, I said I was leaving to go on vacation and then I just disappeared. But you make an excellent point, and as soon as you go, I intend to get in bed and get some sleep. Like I said, you should go do that too. I imagine it's been hard on you without Lee around to help."

There was an awkward and pregnant pause, during which the male's footsteps sounded like he was roving around the room. Was he looking for something? Did the vampires suspect Anton was here?

"Okay, I wanna know what the hell is up with you, Ty."

Shit.

"Siddoh, I don't know what you're talking about. Seriously, I'm really tired. Now would you please get out of here so I can do that resting thing you just lectured me about?"

"All right, Ty. You go ahead and deny it, but I know you, and something weird is going on. I can sense your agitation, and yet you're standing there being all calm and agreeable. You've never been so freaking polite to anybody, babe, not even to me. Not even when we were fucking."

Anton's toes hit the tops of his shoes. "I knew it," he whispered. He wasn't sure when or how he had moved those last couple of paces to the door or put his hand on the knob. He did know he was going to tear that asshole limb from—

"Stop!" It wasn't clear whether Tyra's command was directed at the vampire she'd referred to as Siddoh or if X-ray vision was one of her many superpowers, but the authority in her voice stilled Anton's hand as it was about to turn the knob. "Look, just stop, okay? Siddoh, I was trying to be polite and calm because everyone keeps worrying about my health and I didn't want you running to Thad or sending Brayden to poke and prod at me again. I need some damn space so I can deal with what happened and get back to normal, but I don't need your help to do it, except for you to leave so I can get some rest. Please?"

There was a deep sigh followed by some rustling noises that could have been the two sharing a hug. Anton did his level best to not picture it or anything, but it was a damn good thing *he* couldn't see through the door. As it was, he was amazed he hadn't managed to crush the brass knob in his grip. He swore he could've melted it right then.

There was more talking. Anton didn't listen. *Couldn't* listen. He struggled to breathe, to calm the rage, to control the shaking before he did something really stupid. But there was that old saying about the best-laid plans, and as soon as soon as Anton's ears caught the click of a latch, he barreled out of Tyra's bedroom with nothing in his head except confronting her.

She turned to him with her eyes narrowed and arms akimbo. "Are you out of your damn mind?"

His mouth on Tyra's silenced whatever admonishment she had been working to dole out. They were on the floor in no time, and her body was *perfect* underneath his. Hard and muscular and soft and feminine all at the same time, and she smelled so sweet and delicious. Like winter air and apples. It was so good to have her body under his. A couple of times before his confrontation with Tyra— before her coma—he'd dared to lie in his cot at the shelter and imagine holding her this way. Touching her.

The full bells-and-whistles reality blew the fantasy out of the water.

He was hard and ready, and couldn't hold back from pressing his erection against the giving juncture of her thighs. It was a rush better than any other Anton could imagine when her hips softened, her thighs parting a little to accommodate him. At the same time her lips, which had started out pressed in a severe line, yielded and opened. Her tongue slid against his, her fangs grazing him ever so slightly as he adjusted the fit of their mouths and then moved in for more.

Their bodies melted together. Anton's fingers traveled. They tangled in the springy curls at the nape of her neck, and at the same time his tongue probed and tasted. Ah, so that was the source of the apple scent: gum. It felt so right, so natural to be with her like this.

At least it did until Tyra flipped both of them over and kneed him in the balls.

"Shit." He wound up on his back, disconcerted and nauseous, with her elbow in his chest.

Her hard, dark stare was incongruent with her heavy, ragged breath and kissed-up lips. "What the *fuck* do you think you're doing?"

Tyra squinted at him from across a rack at Milligan's Army Surplus. "What are you, a thirty-two, thirty-two?"

"Awkward" didn't begin to describe the mood in Tyra's home over the past twenty-four hours. The initial period after "the incident" had involved barely speaking. After that, they had made polite small talk as if they were two people waiting at the dentist's office, not… whatever the hell they were to each other.

Finally, they had discussed strategy and timing. Their plans to "lay siege" to his father's stronghold, as Tyra had so lightly put it. She was clearly determined to make this a suicide mission, and he was equally determined to see that didn't happen. After all the talking, they had showered and eaten and tiptoed around each other some more until Tyra had announced that Anton's clothing would not do at all.

In this entire debacle of course, that was their *real* problem.

He shook his head. "If you're asking my clothing size, I don't know."

Now she looked mad. He glanced around for some indication of why. He had been careful not to even come close to touching her since that kiss. Boy, had he learned his lesson there. "What did I do wrong?"

"How can you not even know what size pants you wear?"

Now didn't seem like the time to explain that he hadn't needed to know his pants size during his entire existence as a full-grown adult. He looked around again, this time for signs of a bathroom. "I could go check the tag of these ones I have on, I guess."

She held a pair of black pants up in front of him. "Whatever. Come on, this place is going to be closing soon. Let's get you changed and find something to eat so we can head out. These look about right. Here. I got you a couple of shirts and a fleece jacket as well."

She clattered past him with a bunch of stuff. Admittedly, he hadn't totally been paying attention. Army surplus stores carried a ton of cool shit, and he kept getting distracted. He didn't even know what some of the stuff was. He was checking out a display of shoes when he realized she was at the cash register.

"Shit, Tyra." The blue digital numbers read $158.97. He hadn't been thrilled at the idea of her buying him a pair of pants. But okay, if they ran into a fight, doing battle in blue jeans was less than ideal. Ideal would be wearing his old wizard robes. This? No. Hell no.

"What?" The look on her face was absolutely not to be believed.

"What do you mean, 'what?'" He'd grabbed her wrist in the middle of handing her credit card to an older man behind the counter who was probably more than a little concerned about Anton's attitude. He let go of Tyra so fast she might as well have been radioactive. "For fuck's sake," he whispered, "I can't let you pay for all of that."

"Fine." She rolled her eyes and crossed her arms over her chest. "You pay for it."

He gritted his teeth together. He'd been doing that a lot since meeting Tyra face to face.

"Right, so I'll pay then," she said. She handed the card to the man behind the counter. "We want to get some hunting in before the season's over." She turned back to Anton, a strange closed-mouth smile plastered on her face. "It's our first time going together."

"Well, that's nice." The man behind the counter smiled approvingly as he rang up their purchases. "You know, my wife and I go every year together. She always said she wasn't into it, but when she bagged her first deer, she was hooked. It's a great bonding experience."

All the breath squeezed out of Anton's lungs when Tyra threw a surprise arm around his shoulder. "We'll just bet it is." Mother of mercy, she had strong arms.

"You know, my wife even collects guns and goes to the shooting range with me now. You guys shoot?"

"Absolutely," Tyra replied.

What the hell? Why was she having a conversation with this guy? Wasn't the idea to get the hell out of there? The arm around Anton's shoulder squeezed tighter. "Well, I shoot. I'm trying to get him into it."

"Now there's something you don't hear every day. Little woman'll make a man out of you yet, huh, boss?"

Heat swept Anton's body head to toe. He forced a smile. "You bet."

New conviction to respect boundaries be damned. Two could play at this game. He threw an arm around Tyra and returned the too-hard, not really affectionate squeeze. "Come on, honey. Daddy needs dinner and a beer."

He gave an exaggerated wink to the guy behind the counter.

She smiled tightly and squeezed even harder. If they kept this up, he was going to wind up with a cracked rib. "Sure thing, sweetheart."

He opened his mouth to speak when they left the store but she held up a finger.

Finally, when they reached the car, she said, "'Daddy needs dinner and a beer.' Are you kidding me?"

She was biting her lip, and her cheeks were flushed. Anton couldn't hold the laughter in. So much for being pissed off at her. "Hey," he said, gasping to catch his breath. "I was playing along. What was that about, anyway?"

She leaned her head back and breathed deeply. He tried not to notice how pretty her cheeks were, stained with red like that, and how her chest rose and fell gracefully under the V-neck of her T-shirt. "You never know who's listening or watching. The wizards… well, your… the wizards…" She shook her head. "They're all over the place. And we're starting to suspect that they hide in plain sight. I've never been as good at detecting them—you—them. Maybe because I'm part human." She shrugged. "Better safe than sorry, I guess."

He swallowed. "I guess that makes sense. I don't honestly know what he's got them doing these days. I've obviously been out of the loop." He put a hand on the bag of clothing in her lap. "I'm not happy about this, Tyra."

She honestly seemed incredulous. "What do you mean?"

"You said you wanted to buy me a pair of pants. I agreed to one pair of pants. One. For practical reasons and because I have no money right now. But what the hell was the rest of that stuff?"

If he hadn't known better, he'd have thought she shrank back. "It wasn't that much."

"Tyra, this is more than I've spent on clothes in probably my entire life."

She scoffed and rolled her eyes. That move was already getting old. "You can't be serious."

"Why do you think the wizards wear those stupid robes all the time?" Anton clunked his head back against the window glass. "They're easy to fight in, and they're cheap. Bolt of fabric, and teach a few of us peons how to sew. No need to buy anybody clothes. Bad enough the Master's gotta feed us—*them*—and give everyone a place to sleep."

A hand landed on his knee. Reluctantly Anton met Tyra's gaze, expecting sadness or pity or… he wasn't sure what. What he hadn't expected were the teeth sinking into her full lips, the tiny lift to the corners of her mouth, and the sparkle of humor in her brown eyes. "Do you really know how to sew?"

He jerked. His body was hot again, although Tyra had barely gotten the heat going in the car. Uncomfortable prickles danced over his skin. Her amusing little jab landed squarely in his gut, and suddenly he couldn't sit still. If he looked down at himself just then, he'd probably have seen a hole straight through him to the seat back.

"You know what?" The sound of the clothing bag was deafening when he crushed the plastic material to shove it back into her lap. "I managed to get out of having to cut open one of your brethren a time or two by being useful in other ways, so it's not a fucking joke to me."

Anton ignored her cringe and faced forward. He bit hard on his own tongue to keep from saying more. The sharp bite of his nails digging into his palms and the cold leather of the car seat were satisfying against his skin. Familiar. Pain and discomfort he could handle. He might not like it, but it was familiar. "Let's just get on with the plan, Tyra."

"I didn't mean to offend you."

He thought his head might explode. And how could he be sweating when it was forty degrees outside? "Tyra, I don't really think that makes a difference, does it?"

"Anton."

He shook his head. No. He didn't intend to say anything more on the subject. Letting her know that she had hurt his pride was enough. What if he let on that what really hurt was the continuing idea that he was less-than in her eyes by virtue of his birth alone, and that not a single thing he did would change that? It was far more than he could expose of himself.

"You said traffic's awful this time of day. We should really get going," he said. "C'mon. Drive."

Chapter 7

"WHAT DO YOU MEAN YOU DON'T KNOW WHERE IT IS?" Tyra's grip on the steering wheel was so tight that her knuckles blanched and then turned red. Tension inside the black Land Rover she'd taken from the estate's fleet of vehicles kept climbing even as the sun dipped low in the sky. She pointedly ignored the low growl that was Anton's response.

They wound through the back roads of Ash Falls. Over hills and past farms that weren't very active now because it was January. The sparse scenery scrolled past them, and the more rural things got, the more Tyra's nausea and unease grew. This driving into the middle of nowhere—and the "I'm not sure, it's around here somewhere" crap Anton was pulling with her—were shredding what little trust they'd started to build.

"Do you honestly need me to explain it again?"

Yes, she did. "I'm a little slow sometimes, Anton." More accurately, she still didn't entirely believe him. Checking whether or not he was lying would be easy, if she were willing to touch him. But between the kiss and the strangeness that had happened back at the surplus store? Nuh-uh, no thank you. Not yet, anyway.

He shifted in the seat. "You don't expect me to believe that, do you? You still don't trust me. What do you think I'm doing, luring you into some kind of trap? What, like I've got us tooling around in the woods to kill time until I can rendezvous with the rest of the coven?"

Uh. "I don't think that."

"You do, don't you? Good grief, Tyra, I get why you have your doubts, but I'm doing everything I can here to prove I'm on the level. Sweet Jesus, if I was really out to kidnap or kill you, this wouldn't be the best way to go about it. What about… hmm, I don't know… maybe *when you were in a coma*?"

One side of her mouth lifted in a sneer.

"Or what about the fact that I've spent the past two days crashing in your bedroom while we hashed out a plan to go after my father? I could have snuck out during the day to go take out half the vampires on that estate while you were taking a shower. I could have gone after your king and queen. I mean, come on, what better way to make your kind vulnerable than to take out your leader? Be easy for the wizards to pick the vampires off like frightened rats without the king's military to protect 'em."

He was absolutely correct. That had been the reason Thad was so desperate to find Isabel after their parents passed. Their race had always relied on strong leadership. And she could admit that part of her felt oddly comfortable in Anton's presence. Another part, however, couldn't stop thinking about the very bad ways that this entire situation could go wrong. "I took a very quick shower."

She glanced at Anton in the passenger seat from the corner of her eye. Even in the scant evening light, an angry red flush was clearly visible on his face. Maybe it was inherent in the rivalry between their two races, but boy, they could really push each other's buttons.

"You must trust me on some level or you would have had my head days ago, so I have to wonder what all of this is really about."

"Because I can't afford to be wrong." Tyra's palm slammed the steering wheel. Damn. She hadn't meant to blurt that out. A surge of adrenaline whooshed through her body as the words flew from her mouth, like they were being yanked out forcefully. She shook all over and couldn't seem to stop.

"Pull over," he said,

She did. By God, she actually did. As much as she usually bristled over being told what to do, she jerked the car to a stop right on the edge of a grove of evergreens.

Anton lifted his hand, let it hover, and then pulled it back. Apparently she wasn't the only one who thought they kept tripping over each other. Or maybe he just didn't want her to read him. Not that she would even try right now. She could barely manage her own emotions at the moment.

She looked around. "Where are we, anyway? It looks like we're practically in Maryland."

"We're probably close." He unbuckled and stepped out to look around, leaving Tyra with a disturbingly attractive view of his lower body's anatomy framed by the opening in the vehicle's passenger doorway.

Lord, what was it with her and dysfunctional men? Was she honestly the kind of too-dumb-to-survive female that would find herself attracted to a man who had originally been sent to kill her? Okay, not kill. *Kidnap.* Nearly as bad, in the grand scheme. Hell, there was nothing new about being a female who dug the bad-boy type, but this made her past relationship with Siddoh look like a case study for healthy and well-adjusted.

Light was fading fast. Tyra pried her gaze from the hug of Anton's BDUs on his muscular ass and got out. Funny how she'd never thought of those pants as particularly sexy before. The evening was quiet and peaceful, smelling of pine and snow and far-off fires in cozy homes. It was an interesting counterpoint to the purpose of their presence in these woods. The whole tableau made her long for a warm bed and blankets she could crawl under and pretend none of this mess existed. "So," she said. "Where to?"

"Well, this thing…" Anton dug into his pocket and produced a gold signet wizard ring. He grimaced when it slid over his pinkie knuckle, and Tyra couldn't suppress her own shiver. That ring represented death— either the wearer's or her vampire brethren's—and seeing Anton push it onto his finger like that was hard to make peace with.

"It acts kind of like a divining rod. The portal moves. Sometimes week to week or night to night. We feel around, and either we'll sense some of the higher-up wizards or my ring will lead us to the portal. We find the portal and we find my father." Anton's intense gaze appraised her from across the Land Rover's black roof.

While she met his gaze with confidence, guilt gnawed at her insides. Evil lineage aside, Anton seemed to be a decent guy, and she hadn't given him a lot of choice in what they were about to do. "Anton, just help me find the portal, and then you can go. I don't want you to have to go up against your own father." Okay, so there was still a niggle of doubt. What if Anton's decision came down to his father or Tyra, and he chose daddy dearest?

Maybe the doubt was more than a niggle.

"Tyra," Anton said quietly. God, his voice was so deep.

He came around to the front of the car and faced her. After a moment he lifted his hands, hesitated, and then grasped her shoulders firmly. A flurry of emotions flowed into her: fear, anger, determination, and a massive truckload of very raw *need*. It wasn't sexual, not exactly. More like an intense emotional desire she couldn't quite name, but it manifested in her body as something sensual—and now was so, so not the time.

"I don't think you've been listening. Everything that I have gone through: the wizards leaving me for dead in the woods, letting you drink my blood, watching over you while you were in torpor, bringing you here to find my father. All of it has been because I am trying to keep you alive.

"For that matter, I'm trying to help keep your whole fucking race alive because what my father has done is vile and I am disgusted by it and I am trying to right a *wrong*, here. Now." He stepped back and pegged her with a daring look. "I am coming with you, and that's not up for negotiation unless you intend to take me out right now."

And if she did that, she wouldn't find the portal. *Shit*. Tyra parted her lips to answer, but a white flash and a bang from deep within the woods caught their attention. Anton hauled ass toward it. "Anton. Shit." He was fast, too. Not to mention unarmed. How stupid. She shook her head and took off right behind him, as fast as her supernaturally powered legs would go.

―――∾―――

Anton peered around the trunk of a large tree while two wizards fumbled with what must have been newly acquired powers. They were so engrossed that they had no clue he was there. Seconds later, Tyra bumped into his back and he grunted softly. "If I didn't know better, I'd think you were trying to knock me down," he whispered.

Truthfully, he'd be lying through his teeth if he said he didn't appreciate having her warm body pressed against his back.

Her response was to wrap her arms around his waist and press her body flush against his again. Hell. Even with his eyes trained on the two wizards a few feet away, he was asshole enough to shift accidentally on purpose so that his ass rubbed against her a little more. His dick was nudging against his button fly in no time.

He glanced down in time to see the pants in question disappear from his own view. Okay, it was dark, but it wasn't *that* dark. This must be one of her powers. Most vampires only had one or two, but she had more than that. It was the reason why his father had wanted to "acquire" her.

Ick.

The shock didn't last long. In contrast to the winter chill, Tyra's hands were warm against Anton's cold skin, and her moist lips brushed against his ear. "Shh. I can make it so they can't see us, but I don't have a mute button."

Uh-huh. "Okay." Dammit to hell. They were on their way into what was most likely a losing battle, and he couldn't get his act together. He hadn't foreseen that being a twenty-seven-year old almost-virgin was going to bite him in the ass when he was finally in close proximity with his dream woman... vampire... woman. It was *far* too late to go back in time to bang those hookers his brother had gotten for him. Whatever.

He turned his head. Their lips were uncomfortably close when he said, "If you look carefully, you can see a dark circle where those two are standing. That's the portal. We can wait until they move on and then go through."

"Or we could go ahead and take them out now," she whispered.

He shook his head. "No, we need to be patient here."

"I'm not impatient. I'm talking about taking out two newbie wizards before they go out into the world and inflict damage on any vampires."

Anton turned more so that he could whisper directly into her ear. Much as he tried to ignore it, the move nestled his left butt cheek right into the soft place between her thighs, and the ache behind his button fly got more intense. Tyra, however, didn't seem to notice at all. Perhaps his father had gone about things all wrong with his "males only" policy. If Tyra was anything to go by, women clearly had better focus.

Too impulsive maybe, but focused.

He managed to find his voice again. "You need to keep your powers fully charged until we go up against my father."

Her body got very stiff against his. "There's no 'we' in this. I told you, I can handle your father."

Had she not been listening? He grasped her arm and

dug his fingers in. "You are completely stupid if you think I'm going to let you go in there without me."

"You don't have any powers," she hissed.

Well, he did have the ability to heal. He hadn't mastered it, though, and it wouldn't help him fight. And he hadn't mentioned it to Tyra yet, lest letting her know that he had participated in the claiming ritual would destroy what little credibility he had with her.

The two of them stood there gripping each other in the darkness, their stares locked angrily in the glows from the occasional flash of the wizards practicing nearby. "You're really planning to die in there," he whispered.

He couldn't believe she actually rolled her eyes at him again. "Of course I am. I thought we had established that."

"I thought you were at least going to *try*. He thinks I'm dead. I can distract him. You might be able to take him out before he attacks you."

She held up a hand. Soft fingertips brushed his lips. "If he's as powerful as you say, then you and I don't really stand a chance. My hope is to put him out of business without the deaths of any more of my kind. I don't want any more of us to die.

"And even though I should, I don't want you to die, either. Besides, you keep saying he has been after me all this time. If I fail, I need you to survive so you can go and tell my family. So you can give them the same information that you gave me. Okay?"

His fingers tightened on her arm. "Not okay. We go in together."

"You can't stop me," she said with a lift of her chin.

He pulled her body tighter against his. "Well, I've gone through a hell of a lot so far to keep you safe, and for damn sure I'll give it my best try now. It's bad enough that I said I'd let you find the portal. If you think you're going in there without me, you've got—"

Fiery pain lanced through his body, cutting across his back and the tender, fleshy part of his side. Suddenly it was impossible to breathe, and dizziness descended upon him like some kind of locust swarm. He opened his mouth to tell Tyra to run, to just get the hell out. Maybe if the errant wizard blast didn't kill him, she could come back later when it was safe. All that came out was a faint, raspy groan.

"Shit, Anton. You're hit bad."

The ground rushed up to meet him, and before his face got intimate with the dirt and dead pine needles, the two young wizards turned to advance on their location. Tyra's nifty cloaking device must have stopped working.

That couldn't possibly be good.

Chapter 8

"WHOO! YEAH, BABY." AMID SHOUTS OF ENCOURAGE-ment and flashes of laser light, Alexia managed to do a shot of a Buttery Nipple on the scarred wooden bar without using her hands, while a dozen or so of her new buddies looked on. One of her arms was slung around the shoulders of a bleach-bottle platinum blonde whose sequined shift barely held in the bounty of her gravity-defying knockers. Her new BFF Tanya… Tonya… cool chick, whatever her name was. Terrible clothing choices and the fact that she was kind of a weepy drunk aside.

But Siddoh coming at her from the other end of the bar, and the sour look on his face, meant that the fun was about to be over.

"Shit, Lexi." Siddoh jerked his head and pointed to the burly earbud-sporting males stationed at the far end of the crowded room. "You're drawing too much atten-tion, and I don't want to have to tangle with security. I manage to make those types nervous."

She supposed she could see that. Siddoh was a big vampire. Not quite as tall as Lee but broader and a little more muscular, if such a thing were possible. His disheveled hair and tattoos made Siddoh look exactly like the kind of guy who might start a bar fight. He also looked like the kind of guy not to fuck with, which was why Alexia enjoyed having him along as a drinking buddy. Until he poured cold water on all her fun.

"One more round, Siddoh." She stuck out her lower lip, and for a second it looked like she had him, but the final straw came when a shady-looking guy in a shiny, dragon-covered button-down decided to try and put his arm around Alexia's shoulder. She'd talked to him a little earlier in the night, and she and Siddoh weren't an item, but it was the wrong time to get territorial.

Siddoh pushed his way through the gathered cluster of gin-soaked onlookers, wrapping one hand around the nerdy guy's upper arm and the other around Lexi's. "C'mon, girlie. I'm about to turn into a pumpkin, and I think you are as well."

He pushed Nerd Guy a little too hard, and the man's indignant yell of "Hey, asshole"—plus the flailing limbs that almost knocked over a dancing bar girl—got security's attention. Okay, Siddoh could *not* blame Alexia for this one.

Definitely time to go. The cold gust of night air was exactly what she needed to take the edge off her buzz and her irritation.

Siddoh's impatient growl carried on the chilly wind. "You were having a little too much fun in there. If you keep that shit up, you won't be allowed in the door any longer."

For a minute or so there was silence, punctuated by the frantic clatter of Lexi's high-heeled boots as her short human legs tried to keep up with his longer, faster ones. "You didn't have to come with me, you know. And I'm not the one who almost started a bar fight." Chances were good that he wouldn't respond to that last bit. She'd learned fairly quickly that vampire males refused to be wrong. Come to think of it, maybe that was all males.

When they got to their parking spot, Siddoh beeped the locks on his black Land Rover and held the passenger door open while she sidled past. "Lexi." She stopped in the opening of the door. His expression softened a little. "This area isn't safe enough for you to go out on your own."

She gave him the defensive side of her chin. "I can take care of myself." Back home in Orlando, she went out by herself all the time. She could do it here, too. She didn't want someone spending time with her who didn't *like* to spend time with her. She hated to be a burden.

Her hands rubbed briskly over the gooseflesh rising on her bare arms. Why didn't she ever remember to wear a coat?

He pulled off his jacket and put it around her shoulders. It so dwarfed her that it completely covered the dress she was wearing. Now she looked like a dork. "You're the queen's best friend, Lex. You know full well that Thad would have my balls if I had let you go out alone. It's not the same here as it was back in Orlando. Heaven forbid a wizard spotted you leaving the estate. Besides…" Siddoh took a step back, simultaneously hunching his shoulders and running a tongue around his fangs. "Besides, I'd like to think we've become friends, haven't we? I like hanging out with you."

A smile tugged at one side of her mouth. She hadn't been aware of the tension in her chest that leaked out now. "You seemed mad back there."

He lifted an eyebrow. "Didn't want to have to tangle with security, is all. What's this about? Are you okay?"

Alexia scowled. A lot of things weren't okay, but she couldn't discuss them with anyone. Not even Siddoh, although she felt she could trust him as much as anyone. She was the only human in a microcosm of vampires. She missed Isabel. Sure, they still lived in the same house but now Isabel was pregnant and learning to be queen to a vampire race. And Lexi was jonesing hard for a seven-hundred-year-old vampire who thought she was inferior at a basic biological level.

Talk about culture shock.

At the same time, she knew from past personal experience that bad shit happened when she kept everything inside. She didn't have to give him her life story or anything. "It's just been a rough transition since I came here. I've been thinking maybe—"

"I'm sorry, sweetie. Hold that thought for a second." Siddoh took another step back, pulling a buzzing cell phone from his pocket while Lexi scrambled into the vehicle. "Tyra's calling."

As he flipped the phone open, Alexia rummaged in her purse for a bottle of water and some pills. Dramamine and ibuprofen. Her favorite anti-hangover cocktail. No, it didn't speak well that she *had* a favorite anti-hangover cocktail, but that was a different issue.

"What's up, Ty?" The door banged and Siddoh was a blur of motion, rounding the front of the car and jumping behind the wheel. "Ty, honey. What's wrong?" Siddoh's voice was as tight and controlled as his body language. So unlike his usually laid-back manner. He threw the car in reverse and punched the gas.

Wheels spun on pavement, and Lexi flailed, making a hasty grab for the "oh shit" handle when he braked again and switched into drive just as quickly.

"You hurt, Ty?" Another beat of hesitation. "What

happened? I thought you were on break for a while. Ty. *Ty*." Siddoh flipped his phone shut and stopped a hair's breadth from slamming it on the console. "She fucking hung up on me."

He picked it up again and punched the speed dial. "Hey there, Abel. It's Siddoh. I need you to get over to Tyra's place, stat. Sounds like an injured fighter. I don't have the details." The phone flipped closed, and he chucked it into the console with far more force than necessary. His foot pressed heavily on the gas.

"What's wrong?" The glow of the dashboard instrument panel illuminated Siddoh's white-knuckled grip on the steering wheel.

"Don't know exactly, but I guarantee you it's bad." He cranked the stereo, his fingers tapping in time to vintage Nine Inch Nails as they flew back toward Ash Falls, Virginia.

God willing, Lexi wouldn't puke before they made it back to the estate, because it didn't look like he was going to slow down. Forget about pulling over. "I guess you'll find out soon enough." Her stomach lurched.

"Guess so."

"Siddoh, don't you think you ought to slow down till we get out of DC at least? It won't help Tyra if we get pulled over on the way back."

He blasted through a yellow light before it turned. "They'll have to catch up with me first," he said.

The way Thad was pacing Tyra's living room, he was going to wear a track in the carpet. "I swear, with God and everyone here as my witness, Ty, I am going to kill you myself and bring your ass back so I can kill you again. I cannot *believe* my own sister would do something this fucking stupid."

Thad had hired a new doctor, Abel something or another, in Tyra's absence. Backup to ensure medical coverage for the couple of pregnancies on the estate, as well as the soldiers who might need care. The older vampire bustled around Anton, checking vitals and cleaning up his wounds.

Tyra did her best to tune out Thad and his pacing. She rocked back on her heels, measuring the gentle rise and fall of Anton's chest. The worst of his injuries, an oozing gash that ran diagonally from his lower back to below his right nipple, finally seemed to be drying up. It had taken a good couple of hours.

The tan microsuede of her comfy, overstuffed sectional sofa would never be the same. Nor would the creamy plush of her living room carpet. And there was a chance that a tiny patch of wall in the foyer would need to be repainted. She had lost her footing bringing Anton's body in the door, and she suspected that blood didn't clean off flat latex too easily.

She stood and shook her head sadly. "I tried to tell him to get out of there so he wouldn't get hurt." That he *had* been hurt was doing funny things to her ability to breathe. Guilt, that was what it was. Without supernatural powers of any kind, Anton had been ill-equipped to go into that situation. She should have put her foot down.

Thad's rapid pacing stopped abruptly, and courtesy of his newfound firepower, his feelings on the matter couldn't have been more obvious if he had set her ablaze. Not that she needed verification of his anger. The blast of heat might have knocked her backward if the cold granite counter of her breakfast bar wasn't already digging into her ass. Thad stalked over, fists clenched and temperature soaring. She drew in a deep sigh and let it out slowly.

Here it came.

"You. Bring. A human. Not a human. A *wizard* inside the walls of this estate. A wizard you should have taken care of the *second* you knew who he was." He stopped to rub a spot above his eye, and while Tyra was vaguely aware of the irate heaving of her brother's chest and the muscle jumping in his jaw, it took all of her self-control not to make him move from her line of sight so she could tell what the doctor was doing to Anton.

"And you bring him *here*, Ty, after going out without telling a soul to do what? Try to kill their leader, who has been around longer than you or I have been alive. By yourself. I'm going to say it again: how fucking stupid are you?"

"You said Lee went out on a solo mission to find the wizard leader. I, at least, took backup."

"Lee," Thad ground out, "is older, stronger, and has about six-*hundred* more years of fighting experience under his belt than you do. And yeah, if you had stopped to think before running off into the night kamikaze-style with your new enemy boyfriend, you would have realized that your little mission to kill the wizard leader was pointless. Not even Lee was able to get it done."

Tyra's eyes flicked up to the stamped pattern on her ceiling. "He isn't my boyfriend. Besides Lee didn't have inside information." She gestured to Anton.

"You know what, Ty? Save it. I have to get ready for an Elders' Council meeting, and frankly I can barely stand to look at you right now." Thad jabbed a finger in Anton's direction. "If he so much as causes a paper cut around here, I am holding you personally responsible. And God help you if a single one of his brethren shows up on our doorstep because he blew the whistle on our location." He thrust both hands into his short, dirty blond hair. "Jesus Christ, Ty, we've been safe in this location for over a century, and now we're at risk of you bringing it all down like a house of cards."

The thought made Tyra squirm, but damned if she'd ever voice her doubts to Thad. She *had* to believe that Anton was on their side. But she acknowledged, if only to herself, that it was one serious motherfucker of a risk.

"I told you, Thad, he isn't like that. They tried to kill him because he wanted out." Okay, so that wasn't exactly accurate. She'd been forced already to lay most of her cards on the table. Otherwise, there was no good way to explain where she'd been or how Anton had gotten injured. But that he'd nearly died in an effort to protect Tyra because the wizards were out for *her* specifically? That would only make Thad more nervous.

Thad's mouth opened like he was about to respond, but a pained moan from the couch shut it again.

"And how are we feeling, sir?" That was the voice of Abel, who seemed to have a rather jolly disposition. Probably a necessary attribute for tending to cranky, injured vampires all night.

Anton mumbled some sort of response to the doctor.

Tyra should have been able to hear it, but the roar of Thad's lecture made it impossible to catch a word. She took a step, ready to push past Thad so she could get a look at Anton, but her brother was still staring her down with murder in his eyes.

Thad sucked in a breath and pointed toward the sofa one more time. "For everyone's sake, you better pray to whatever deity is listening that you're right about this guy." He drew back, pointing in opposite directions to Lee and Siddoh, who until that moment had been standing so silently on opposite ends of her living room that she'd forgotten they were there. "I'm posting a guard on him," Thad growled.

Well, she should have expected that.

"Lee, you're coming with me. Siddoh, take the first watch with our guest here." Thad's sneer of distaste was impossible to miss, if for no other reason than that it was completely out of character for her once mild-mannered brother. Clearly, a lot had changed.

Lexi, who had come in with Siddoh, was backed into the corner of Tyra's living room between the entrance to the underground tunnels and the coat closet. They'd been on the way back from somewhere. Alexia still wore Siddoh's jacket and a very wary expression. Tyra couldn't blame the girl for giving Thad a wide berth. Aside from bending down to remove her foot-murdering high-heeled boots, the human hadn't moved.

The small blonde almost shot into the air when Thad snapped his fingers in her direction. "Alexia, come back to the house with us. Isabel could use the company."

Siddoh gave a curt nod to his king as Thad, Lee, and Alexia left the room and then resumed a watchful and ready stance by the front door. His eyes were flat and firmly fixed on his new prisoner.

Apparently Thad wasn't the only one who couldn't stand to look at her.

Chapter 9

Anton breathed slowly and carefully, a controlled in and out that served both to lessen the stabbing pain in his side and to delay announcing to the room that he was conscious. His ears worked fine, but his brain was still churning through sludge. The gist was perfectly clear: Tyra had told her brother who Anton was, and the shit had hit the fan.

It was a little hard to believe that he wasn't dead yet. How much time had they wasted while the doctor checked him over and the king read Tyra the riot act? Hours? Not that Anton was going to point that out, but instead of spending half the night and precious vampire-strength painkillers, they could've cut to the chase and more expediently done what everyone there knew they were probably going to do to him anyway.

But then none of that mattered because Tyra was close, the heat of her breath puffing against his cheek. The muscles in his neck twitched and burned with the urge to turn toward her. To open his eyes so that he could gauge the expression on her face. Maybe he could give them all the information they wanted and skip straight to the part where they killed him. He wasn't afraid to die, but he'd be happy to take a pass on more torture.

A shadow fell over his face. "Anton."

The whisper caused a gentle flutter of Tyra's soft, damp lips against Anton's outer ear. Another puff of breath curled around the base of his neck and sent a shiver down his spine. His breath caught. Dammit, Anton wanted to look at her face. But that male—the one who had been here before, and whose voice had been colored with tones of possession and familiarity—was still in the room.

A warm puff of Tyra's breath hit Anton's skin. "I'm sorry I had to tell them. There was no other way for me to explain why I'd been with you. How you'd been injured."

The brief frisson of excitement was chased down by a full-scale stiffening of his body of an entirely different variety. He groaned at the pain it caused. "Why did you even bother?"

Now Tyra stiffened, throwing off the kind of angry heat that one might expect to experience from, say, a sudden nuclear explosion. "That's some gratitude you've got."

Gratitude? "Either way I was dead before we set out at the beginning of the night. Why prolong things?" He breathed the words in a low tone that, God willing, only she could hear.

"What the hell are you talking about? I saved your life out there," she hissed.

Goddamn, he was too hurt and exhausted for this shit. "Do we really have to rehash this? They're going to kill me as soon as your brother has all the information he wants from me."

"You saved my life. Thad will understand. I'll make him understand."

"No *way* is he going to give a shit about that, honey." The volume of both their voices had risen, but Anton didn't care. He was sweating now, his body vibrating intensely with an unfamiliar rage. He finally gave up the ridiculous pretense and opened his eyes, turning his head slightly to face her. Brown eyes flashed only inches from his own, dark and full of fire.

Tyra's jaw clenched, her lips pressed together into a thin line. "I am not your hon—"

A shrill whistle cut through the electricity between them. "Sorry to interrupt the love fest, Ty, but I'm gonna have to ask you to stop talking to the prisoner."

Tyra rose to her feet, whirling to face the growling Siddoh. She vibrated with even more rage than Anton. Thankfully it was no longer aimed at him, but at the beefy vampire across the room instead. "He isn't a prisoner, Sid."

The large vampire—Siddoh, his name was?—cut her off with a snarl. "You are fucked in the head, Ty, if you honestly believe that. Thad wouldn't have me standing here if he weren't. Son of a bitch is lucky he isn't being held in an interrogation cell."

An excruciating pull in Anton's side made it a fight to sit up. Still, he gritted his teeth and pushed forward. He would not stand for Tyra being treated like that.

"Siddoh, he kept me safe for almost two weeks. You have no grounds upon which to treat him like a criminal." Tyra advanced fearlessly toward Siddoh, shoulders squared and head held high. Her loose curls were in wild disarray from the wind outside, which only made her seem more feral as she challenged the big vampire. She looked for all the world like she was ready to take him on in any way necessary. She was gorgeous like that.

Siddoh stepped forward as well. "Which *might* mean Thad lets him die quick instead of slow."

Anton stepped forward, panting through each stab of pain. He ignored the damp trickle down his side. Siddoh and Tyra were toe to toe now, two hot-tempered vampires coursing with barely contained fury.

"No one is killing him. I am Thad's sister, for chrissakes, and I am telling you—"

"You aren't shit anymore, Sister. He is our enemy, and he's in serious trouble just for being here." Siddoh's mighty bellow was accompanied by a shove of his ugly, meaty hand against Tyra's shoulder, sending her back a few steps.

Oh, hell fucking no. Before he even thought it through, Anton had launched through the air, ignoring the head-spinning nausea and the scream in his side. "Don't you touch her!"

Shit. One second Anton was launching himself at a seething wall of vampire, and the next, Siddoh had disappeared entirely. The blow came from behind. White light exploded behind Anton's eyes, and the plush white of Tyra's living room carpet smacked him in the face. He followed the sound of boot steps, pushing away from the floor to confront Siddoh again, but a powerful wave of dizziness pulled him sideways.

"Anton?"

Tyra's hands were warm and reassuring as they pressed gently on either side of his face. Once again he was bleeding from somewhere. The fresh, bright red against the white fibers struck him as bad, but through his rattled brain and the ringing in his ears, Anton couldn't make sense of it.

Someone tried to help him up. Tyra. Boy, she smelled good. "Anton. My God, Siddoh, what did you to do him?"

Anton groaned, and the angry voices faded away. Everything was so blurry all of a sudden. So much for being the white knight.

———

"Oh God. Oh God. *Fuck*." Thad's fingers clawed at the sheets. He stilled, his release coming just as Isabel bent over him, fangs extended, to rip into his flesh. Sore and spent, he lay still and let his breath come under control as his blood flowed freely. Likely he was bruised head to toe.

Isabel sucked hungrily, and after taking her fill and lapping at his wound, a trickle of his blood still leaked from the corner of her mouth. Her hair was wild and full, flowing over her shoulders. Ten points of pain, five on each arm, told Thad her nails were still embedded in his skin. The pregnancy had turned Isabel's need, both for his flesh and for his blood, into something base, carnal, and altogether primal. Thad fucking loved it.

"Did I hurt you?" The languorous sweep of Isabel's tongue over that stray rivulet of blood and the catlike curve of her lips showed that his female knew just how much he enjoyed these wild lovemaking sessions. He brought his wrist to his mouth to seal another leaking puncture with his own saliva.

"Of course you did," he murmured to his mate. His body was leaden and wrung out from the frenzy, which had been just exactly what he needed. The world outside their bedroom door was more than he could handle on so many occasions, and given that handling it was exactly what he had pledged to spend the remainder of his days doing, he reveled in knowing that one thing he could do for certain was please Isabel.

They'd come such a long way together in such a short time, with Isabel changing from the party girl who had run away from him when he'd first found her to the trusted lover and confidante he now had.

Isabel curled against Thad's side. He lazily combed his fingers through the soft auburn waves of her hair and then trailed his fingers over her damp skin. Foggy mist hung in the air, a result of their union. When the two of them made love, Thad's power of fire and Isabel's ability to produce ice came together in a most explosive way, sometimes producing a light mist and sometimes enough steam to turn their master suite into a sauna. The drawers in each of the two bedside tables were already starting to stick, as was the door on Isabel's closet.

Perhaps they needed to replace everything in the room with deck furniture.

"Feeling any better?" His mate ran a lovely, pale manicured hand over his chest. Thad sighed into the touch, bringing the hand to his lips so that he could kiss and lick the salty sweat from her fingers. An essence of something sweet, like vanilla sugar, lay on her skin as well.

One more deep, bolstering breath and Thad nudged Isabel to the side. He needed nearly every spare ounce of energy to get his ass out of the privacy of their curtained, walnut four-poster bed. He hated the loss of Isabel's warmth.

"Better?" He shrugged and bent to retrieve a discarded pair of black fatigues and a rumpled shirt from the floor. "You popped a button, love." He smiled wryly and tossed it into the special bin the maid had placed beside the dresser for damaged clothing in need of repair. Most fighters had such a bin. Fighting was a messy business, after all. But Thad's bin had never seen as much action as it had since he'd stopped fighting and mated with Isabel.

"A little more relaxed, at least?" Her brow furrowed in that way it did when she was worried, creating an amusing topography of hills and valleys on her face. Thad leaned down to kiss the spot above her nose where the deepest of the frown lines ended. His hand smoothed over the skin, willing it back to normal. His finger traced carefully over a scar on her throat from a childhood accident. She regarded him thoughtfully with green eyes, one clear but one cloudy from that same accident that had left her an orphan.

"A little. Thanks." Though even as he said the words, responsibilities that lay just outside their door came barreling into his mind, causing his muscles to draw tight and his heart to beat faster.

Thad deliberately turned his back while he donned his pants and rummaged in his smaller closet to find a clean shirt. When at last he was dressed, socks on and boots laced, he chanced a look at the bed. Isabel's expression was deadpan, and her arms were crossed over her ample breasts as she sat propped against the headboard.

That otherworldly left eye narrowed at him from across the room. "See, I know you're not trying to bullshit me, Thad, because I just drank your blood."

Uh-uh.

Hands on hips, Thad shook his head slowly. "I'm not

trying to bullshit you." He dropped his chin to his chest and sighed. "I just can't wrap my head around what Ty was thinking in trusting this guy. I can't fucking believe—" At Isabel's visible wince he stopped short and lowered his voice. Her preternatural hearing was off the charts these days.

"Sorry. I just can't believe Ty was stupid enough to bring an enemy into our midst like that. And then there's Lee. After seven hundred years he makes a boneheaded move like leaving her with this guy for more than a week? I don't know what to do with any of it. I can't let it go unanswered."

"You said this man protected her."

"Wizard," Thad ground out.

"Okay. Wizard." After a nasty smirk aimed in his direction, she rose from the bed so she could slide into her robe. Thad's annoyance died away and his heart clenched at the sight of her voluptuous curves disappearing beneath layers of peachy satin. "So this supposed wizard helped her. He offered her blood and protected her for days while she was in torpor.

"Lee, your guard, your friend, who has pledged his life to keeping your family—*our* family—safe, took an incredibly dangerous mission upon himself. He used those centuries of experience to make a judgment call that he was leaving Tyra with a concerned individual so he could try to finally kill the monster who most threatened not just her life but the lives of all of our kind.

"There must have been no malevolent aura about this man. Lee is old enough, strong enough, that he would have sensed it, even if it were subtle. For that matter, Tyra can read emotions. She ought to have felt it if this

guy was dangerous to her. I know she's impulsive sometimes, but your sister is not stupid. I can't see her putting
herself in his grasp at her most vulnerable healing time
if she sensed any kind of danger from him."

"Isabel…"

Isabel silenced Thad's protest with one lift of a finger,
and he stifled a growl. She was with child, of course, but
there were limits to Thad's patience, even with her. He
strode impatiently back and forth across the length of
their bedroom.

"So that means probably this wizard was telling the
truth about his intentions. Maybe he really was trying to
help Tyra find the secret lair or whatever, not lead her
into a trap. And maybe he really is willing to help us."

Thad scrubbed a hand over his face. "The fact that he
saved Tyra's life is why he's under guard in her house
and not locked in a solitary cell across the estate. But I
cannot just ignore who and what he is, or the fact that
Tyra kept pertinent information from me."

Suddenly Isabel was behind him. Warm arms,
breasts, and gently swollen belly pressing. She wasn't
very far along, but vampire pregnancies progressed
quickly. Feeling evidence of his offspring inside her was
a turn-on. His cock swelled slightly despite his exhaustion. Despite the fact that it hadn't been long since the
last time.

"What are you going to do if it's something more
serious with this male than just saving her life? After all,
we both know how grateful I was when you saved my
life not so long ago."

The very memory of Isabel's gratitude the night he'd
saved her from being kidnapped by wizards kicked his

body temperature into high gear in a very pleasant way. Thad turned into her embrace. Her lips were warm and soft against his when he claimed her mouth. A trace of his own blood lingered when his tongue swept inside. If only he could kiss her forever, or at least until this whole terrible business with Tyra and that wizard got straightened out.

"Jesus, Isabel, I really hope you're wrong about that. If she is involved with this wizard intimately, it's even less likely that I can trust her judgment."

Isabel pulled away, and for all his power and station, he fidgeted uncomfortably under the intensity of her stare. "When you met me, you didn't know me. I was a stranger. A prophecy brought you to me. What if someone had told you then that I couldn't be trusted? That your assessment of me could not be counted on because your belief in the prophecy had clouded your judgment? Or if somebody had suggested that I was an unworthy queen because my best friend was a human?" Her breath caught on a sob. Thad reached to comfort her, but she held up a hand. "Or that I was a danger to our race because I got myself captured by wizards and ended up getting one of your fighters killed in the process?"

Thad's heart ached. For Isabel's pain and guilt, and for his own loss of a good friend and a good soldier. His arms reached for her almost automatically. The flesh on his fingers itched to thread through her soft mane of hair and pull her tight. But he would always wait for Isabel to come to him, like a wild animal that could never be tamed. When she remained a mere arm's length apart from him, and at the same time worlds away, Thad sighed with his arms akimbo and his head dropped back onto his shoulders.

"Okay, I see what you're trying to get at, but it's a very different situation, Isabel. And fair or not, I'm king and Tyra isn't the one in charge. It still falls to me to make these decisions. If she is wrong about this wizard and his intentions, then our race is in far greater jeopardy than it has ever been. And the blame will lie on my shoulders, not hers."

Isabel's arms crossed over her chest, and her expression changed to one that Thad could not give name to but had quickly learned to recognize. Whatever was about to come out of her mouth would be exceedingly reasonable and would somehow at the same time make him want to put his fist through a wall.

"So talk to him, Thad. I don't mean sit him down and interrogate him, I mean talk. You're a good judge of character, and if you need to get your own warm and fuzzy that Tyra is judging him accurately, then this is the way to do that. And talk to *her*, while you're at it. I suspect you've done nothing but yell since she's gotten back. She's made some mistakes, but she had good reason for them, so find out what they were before you convict your own sister."

Thad's jaw cracked. "Yelling isn't all I've done."

The quirk of Isabel's eyebrow made it exceedingly clear that she didn't believe that. "Talk to her, Thad."

In the midst of letting out the longest breath he could manage, Thad's jaw cracked painfully again, and loudly enough that even Isabel winced. His gut soured and knotted. His mate was right. Still, his pride could not countenance being told how to handle this situation by her or by anyone else. Wisely, even Lee and Siddoh had refrained from offering their two cents.

Tension spread throughout his body despite the marathon lovemaking only minutes before. That Isabel could feel his anger was as clear as the nose on her face. She held his gaze with an unwavering stare. If they tried to make this a contest, they'd be here all night. Thad growled and spun on his heel. "I have the Council meeting."

"Thad." He'd just reached the door when the soft warmth of Isabel's body pressed against his back. Her arms wrapped around his. They breathed together like that, totally in sync, until Thad's muscles unwound again. "It isn't you against everyone. I'm trying to help."

He turned over his shoulder to kiss her. "I know," he said.

Chapter 10

TYRA'S FANGS SANK INTO HER FLESH. PAIN SHOT FROM her wrist to her elbow, and disbelief at the sight of her own blood stunned her for longer than it should have. The heavy, slow thuds of her own heart echoed loudly in the quiet of her bedroom.

Ouch. She'd never bitten into her own vein, and she wasn't holding on to another body to ground herself, so her fangs didn't hit their mark cleanly.

Anton mumbled incoherently but didn't exactly answer her. Not that she'd expected him to. He'd been barely there for most of the day, aside from occasional restless flailing and a more recent bout of shivers. The shivering was somewhat contradictory, given that he was sweating so profusely that he'd dampened her nicest thousand-thread-count sheets and his forehead was hot to the touch.

Thanks to her hesitation, fat drops of blood hit her silk duvet before she managed to position the flow over Anton's mouth. Between this and the living room, her house was starting to look like some kind of war zone.

"Okay, Anton." Her fingers brushed lightly over his lips to pull his mouth open. Her index finger had a jagged nail, and she didn't want to scratch him. Silly as *that* was. The doctor had given him a sedative, but he was moving more. Hopefully that meant he'd be able to drink on his own. "You helped me, so it's time I return the favor."

While the blood drizzled in, Tyra looked out through the cracked window blinds. The sun would be going down soon. Just before dawn, she'd forcibly removed Siddoh from the house and moved Anton to the bed so he could rest more comfortably.

Despite her assurances that she'd call when Anton was awake, she was dead-certain that someone would return at dusk and it wouldn't be pretty. But Anton's condition had worsened over the day, and the doctor had bluntly stated that he didn't know a thing about how to treat a wizard medically. Why would he, after all? They'd never cared about healing one before.

Tyra was short on time as well as options.

"Come on, Anton. Work with me here." Her fingers slid over his throat in the hope that would encourage the first swallow. He coughed and sputtered. *Jeez, don't kill him, Ty.* The wet sounds of his throat working were far more satisfying than they should have been.

Along with the hot, tight seal of his mouth against her arm came a slushy, cold sensation of fear. It pushed along her arm and spread through her body like a moving glacier. She'd never experienced anything quite like that from anybody before. But then there was another hard gulp. And another.

Her relief was immense and dizzying. Anton groaned in his half sleep and swallowed again, tipping his head unconsciously and sliding his tongue on her skin for better suction. His breath deepened audibly, and his bare chest rose and fell with the effort. Something deep and primitive and fiery stirred inside Tyra. Something she'd never experienced before.

She knelt there by the bed, her breath coming in

shallow pants while her free hand gripped a fistful of duvet. "Oh hell."

Sometimes the blood exchange was sensual, sure. But this… a rush of desire chased Anton's panic, melting the icy slush as it flowed from his body into hers and pooling deep in her core. It couldn't even possibly be something he was conscious of.

Anton sucked harder and Tyra gasped. A part of her was embarrassed at having such a very base response, even though nobody was there to witness it. Not even him, actually. His eyes were still closed, and though he reacted physically, he clearly was still on a different plane somewhere.

She closed her eyes and shifted a little, thinking she might clear her mind or find a position where the seam of her fatigues wasn't pressing in such a stimulating way. But when she opened her eyes again, everything was even more muddled. It wasn't clear anymore what was her own physical need and what was channeling from Anton.

Her hand wandered from the bed across his face. A coarse dusting of stubble coated his jaw and chin. His cheekbones were prominent, his nose almost patrician. His chin was square, with a slight divot under all the stubble. In sleep, with his impossibly long eyelashes, he didn't look like someone capable of great evil. Or even the offspring of a great evil.

It was incomprehensible that he'd done so much to protect her. That he could claim to love her. He didn't *know* her. But the way he'd charged Siddoh. For *her*.

Damned if that didn't *do* things to a female.

She settled her hand in the center of his chest, just

under that soft ridge of scar tissue. Even in his sleep his face was actually rather handsome. "You do manage to make a girl feel precious," she murmured.

───∾───

Thad had only visited the Elders' Council a handful of times—once when presented on his eighteenth birthday as the future heir to the throne, a few times as an observer during his father's rule, and once a week earlier to present Isabel as his queen.

This time, he stared out at the crowd of old vampires situated around the terraced, amphitheater-style room with awe more than fear. The long walnut table in front of Thad would have been where his father sat as Thad's closest advisor for maybe a century, perhaps even more, before he should have been forced to fly solo.

Best-laid plans.

He gripped the edges of the podium hard to keep his fingers still on the lacquered wood. "I want to thank you all for coming tonight." Everyone looked so serious. Thad worked to keep his body language easy and calm. No need to make matters worse. Holy effing Christmas, these folks would all shit kittens if they caught wind of what was brewing back at the estate. "I'd like to keep this meeting brief. As we make the transition from one leader to the next, things may be rocky. After tonight, though, we can return to regular semi-annual status updates."

Lots of nods and murmurs. A few hundred in the room, probably. Many empty chairs scattered around. Their numbers were dwindling to so few.

To the far left, at the end of one of the long tables, a

male stood so fast that his silvery braid of hair flopped over his shoulder. Thad recognized Elder Grayson as the father of his house manager, Ivy. The guy lived on the far residential quarter of the estate and Thad had seen him around. Seemed kind of quiet and solitary, though, and they'd never spoken much.

Not tonight. Tonight, Elder Grayson was troubled in his demeanor and tight in his carriage, but he clearly had a lot to say. "Highness, I would like to bring to the table two issues of great concern." He spread his arms wide and stepped onto the tier of seats above him, apparently intent on roaming the room while he made his request. "I imagine you can see that our numbers are few these days. Lots of empty seats at tables that once were full."

Thad nodded. "Our numbers are down society-wide, Elder Grayson. This is my highest priority and has been from day one. I have a meeting scheduled with my military to discuss proactive measures as soon as I leave here." It was sort of true, anyway.

The man nodded, flipping his braid dramatically over to the other shoulder. Was it very heavy? "Of course you do, sir. Only, we on the council feel that it is important for us to step up our efforts as well. You're such a young king, after all."

Thad's squeeze on the podium made a tiny squeak that echoed in the large room. Beside him, Lee shifted and tensed. They should have known this was coming. "My father was young once too, Elder Grayson. He led effectively. I have every confidence in my ability to do the same." He drew up, shoulders back, spine so straight that they could have stacked books on the top of his head like a damn debutante. No way would these old bastards would ever see him sweat.

Elder Grayson's erratic pacing was causing agitation in the room, and Thad suspected it was intentional. Heads swiveled back and forth; voices mumbled. What was going on here? Weeks prior, when Thad had been on the quest to fulfill the prophecy that would lead him to Isabel, there had been rumors that some on the Elder Council wanted to overthrow his rule. Perhaps it was more than just rumor.

"Elder Grayson, do you have a point to make here?"

That stopped him, at least for the moment. Elder Grayson cleared his throat and managed something almost like a bow. "Yes, sir. I'd like to propose increasing the frequency of the Council meetings."

Thad almost pulled a Tyra and rolled his eyes at the elder. "And?" Because without a doubt, there was more.

"The Elder Council is so much smaller than it used to be. We could regain our numbers by lowering the age of induction. Say, from one thousand to eight hundred years of age."

Lee coughed quietly. Thad's first in command, who rarely broke a sweat, now radiated tension. "No way. Table it, Thad. Fucking table it."

Over the murmurs in the room, Lee's hiss of a whisper couldn't have been heard by anybody but Thad. There was no time to discuss the whys and wherefores of his guard's vehemence, but Thad nodded in agreement. No way would he give his assent now, and Lee didn't ask him for much. "Elder Grayson—"

"In addition," the elder continued, "we would like to revisit the issue regarding human-vampire interaction.

We believe that our mixing with modern society and the human world continues to be the greatest risk to the safety of our species and should not be summarily dismissed."

This was not going to fly. Thad pointedly stepped back from the podium and folded his arms, waiting. It was not only rude to interrupt the king while he was speaking in front of the Council, but it was against the rules of conduct. Unquestionably Elder Grayson knew this.

Lee leaned to the side. "Either he's testing you or just being an asshole."

Thad smiled a little, maintaining eye contact with Elder Grayson. He made certain to show a friendly hint of fang. "Both, maybe," he said under his breath. When the ambient murmurs of agreement and disagreement had ebbed, Thad stepped forward. "I won't have you talking over me, Elder Grayson. Before I respond, do you have anything else of dire importance you'd like to request?"

There was a responding confused frown. Elder Grayson shook his head. "No. We just want to be sure that you have adequate guidance—"

"Good. Then perhaps you'd be more comfortable in your seat." Thad glanced at his watch. *Stand still. No finger tapping. Keep your hands out of your hair. Whatever you do, don't throw a fireball at anyone.*

"I meant it when I said I needed to keep things short tonight. I came here to announce to you all that your queen is with child." He ignored the raised hands of those who wanted to ask questions. "My place, especially during these first crucial weeks, is with her. I did not come tonight to have a long conversation about a topic that had already been laid to rest."

He held up a hand when the mumbles and grumbles rose louder. "Obviously, I want to hear your concerns. Let's schedule a special session so that we can discuss these matters properly. Elder Grayson, I will have your daughter send out a notice with the details. Thank you."

He gave a nod to the crowd and signaled Lee, who led him out. Thad had left no room for questions or negotiation. The real issue, of course, was that he needed time to get his head together before discussing these issues. Find out what the deal was with Lee. Thad truly didn't see a need to lower the age at which upper-class vampires and soldiers retired to the Council. Elder Grayson's logic struck him as half-baked at best. Still, this political stuff was going to be a minefield, and clearly some members of the Council had designs on using Thad as a sock puppet, thanks to his youth.

That'd be a cold day in hell. He might be young, but sure as hell, he wasn't stupid.

Chapter 11

STRAWBERRIES.

It was a sad and crazy fact that Anton hadn't tasted a fresh strawberry until the day before being released from the hospital. He'd stayed there after being left for dead by his own supposed family. By God, he had delighted in every sweet, tangy bite.

Dreaming of them now was so vibrant that the flavor filled his mouth, accompanied by something richer. Something delightfully bitter, like a dark chocolate. He'd had some of those in the hospital too, both thanks to a patient in the next bed sharing a gift basket with him. He moaned at the delicious combination of flavors.

There had been nightmares, too. Vivid images of his father and the torture he'd received at the man's hands, and of Tyra being held captive. Tied down like all the other vampires had been, while his father approached with a sternal saw in hand and something unseen held Anton fast. Helpless.

No amount of fighting had been enough to get him to her in time. He could still hear her screams and smell her blood. The scent was still fresh in his nose...

Something clogged his throat. Anton sputtered and was forced to swallow. It had smelled remarkably like... like...

Anton forced his eyes open. Tyra's gaze made contact with his for just a second before she brought her wrist up to her mouth. Then the warm, comforting weight of her other hand landed on his chest and the cock in his pants throbbed harder.

Good grief, he'd woken from sleep aroused plenty of times, but usually not from a nightmare. How odd. And that succulent flavor lingered in his mouth, even as he shook off sleep. A lick of his parched lips, and the flavor burst on his tongue all over again.

Suspicion dawned when Tyra ran her tongue across her wrist. A drop of blood lingered at the corner of her mouth, and he gave no thought to reaching up and sweeping it away with his thumb. Or to licking the residue. He just did it. For a few beats his eyes closed again. It was the same flavor.

He didn't have words to thank her for the gift she had just given him. "You gave me your blood."

Her head tipped to one side. "You did the same thing for me."

Anton inhaled deeply. Suddenly, he was so warm. His veins sang with energy. Power. He had felt this before. Twice. Two terrible, awful, hideously sickening times when he had participated in the ritual of cutting open a vampire and eating the heart to claim its power. Despite the increase in his body temperature, the memory made his stomach lurch and his body shiver.

"Do you need a blanket?"

He shook his head. It made his brain slosh a little, but he would not show Tyra. He wanted nothing more than to be worthy of her. "I'm fine." He blinked and met her gaze. Those eyes were just beautiful. So dark and vast. "You shouldn't have wasted your blood on me."

Her brow furrowed, but she didn't answer. Instead the

firm weight of her hand slid across his chest. The touch burned his skin, moving over one painfully tight nipple and down his side. The heat turned to shivers again and Anton pressed his lips together hard, determined not to release the undignified whimper trying to claw its way out of his throat.

One jagged fingernail scraped near the wound on Anton's side. The bandages plucked a few hairs when they were lifted, but Tyra's palm was there immediately to soothe the pinch away.

Anton realized he was holding his breath. For what, he wasn't quite sure.

"You were hurt so badly. The doctor said he wasn't sure what to do for you, since you're not a vampire. I wasn't completely certain it would work, but I figured it had to, right? See, now it's already healing," she said.

Her hand dipped lower, conspicuously close to the waist of Anton's pants, and the rest of his blood went south with dizzying speed. Shit. He could barely control himself in her presence, let alone when she touched him like that. For the love of mercy, what would he do if she actually touched him further down?

Anton's cock was hopeful that they might have their answer when her hand stilled. "Anton?"

He almost didn't hear her over the sound of his own thoughts. A rush of breath left his lungs and didn't return. He placed a hand over hers. "Tyra?"

"Why did you help me?" Her voice was unusually soft. Breathy.

His fingers dared to close around hers. "I told you why."

"But you…" Her head shook, a slow back-and-forth, like she was suddenly very tired. "You just don't do that sort of thing. You don't fall in love with someone you've never met. You don't sacrifice yourself for them the way you did."

Anton squeezed his eyes shut. The late-afternoon sun was coming through the blinds and hitting him right in his face. His head throbbed like crazy. So crazy that he almost forgot how hard he was. Almost. Damn, what he wouldn't give to sink into the bed right now.

"Tyra, can you close the blinds? I get these migraines, ever since my head injury." Thanks to his father.

"Sorry." She stood to pull the heavy drapes over the window, and almost immediately the room was blanketed in darkness.

Anton expected to need time for his eyes to adjust, but his vision was startlingly acute. Sharp enough that when she eased next to him on the mattress, the widening of her eyes and the frantic tick of the pulse at the base of her throat were immediately apparent. His mouth was as dry as the desert. More of her blood would surely quench the thirst. And what did thinking that say about him? Maybe he was no better than any other wizard, if he was thinking things like that.

For fuck's sake, I can't be like my father. I can't be.

"Tyra, I don't think you should be so close to me." Her chest rose and fell under the fitted V-neck of her T-shirt. If he had fangs, no doubt they would have gotten longer. That neck of hers was gorgeous. Long, smooth, and golden. A single, wispy curl clung to it near her pulse point.

She bit her lower lip. "Anton, how can you say you fell in love with me? You didn't know me."

He *had* known her, though. He'd hidden near the

shelter and watched the way she'd interacted with humans for weeks on end. Day after day he'd witnessed who she was through barred windows and when she ventured outside. The way she carried herself. With confidence, but always with care and compassion. The way she melted when someone—a child especially—smiled at her. Probably because as much as she cared for people, she never stopped to let anybody care for *her*.

He gave in to his longing to brush that stray curl from her neck with his thumb. He let his palm linger against the softness of her skin. When she allowed his hand to stay without complaint and silently held his stare with hers, his breath rushed out with dizzying speed. He shook his head.

"I know it sounds psycho. Considering how I was raised, maybe I don't really know what love means." His breath came deeper and faster as she allowed that same hand to trail down her neck and over her shoulder. Her arm. Such an amazing rush, that simple touch.

"Look, I just know that when I was assigned to watch you, I saw someone who was far beyond good and giving. I remember a little girl that you pushed on the playground swings at the shelter and stuff. I hated who I was, and you were… I couldn't sacrifice you to my father's disgusting cause. I just couldn't."

He sighed deeply and scrubbed a hand over his face. Warm, soft lips brushed over his. *Oh God*. Kissing back was the most natural thing in the world. He licked gently against the seam of her mouth. Hooked an arm around her waist and pulled her tan body on top of his. Her groan mirrored his own when her pelvis ground against his hard length—it was *so* good. He was gonna come in his pants if he wasn't careful.

"Tyra," he mumbled against her lips. God, they were so soft. And sweet. She must have been chewing gum again.

"Hmm?"

"What changed your mind?"

"All those things you were saying…" She shook her head. "I'm not sure myself at the moment."

Right. Who was he to question her abrupt one-eighty when he was about to get *laid, for heaven's sake?* But she deserved to know first. "Tyra. I really have to say something." She dipped her head to trace one fang around his nipple before sucking it into her mouth. "Oh God, that feels good. But… listen, I'm… you should really know that…"

She sat up. "What is it? Are you in too much pain?"

He shook his head. "No. Like you said, it's already healing." It was amazing how fast. And he would ignore a little pain for this.

Oh boy. He was really about to screw the pooch here. *You have no fangs. No fighting powers. Your kind has been killing hers for centuries. You have absolutely no clue how to please her physically. What do you have to offer her, Anton? Not a damned thing.*

"I haven't done this before, Tyra."

Tyra blinked at Anton, who seemed both hopeful and afraid at the same time. "You haven't done what before?" Not that she was clueless, but they couldn't afford any miscommunication here.

He coughed and cleared his throat. "I haven't… been with a woman. A female."

How was that possible? "Have you been with males?"

Anton coughed again. More of a choke this time. "Of course not."

"There's nothing wrong with—"

"God." More coughing "I like females. I like *you*." As if to illustrate, large hands grasped her hips. He was still hard, and he pressed himself against her between her legs, just enough to drive his point home.

Oh mercy. His admission had sobered her up from the buzz of exchanging blood and reminded her that it could be nearly suicidal to sleep with him. But the way he was touching her? Turned out she wasn't quite as sober as she'd thought. She met his smoky gaze. "You're serious. You're a virgin? Aren't you in your thirties?"

Anton held up a hand. "Twenty-seven, roughly. At the risk of sharing more than I should, I did once allow a prostitute to, you know, service me orally. But I haven't had… sex, no."

She shivered. The room was cold and this conversation was strange. Come to think of it, no lover had discussed his sexual history with her. "Why?"

Almost with resignation, he pushed her to the side until she sat next to him in the bed, rather than on him. It was probably better that way. "All roads lead back to my father, I'm afraid. Sex was only to procreate, and only with the lowest of the low. To ensure not just the genetic anomaly that allowed us to absorb powers but also the… more psychopathic tendencies, I guess. Whores and addicts mostly, because they're easy to find. Since I wouldn't go looking for them, I had two brought to me.

The first was too young. I paid her to pretend. I did let the second... service me, but never... never...

"I didn't want to bring more of me into the world," he said finally.

Tyra's chest ached. What a thing to say.

She didn't realize that Anton's hands were still on her until one of them moved. Callused fingers caressed her cheek with startling gentleness. "Then I saw you." His thumb brushed over her lips. "And I couldn't fathom wanting any other female."

Well, good grief, if that didn't just make her heart melt.

Hardly a thought passed through her head before she turned toward his palm and planted a kiss in the center. She leaned back and studied him. His square jaw and full lips, his scarred collarbone... His demeanor seemed mild at times, but the whole look screamed sexy bad boy, and she couldn't deny a dangerous attraction to that. Very dangerous, if it turned out that she had read this whole situation wrong.

No. No, she wasn't wrong. Just wasn't. There was no evil aura. No malevolence that she could detect in his emotions. And he had saved her. Saved her, when he could have just as easily have taken her home to reap whatever reward his father had offered for her capture. And sex could be a very comforting thing. They deserved some comfort after everything they'd both been though, right? Anton especially.

Hard to believe such a sexy bad boy hadn't been with a female before.

Thad will be furious.

She didn't care about Thad just then.

Tyra smiled slightly at Anton, who returned the gesture after a moment of confusion. The smile lit up that brooding face of his. "You're so handsome when you smile," she murmured. Slowly, she leaned forward to kiss him, at the same time reaching down toward the button of his pants.

Chapter 12

DON'T COME. DON'T COME. DON'T COME.

The barest flutter of fingers over the head of Anton's cock, and already he was about to blow. That wouldn't do at all. Thoughts whirled in his head like a tornado, and he reached desperately to grab one. To have something to focus on so that he could hold back at least long enough to get Tyra naked, for heaven's sake.

It was amazing, the clarity with which he could make out her features, even in the dark of the room. Tyra's ordinarily rich brown eyes had gone darkdark*dark*, her lids hooded, and that gaze never left his as she divested him of his pants and socks.

She slid forward to cover Anton's body with her own, and despite the warm softness and please-god-kill-me-now of her still-clothed body, he couldn't stop himself from pointing out: "The last time I tried to kiss you, you almost made me sing soprano."

She kissed him. Her lips made a warm, smooth, whisper-soft caress against a mouth that barely deserved to say words to this female, let alone worship her with his tongue as he so longed to do. "Anton, if you don't stop talking, I'm likely to remember all the reasons why this is such a God-awful idea."

Right. A foreign-sounding growl emitted from the depths of Anton's throat. His hands thrust under her shirt, pushing it up to her shoulders. "Your skin is amazing." It was. Smooth. Soft.

That seemed like a better thing to say.

His hand caressed the back of Tyra's neck and she moaned, honest to God moaned, and after some thrusting of hips and pulling of hands, with lips meeting sporadically in between, his female was naked and writhing underneath him. His female. *His.*

Anton's hands were everywhere. The tips of his clumsy fingers ached to touch every smooth inch of her. He stroked, licked, and nibbled. Starting with her gently toned belly and easing up to the luscious swell of the most perfect breasts that heaven or earth could have possibly managed to produce.

His pulse surged and his cock throbbed harder when a tiny taste and a puff of breath caused one round, smooth-skinned peak to tighten and wrinkle into a hard point. He ignored the stab of pain in his side when he twisted to worship the hourglass curve of her side and the roundness of her ass and her hip, which were as creamy and delicious-looking as a warm cup of tea flavored with just the right amount of milk. Her legs, parted around him, were long and firm. And between those legs... dear God, he was almost afraid to look, much less touch.

This female—this amazing, beautiful, perfect angel. This warrior in such an impossibly feminine package. She deserved to be touched by cleaner hands than his. Hands that had never done what his had. But even as he thought it, one palm slid closer to the mound of her sex, delighting in the startling softness of the curls he found there.

"I can't believe this." It was the most unmanly thing

he could have possibly said, but damned if it wasn't true. All the times he'd watched her and fantasized… never in a thousand lifetimes could he have imagined being given the gift of this woman's body… her blood… *her*.

"Anton," she whispered in a low, husky voice as she placed a hand over his, the one at the juncture of her thighs, and—*Oh God*—thrust it, pointer finger first, into a moist heat so exquisite he very nearly passed out.

"Tyra." Without further instruction on her part, Anton burrowed a thumb into those tight, damp curls to find the sensitive nub inside. This much he knew about. A tiny whimper told him that he'd found the right spot.

Anton thought he very well might die like this. With his head so light and dizzy, and his fingers curling and thrusting inside the most amazing place he had ever known. The nerves of his skin and even the blood in his veins were lit like an overstrung Christmas tree. Some kind of amazing shiver and tingle flew through him, and when he dragged his stare from the action at his fingertips to the molten chocolate of Tyra's gaze, the tie between them was clear.

That cool rush flying through him was Tyra. Her blood. Her pleasure. How could he have forgotten that they were already part of each other? The infinitesimal jerk of Anton's body over that stunning remembrance brushed his desperate, hungry cock against the hand working her core. With no warning, the orgasm he'd fought so hard to push away was back and a mere fraction from release.

"Anton, no. Stop." Amazing how things could change in only a fraction of a second.

Tyra's strong grip wrapped around his wrist. Pushed

his hand away. Immediately his entire body chilled, as if the heat between her legs had been the only thing keeping him warm. "Did I do something wrong?"

"No," she gasped. "God, no."

Oh, thank fuck. He had barely begun to process the dizzying relief, to grasp at the intense joining of their auras, their spirits, or whatever the fuck it was, when a pair of deceptively soft hands landed with an iron grip on his shoulders.

Before Anton could blink, he'd been pulled, flipped, and mounted. The breath left his lungs in a mighty *whoosh* the second his back hit the mattress.

Now *that* was a female.

"Wait." Hands on Tyra's hips, Anton squeezed his eyes and gritted his teeth, willing his body under control with every fiber of his desperate being as she straddled him. Just one slip of his hands and he would be inside of her…

"What's wrong?" With her curls matted against her wrinkled forehead and her body poised above him, Tyra was absolutely without question the most amazing thing that Anton would ever see in his lifetime.

Not one damned thing was wrong. She was amazing. Fucking amazing. "What about… can I get you pregnant?"

"No. Only at the full moon."

A slight shake of her head, and that was all Anton needed. Tyra's gasp and Anton's, thanks to a God he wasn't sure he believed in, collided in the air at the same time his hands released her hips and allowed their bodies to join.

Holy, holy, *holy* shit. He could have died right then and there, and he would have left the earth the happiest man ever. Tyra planted her hands on his chest. Sweat made her fingers slide just a little, just enough to get his nipples hard before the bite of her nails sank into his flesh. His head dropped back with a hiss. The ride was… unbelievable. Both of them were breathless, their stares locked firmly with each other's as Tyra's body rose and fell, milking him for all he was worth.

Anton bit down hard enough to crack his teeth. He would not last long. Dear… fucking… Lord.

His heart skipped a beat when a thunderous bang sounded from beyond the door. Someone was knocking on her front door. Dammit, he really hadn't meant it about dying right then.

"Tyra!"

"Shit." Rather than stop, as Anton assumed Tyra would, she sucked in a breath and sped up.

"Tyra, that sounds like the king."

"Shh." Tyra folded forward so that their bodies were flush against each other and her lips met his. Long fingers pulled his hands from her waist and threaded their fingers together above his head. Slicked with sweat, their bodies slid together, their breath sawing and mingling so loudly that Anton barely heard the bang of Tyra's front door slamming open and then shut again.

Barely.

"Tyra."

"Shh."

The muscles of Tyra's sex squeezed as if to drive home her point, and Anton was no idiot. Or he was, but he did as she instructed him and shut up. He blotted out everything else, including the vampire king outside who was likely about to kill him. His world narrowed to nothing but two sweat-slicked bodies and Tyra's golden face. Their noses bumped together as she moved, faster and faster, gasping louder.

He was so close, but he wanted to know that he'd pleased her.

"Tyra." The bang on the bedroom door came just as Tyra's body shook, her head thrown back in a silent scream of ecstasy. Anton's split second of turning his attention over her shoulder to the door made him miss the strike of her fangs.

The pinch was exquisite, so unlike the pain of before when her life had been on the line and he'd been afraid for the both of them. So fucking amazing that with the first suck of her lips at his vein, he shuddered and thrust hard. He spilled inside her as the pounding went on outside the door, and everything went white behind his eyes.

"Oh hell, yes." For the next few beats of Anton's heart, he and Tyra were alone inside a quiet, imaginary bubble. The forces outside the door were nothing but a distant echo as he wound his arms around her back and held on. Feminine muscles rippled gently beneath his hands as she sucked, licked the wound, and rested her forehead against his.

Their hearts thumped in perfect time with each other.

"Shit, I shouldn't have done that. You're still healing."

Then reality returned with a loud, angry rush. He took a deep breath. "No. I feel amazing. Better than I can ever remember." He really did. That blood of Tyra's must be powerful stuff. Even though he'd been injured, and even after the physical exertion of lovemaking, he'd never had so much energy.

Another series of loud bangs sounded from the other side of Tyra's bedroom door. "Tyra Yavn Morgan, I swear to God, if you don't open this door in the next thirty seconds, I'm gonna break the fucker down and I don't give a damn what you're doing in there when it happens."

Anton realized the harsh rumble that filled the room was coming from him. No way was anybody going to see her the way she was right now. No way was he going to let the king lead him gently to the slaughter. This was his female. He wasn't leaving without a fight. Most importantly, there was his father to kill.

"Shit," she murmured again and slid off, leaving him cold. She raised her voice and said, "Just a second."

Anton's hand stilled hers when she reached for her shirt. "I'll go. We both know he wants to see me," he said. His large hand caressed her smaller one and moved in to kiss the remains of his blood from her lips. "No worries." He smiled and ran a thumb over the worry lines on her forehead. "He's not going to kill me out there in your living room, right?"

The corners of her mouth lifted slightly. "Hope not. That carpet's taken enough of a beating."

He placed a kiss on her shoulder and made a hasty grab for his pants. "We'll talk later."

They absolutely fucking would. Anton might not have a clue what love was supposed to be, but he sure as fuck wasn't going anywhere without a serious fight. The way they'd been so *in tune* with each other just then? It had to be something real. It did. If only they had time…

"No. I'm not sending you out there alone." She swung her legs over the side of the bed and leaned down to gather her clothes from the floor. "I'm not trying to insult you, but it wouldn't be right."

He couldn't help but stare for a moment at the long, graceful curve of her back while she bent over. Her neck was so long, and her hair was curled and scrunched from the sweat of their lovemaking. He swept it to the side to give one last kiss to that intimate piece of real estate before going out to confront Thad.

Oh no.

Anton's vision, sharpened even in the dark by Tyra's superior blood, landed on a mark just below her hairline. A strawberry-colored birthmark in the crude shape of a heart. He had one like it just under his own hairline. All wizard offspring did. Some sort of magical marking tagged in their DNA, or whatever. Anton wasn't sure how that worked.

Tyra opened her eyes again and sat up straight. The slight smile fell from her face, replaced by a look of worry. "Anton, what's wrong? He won't really kill you. I wouldn't let him even if he tried."

He shook his head and schooled his features, leaning to place one last kiss on her satiny smooth cheek. "No, I know. I want to do whatever I can to help your kind. He'll see that. Please stay here. He needs to see that I can face him without you." He made a hasty grab for the doorknob behind him, suddenly anxious to reach the living room where Thad was likely waiting.

Anything to avoid telling this beautiful, fierce vampire warrior that she wasn't part human, after all.

She was part wizard.

～

Finally, the crying had stopped.

Xander slumped in Eamon's comfortable leather chair. The sound of the central air kicking on was almost deafening, given the extreme silence now that the baby was no longer wailing. His phone clicked softly, the keyboard and screen flashing each time he slid it open and shut. Until he became too agitated by the flashing lights, and then he'd pause and start all over again.

Exhaustion and blood hunger made his eyes very sensitive to the bright light from the screen.

Flay had called. Word was spreading across the estate of some craziness about a wizard being brought into their midst by Tyra, King Thad's sister… Ugh. He scrubbed a palm against his forehead. He barely remembered their conversation already and it had been… what? He checked the phone. January 7… close to midnight. Flay had called barely an hour earlier. Something big was going down; that much was clear. Tyra had brought this wizard in as a potential weapon—sounded like maybe a big attack was planned. More and more lately, he was wishing he could be back out there, be part of the fight again.

The bedroom door clicked open and Theresa stepped out quietly, baby monitor in hand. Her hair hung down her back in almond-colored waves. Today's dress was red. More of a somber burgundy, really, but its color drew attention to the fact that her skin was unusually pale. A creamy ivory, when it should have been more of a honey tone. When she turned to smile at him, the circles under her eyes were even darker than they had been the evening before, and the one before that.

She sank into a matching chair opposite his. "You look worn out."

Quite possibly, sadder words had never been spoken aloud. He managed what he could of a smile. "Says the female who just gave birth?"

She had the decency to look chagrined, at least. "Just trying to be polite."

"I put a glass of water over there for you, next to your chair." He gestured toward the walnut end table at her elbow. "The midwife and the doctor both said it's vital that you keep up with your fluids while the baby is nursing, remember? They said water, juice, herbal tea… *blood*."

Maybe it was the condensation on her water glass that made it slip from her hand just as she lifted it to her lips. She muttered quietly and returned the tumbler to its coaster. "Xander."

They had been dancing around the topic for a couple of days, but finally there it was. Xander found it hard to look directly at her, so instead he rubbed his forehead and studied the small table on which her drink sat. It was bold and dark. Classic, with clean lines like the rest of the furniture in the room. Everything, including the Panasonic plasma-screen television and the unfussy cabinet it sat on, spoke to how much time Eamon had spent in this room before his death.

Jeez. *Jeez*.

Xander squared his jaw and forced himself to meet her amber-eyed gaze. "Theresa, nobody knows better than I do how difficult it is to move on."

"I won't do it." Her voice was barely a whisper, kept low so as not to wake the baby, but the fierceness of her conviction was unmistakable.

Xander sighed. As a vampire, as a warrior, he

respected and honored her resistance to drinking from someone other than her departed mate. Before Thad had posted him to guard Theresa, Xander had given consideration on more than one night to stepping outside his door and running until the sun rose and burned him alive. But this… he couldn't let her do it.

Only a few days out from the birth, and she was exhausted. She was healing but too slowly. And as much as it might pain her, she had a tiny infant who was relying on her for care. They didn't have the luxury of waiting for her to be at peace with drinking from someone other than Eamon. So he did something he had never done for anybody.

He got down on his knees. "Theresa. Please."

"Xander. My goodness, get up." Her face flushed and she covered it with her hands. Embarrassment, probably.

Well, that made two of them.

He nudged his way alongside her legs. Pressed as close to her as he dared. Carefully, like he was approaching a frightened woodland creature, he used the barest pressure to rest his fingers on her cheek. "Theresa, you have a helpless baby in there that has already lost his father." He closed his eyes against the memory. "I was *there* for the birth, Theresa.

"Remember all the blood? Remember how you were in labor from Sunday to Tuesday, and by the time he arrived you barely had the energy to push him out? Just how long do you think you can continue caring for Eamon's namesake when you barely had the strength to get through bringing him into the world? That child can't afford to lose his mother, too."

He had her. When her face crumpled and a tear slid

down her cheek, he was forced to blink back the moisture pressing in his own eyes. The pearl button of his cuff flew to who knew where when he yanked up the sleeve. "Theresa. You have no idea how sorry I am." *This is hard for me, too.*

The room was ominously quiet, save for the heavy beat of both their hearts, the tick of the hallway clock, and the tiny, tiny snores coming from the baby monitor. "I know," she whispered. "I know. I just don't think I can."

"He'd understand," Xander said. "And he'd want you to take care of yourself. Of your family." That much was true. He brushed his fingers against her face once more. This time, his wrist brushed against her lips.

When her mouth opened and her fangs sank in, he closed his eyes and rested his forehead against hers. Tried to focus on the gentle suck of her lips, the delicate sweep of her tongue, the brush of her long hair against his hand.

He tried not to notice that it was all so different from what he was used to. The size and shape of the body, the fact that she was sucking at his wrist instead of his throat. The crushed velvet dress that was soft underneath his left hand. Tam hadn't worn dresses much at all.

His biggest failure was in blocking the room itself. In his heart, Xander knew he was doing this for all the right reasons. But the warm, soft, pink lips of a fallen comrade's mate on his skin as she sat in a leather chair that still held the scent of its old owner—and as Xander knelt on the dark brown carpet next to a rattan basket of never-to-be-read-again *Sports Illustrated* magazines—brought it all into vivid mental focus, even though he tried for it not to be. For all of his guilt, he might as well have made love to Eamon's mate on top of their oval coffee table.

I'm so sorry, Eamon.

Xander held his body so still that his muscles ached. He needed to get out of this house. Back to helping the fight against the wizards. Maybe to find out what was going on with this rumor about a wizard Tyra had brought in. Or finally to take that sunbath he kept pondering. Either way, he'd gotten Theresa to feed, and once she was out of the woods, his usefulness here had passed, right?

Just then, lights flashed on the nearby monitor and the baby cried.

Chapter 13

SILVERY BREATH GHOSTED IN FRONT OF ANTON AS HE trekked across the crunchy, frozen estate grounds to a small stone building situated conspicuously on the dark edge of nowhere. Thad and Siddoh flanked him, and accusations rang thick and loud in the air around them all. *Good times*.

Anton growled and shoved against Siddoh's meaty vampire mitts when they reached for him at the doorway. "I can walk through on my own." He ducked slightly and turned to shove again when Siddoh struck from behind. Those opposing forces made him stumble, and his back hit the nearest wall with a lung-punishing "oof."

The dimensions of the place were little more than about double by triple Anton's arm span, and there was nothing inside except some old, rusty bolts and chains hanging from the wall. Dust and dirt and dark stains covered the floor. A thick, metal, windowless door was the only exit, and it clanged shut ominously in their wake. Not hard to guess what this place was used for. The primary directive was to convince them to keep him alive.

Upon leaving Tyra's bedroom, he had planned to make nice with these guys. Too much aggression would send the wrong message, especially right now. Give them the excuse Siddoh was unquestionably looking for, with his jealous, glittery eyes narrowed at the fresh bite on Anton's throat and his nostrils flared at the lingering smells of sex on skin.

Yet there were limits to Anton's patience. He jerked his chin in response to the threat in Siddoh's cracked knuckles and retracted arm. "Do it. G'head." His own father had tried to kill him not so long ago. What fear could these vampires really hold? Anton was firm in his conviction that he would not go down without a fight— not without making every effort to protect Tyra— especially knowing what he knew now about Tyra being part wizard. God, how could that be?

"Cut it out, Siddoh. That's not what we're here for." That was Thad. Anton might have thanked the king for rising to his defense, had the guy sounded the least bit sincere about it. The young vampire leader stood quietly in the center of the room, his arms folded over his chest, his stare sharp and narrow. Siddoh, angry and restless, paced between them like a wounded animal.

The king stared Anton down until he felt like he was about two feet tall. "I'd tell you to get comfortable, but there's not really any point in that."

"I guess not." Anton assumed a similar stance. Feet planted, arms crossed, jaw set. It was understood that they saw him as the traitor here, and they had every right to see him as such. In a way, though, Anton was angry too. All of this had been to protect Tyra. To help their kind. And the chances were good that they would never believe him. Patience? He'd spent the better part of thirty years biding his time for an escape from the dark, empty life that being born a wizard had given him. He was fresh out of patience at that moment.

"Okay." The king eyed Anton intently, his hands

casually caressing the butt of a dagger at his waist. "So tell me everything you know. Every bit of inside data, every possible weakness, everything. No matter how insignificant. I was already in need of a damn good reason not to kill you, and that was before you slept with my sister. Hell, I almost killed *him* for that." The king jerked his head toward the bulky, restless male.

Aha. So Anton had been right. Siddoh snarled, though whether at Anton or at the king himself was hard to say for certain. Surely, though, he wouldn't snarl at his own king. Then again, Anton would have snarled at his own so-called king. So who could tell?

He wiped a hand over his face. "I already gave Tyra every bit of the information I'm about to give you."

"That's just great. If I didn't hear it myself, it didn't get said."

Yeah, yeah. "I just want to be clear. I understand that having me here inside your compound is uncomfortable, and I realize that for the safety of everyone here you have to proceed carefully. At the same time, my foremost concern is for Tyra, and I am not going to roll over quietly just because you threaten me. I've seen a hell of a lot worse from the wizards than I could ever see from you."

Anton stepped back. He planted his tongue against the roof of his mouth and breathed out to keep his jaw from clenching and his teeth from grinding together. He folded his arms over his chest as much for warmth as to put a buffer between himself and the five hundred pounds of angry vampire. If he looked defensive, oh well.

"So. My father rules the wizards. You've got that

much, I guess. It's kind of a ragtag bunch, but they do follow and look up to him. To a degree, he trains them to be that way. He tries to start them young, usually when they're still children, to ensure total compliance, and he breeds them to be predisposed to the personality traits he's looking for. Except in my case, I guess, it didn't work."

"Nothing we didn't know before," Siddoh growled.

The king held up a hand. "Continue."

Where should he begin if not at the beginning? The king had said he wanted to hear everything. Anton started again. "Part of what we're supposed to do— what the wizards are supposed to do—is propagate the species. Find 'suitable' women. Dregs of society. Throwaways. The wizard males impregnate them, and all beings with wizard DNA are born with this mark on their hairline." With a small turn of his head, he gestured to his birthmark. Tyra's. Hell…

The king cleared his throat. "What of the females?"

Anton straightened. "My father was of the belief that they weren't of any use to him, I think. He discarded them or left them alone. I'm not sure why, but I hear that they tend to die young." *Tell him. If something happens to you, he can keep Tyra safe if he knows. But what if he hates her? Holds it against her? Shit.* The words wouldn't come.

"So my father—I know he's been around since the early days of your father. He came here from Armenia after your kind did." He tipped his head forward to indicate Thad. "And I know he looks down on your species. I don't know if he sees you so much as an enemy as he does cattle. You're food. A power source.

"That's just an observation I've made over my lifetime, which is about twenty-seven years, I guess. It's
hard to say for sure because we don't exactly celebrate
with cake and ice cream growing up in the wizard clan."
He laughed, an awkward, nervous laugh because—
well, damn, something had to give. At least he sure as
hell thought so. Apparently he was the only one who
thought so.

Siddoh kept right on staring. The king shifted his
stance, blinked, and waited.

Anton licked his lips. "Someone found out about
Tyra. She's unique in her ability to absorb multiple powers the way we can?"

Thad nodded tightly. Understandable that the information exchange was only going to go one way. Really,
though, this was like pulling teeth.

"Anyway, that's what we—that's the assumption that
the wizards have operated under—that vampire powers
are biologically inherited. Somehow Tyra absorbs them.
The way we—they—do. She doesn't have to go through
the sacrificial ritual of eating the heart the way wizards
do. Master wanted to study her to figure out why. I get
the feeling he's losing his grip on things. Somehow, he
doesn't command the same kind of loyalty he used to.
It's a perfect time for you to take him out. If you can,
you might be able to wipe out the clan entirely."

The king nodded. "We've noticed more of an 'every
man for himself' mentality lately. More attacks on our
kind, too. Less rhyme or reason to them. Used to be we
could predict patterns, but not lately."

"Wish I could help you there. For obvious reasons,
I'm not in on any plans of late." Anton rubbed his

forehead. He had trouble focusing since the head injury, and he was under a little pressure here. It was hard to know how to even address the king. "My lord…"

"Whoa. Okay." The king held up a hand. "Thad is fine. Until you piss me off, anyway."

That remained to be seen. "Okay, Thad." *He needs to know. Tell him.* "Listen…" Anton cleared his throat. "That mark I just showed you on the back of my neck? Tyra has one." His body went rigid then, waiting for the fallout. Would the king leave him here in this stone shed? Would Siddoh gut-check the messenger?

The surprising thing was that the king was *not* surprised. His hands went to his hips, and with a slight nod, he dropped his chin to his chest. It was Siddoh's startled murmur of "fuck me" that made the cinder block–walled room get colder.

Anton's eyes widened, heat rising in him again. "You *knew*?" They'd known and not kept an eye on her? What kind of a two-bit moron was this king?

Thad licked his lips. He seemed to absorb Anton's countenance like he hadn't seen him before. "I only found out recently myself. Tyra's older than I am. We thought for years that her mother was human." Thad shook his head sadly. "Tyra's mother disappeared long before my father mated with my mother. Nobody ever questioned the story."

"Fuck me," Siddoh muttered again, louder this time. The larger vampire ran his hand through his hair, which made it stand out all over and made him look like some kind of mad scientist. He held his hand in front of himself then, looking at it. Then he looked at Thad and Anton. "Her powers. She absorbs them when she feeds."

His nodded vigorously. "She can turn invisible like I can and read emotions like that douchebag she dated a few decades ago." He looked up. "Why didn't someone think of that?"

"We didn't want to." The king, who had started his own little loop of pacing, stopped and pressed his eyebrows together until Anton thought the deep crevasse between them might open up a magical portal to another world. He advanced on Anton and shoved two fingers hard into the wizard's chest. "You haven't told her, have you?"

"No. I figured it out about the same time you were threatening to tear down Tyra's bedroom door. Telling her then wasn't right. She identifies strongly with being half human. Woulda freaked her out. In case you haven't figured it out, my goal here is to *help her*."

Thad nodded. "You did protect her when she was in torpor, and you have my thanks for that. It's the primary reason you're getting this much leeway. Though I'll admit—how you pulled one over on Lee, I'll never know."

Rage boiled in Anton's gut. "I. Am. Not. *Evil*. He believed I could be trusted to watch over her because I *could* be trusted to watch over her. Think about it. We know that you can sense us—" Shit. *Shit*. "I know you can sense *wizards*. I know it's an innate vampire ability to sense the evil aura projected by wizards. I was there to protect her, and an honorable male knows another honorable male. I'd think you would be able to do so as well.

"Now." Anton's fist slammed his open palm. He was burning up, and he did some pacing of his own. He ignored Thad's look of frustration and Siddoh's weak attempt at an intimidating growl. He needed to *move*. "Do you want the information that I gave Tyra about how to find my father?"

———⟶⟶⟶———

"Thad." Tyra's fists stung, but she pounded the cold, steel door even harder. "Thad, open the fucking door. I swear if you hurt him I will make you sorry."

Footsteps crunched behind her. "Evening, Tyra."

She whipped around. "Flay. What are you doing here?" Her fellow fighter didn't answer, but he was fully armed and ready for battle. Gary pulled up next to him, followed by what appeared to be all of the off-duty patrols for the night. Gary handed Flay a duffel, and the contents clanked and shifted, "What the hell is going on?"

Gary was a human lie detector. Human, not wizard, but maybe that was close enough. What if Thad was planning to use Gary for some sort of interrogation? She should never have let Anton leave her room alone.

Flay looked like he'd swallowed a handgun sideways. "I'm sorry, Ty. I'm not at liberty."

What the hell did Thad have planned? The lapels of Flay's jacket were cold in Tyra's clenched fingers. "Look, Anton is on our side. He has done nothing but help us. I swear I'll kick your ass if you hurt him."

The door groaned and creaked open. Siddoh's bulky form filled the entryway of the small interrogation space. He shoved Anton through the door ahead of him. "Tyra, you need to back off and let us do our jobs, honey."

"Don't 'honey' me. This is my job too. Or have you forgotten that?"

Thad stepped out. "You've gotten a little sloppy about it lately. Or have you forgotten that?"

She looked over the group, trying to get a read on things. They were armed and ready to head out. Someone had handed Anton a jacket. Her gaze narrowed at Thad and then swung back to Anton. "Oh my God. You're going after your father again."

"Tyra, you aren't safe as long as he's alive."

She scoffed. "I've been taking care of myself just fine since long before you showed up, thank you very much."

Thad came forward. "Ty. None of us are safe as long as the wizards have a leader." His voice was quiet. Precise.

"Thad, who's to say that if we yank his father out of power, three more won't grow back in his place?"

Thad rubbed his eyes. Annoyed? Yeah, well, so was she. "And there's just as much chance that if we wipe out the queen, we wipe out the hive. Come on, Ty. This is stupid. You're just pissed because you didn't get a crack at killing him yourself, and you know it."

She took a glance at the peanut gallery. There were about a thousand ways she'd rather have this conversation than in front of an audience. "Well if he's after me, don't you think I deserve a crack at him?"

"Sure. But he's after all of us, and we have to think of the greater good here. And you're not back at a hundred percent yet."

"I can fight, Thad."

"You just came out of suspended animation not long ago."

"I'm healed from that. You were there when Brayden gave me the go-ahead."

"Apparently your poor judgment needs more time on

the bench. You tried to charge into a den of wizards with nothing but this asshole here as backup." He gestured to Anton. "No offense."

Anton shrugged into his jacket. "None taken."

"Thad, there was no way you were going to trust him to give you valid information."

Thad sneered, his fangs bared slightly. "No question, bringing a wizard into our midst was risky and stupid and something I would never have allowed, had I known about it. Does that mean I wouldn't have gathered and tried to use his information?" He jabbed his finger in the direction of the assembly of soldiers. "You tell me what it looks like I'm doing here."

He folded his arms over his chest and nodded to Siddoh. "Report hourly, whether or not there's action." He stepped up to Anton, almost as if they were squaring off. "And if he puts a single toe out of line, disable him."

Anton didn't even blink. Siddoh tapped Anton's shoulder and motioned for him to walk ahead, which he did without question. No word, no look back at her. *Stand up for yourself, dammit. He just gave Siddoh permission to kill you.* "Anton…" Her heart squeezed and flopped around hopelessly inside her chest, like a fish unable to find water. There was really nothing to say, was there? Not now, certainly. Not in front of everyone.

Maybe not at all.

Thad moved closer, and his blue eyes stared expectantly. Daring her to argue more. The group moved out, taking Anton along with it. Anger boiled up and she bit the inside of her cheek. The tang of blood hit her tongue.

Finally, Thad sighed. "Why don't you come back

to the house, huh? Have something to eat. We can talk strategy, and if Siddoh calls in, you'll be there to hear about it."

Tyra couldn't seem to make her lips move. Her feelings toward Anton were muddled. The sex had been… she didn't have the words. That he'd walked away without so much as a glance back twisted like a serrated knife in her gut. It had been his first time, right? Hadn't that been special? She'd thought that the intense, indescribable emotion that flowed between them when they'd made love had been mutual, but maybe she'd been so wrapped up in herself that she hadn't read his experience properly. Or at all. It took a little focus to read another's emotions, and Lord knew her blood was not all in her brain at that time. But for once, she'd hoped sex like that had meant more.

Like crazy, she hoped so.

Thad shifted. A hand landed on her shoulder. "Tyra. I understand why you want to go, but you're too close to this."

"And Anton isn't?"

Thad shook his head. "Of course he is. But he's got information that you don't."

Tyra's breath ghosted in front of her. She jammed her hands deep into her pockets. The team left across the frozen grass to load up and roll out, and Tyra grew sicker with each collective footfall on the grass. With fear… with dread… with doubt. Now that the warmth of her bedroom and the feel-good chemicals from having sex had all floated away, she found herself wondering things about Anton that she shouldn't be.

Could his good intentions overcome his biology?

Thad nudged her shoulder. "Actually, he's got some balls if you ask me."

She rolled her eyes as she turned to face him. "I didn't ask you."

He laughed mordantly. "I just gave Siddoh the go-ahead to end him if he did anything suspicious, and he didn't react. Pretty hard core. Or stupid."

"I swear, Thad, if he gets killed—"

"If he gets killed, he knew what he was signing on for. I love you, Ty, but my greater duty is to the thousands of vampires still alive on this planet who are in danger of being killed off by an enemy race. If I can use him, I will use him. And if he turns out to be playing both sides, I'll fucking kill him."

Not a damn thing she wanted to say in response that would be productive.

Thad's eyes all but shot daggers at her. The team was long gone before the two of them gave up the stalemate and walked back to the mansion in silence. There was too much anger and mistrust between them to say a word.

Chapter 14

"XANDER, I TRUST YOU."

"No." Xander's harsh tone put a stricken look on Theresa's already strained face, and he immediately cursed himself. He took a deep breath and calmed his tone, even as his gut cramped and twisted. "No. Theresa, it isn't safe."

"Xander, I still talk to the other fighters' mates. I know what's going on out there. I just heard that they're pulling reserve fighters to go after the wizard leader. There's a rumor about a wizard on the estate who has offered his help in finding where they hide. Even without that, for weeks now there have been increased civilian attacks downtown. They need you out there. You want to go, too. I can tell."

He ran a hand through his hair. They were on the back patio; Theresa was hanging clothes on a series of folding racks while the baby slept bundled under about a foot of knitted blankets in a wicker basket on the patio table. It was winter, and it wasn't as if the female didn't have a dryer or the money to run it, but she insisted on line-drying her clothing now that she was healed up enough to get around with the basket. Some vampires clung to the old ways, sure, but this? Fucking odd was what it was.

The baby slept with his tiny fists balled against his cheeks, lips pursed as though even in sleep the kid was ready to kiss somebody. Every time Xander so much as looked at the tiny thing, it ripped his heart out anew. Eamon would have fallen in love immediately.

Xander sure had, but he was just an interloper here and didn't belong. He'd overstayed as it was. Still, he was stuck in some kind of uncomfortable limbo—that baby was just so damned small and he was needed on the front lines, but something kept whispering in his head that he was needed here more.

He'd waffled on the blood issue for too long, and now… well, he'd been handling his shit, but if he sank his fangs into Theresa or anyone else, he was taking a huge risk. And his host was taking a bigger one. "Theresa, it's been months since Tam was killed. I…" Shit. A sob tried to sneak its way out, and he pressed his lips together firmly enough that his fangs, which had already begun to lengthen at the mention of feeding, poked into his bottom lip. He focused on the baby, whose eyes fluttered and rolled, hands occasionally opening and closing, lost to some dream about who the hell knew what. "I could kill you. I already told you, I'm not leaving that kid down another parent."

She sighed. Almost an exasperated sigh, like that of a mother impatient with her child. "Is that what you think? Seriously, Xander." She draped an itsy-bitsy bodysuit and a pair of rainbow-colored leggings over the rack and walked over to him. It was a breezy night. Her warm, honey-colored hair was pulled back into a loose pony-tail. A few strands had pulled free and blew across her face in the night breeze. "I know you were ordered here to watch over us, but I'd like to think you and I have become friends."

He ducked his head. "Of course we're friends." Hours and hours of Theresa on bed rest, nothing to do but talk, how could they not have become friends?

She bent her knees and weaved back and forth a little, looking to make eye contact with him. "So you trust me, right?"

He'd always hated that question. They'd gone through that shit in training: "You trust me, right? Okay, so go ahead and fall backward, naked and bloody, toward this pool of UV light and piranhas. Don't worry, man. I'll catch you." He couldn't hold back the low growl. "Theresa, of course I trust you. What the hell kind of question is that?"

She shushed him and looked pointedly over at the little one, who had squirmed and rubbed a fist over his eye mid-sleep. "So trust me when I say that I can be sure you won't hurt me, okay?"

He was dimly aware, just then, that he didn't even remember the exact date. But it was sometime after the first of the year, which meant it had been a good six months since he'd last drunk blood. Six months was an okay time period for most vampires, but for a fighter it was a long damn time. And since giving Theresa his blood, his hunger had increased exponentially.

He was in pain. He was damn tired. After giving serious thought to offing himself, he'd realized he didn't want to go out like that. And deep down, he knew Tam wouldn't have wanted him to do it. And tonight… he drew in a deep breath. The fight was a long way off, but still he could practically smell the blood in the winter air.

He missed it.

He searched Theresa's face, but his body had already decided. His feet moved forward, and his fangs filled his mouth. His fingers curled, ready to grab for her. Just as he stepped into her physical space, her delicate hands came against his chest. "Sit."

Xander bristled at the command, but his ass hit the cold surface of one of those chaise lounge thingies faster than he could think. She sat next to him, slowly and carefully, and then it was all over.

He struck fast, and he struck hard. Her body was warm and comforting and pliant beneath him, and her blood was tart with hints of blackberry and walnuts. He loved the taste of walnuts; he could eat bags and bags of them until painful bumps popped up all over his tongue.

He drank until he went blind from the pleasure of it. Until the ache in his gut eased and beyond it. Until the ever-present ache in his injured shoulder disappeared and his veins sizzled with a vitality he'd begun to think he'd never know again. He drank until the body in his arms went slack and heavy, and somewhere in the distance a baby cried.

Stop.

But the blood was rich and delicious and slid down his throat so easily, and once it was there in his throat there was nothing to do but swallow, and then more was there in his throat, and then... *Stop.*

He gripped harder. His nails dug into soft fabric even though his host wasn't putting up a fight. The baby cried again. He'd known this was going to happen. He never should have agreed to this.

Stop.

A hand brushed over his forehead, and his eyelids got

very heavy. He yawned, his mouth stretched wide, and his tongue extended to lap up one last taste of berry and walnut. It was as if he hadn't slept in days and days. Had he? He couldn't remember. Why couldn't he remember? His body seemed to weigh a thousand pounds.

The baby cried again, but this time its wails died down, answered by a sweet lullaby of some kind. Brahms? Theresa had such a lovely voice. It was his last thought before the world went dark.

Anton was staring at an empty stone-walled room.

They'd found the portal to the wizards' den. They'd made it inside, and they had found a whole goddamned lot of abso-fucking-lutely *nothing*. Not one wizard. Not one. Not even his father, who as far as Anton knew had been too paranoid to leave his stupid evil command center in a good year at least.

"I don't understand," he murmured.

A small group of vampires shifted and muttered behind him from just inside the portal entrance. The air inside the empty stone-walled room was cold but stagnant. The immense silence was peculiar. In all his years, this dungeon-like hideaway had always stirred with activity.

This didn't look good.

The big one, Siddoh, stepped up next to him. "You're sure this is the place?"

"Dead certain. Take a deep breath." He'd gotten used to it over the years. Even now, to some degree, he could filter out the smells from the blood sacrifices that were done down the hall from the assembly area where they now stood. After having been away for a while and breathing fresh air, though, he thought the air here seemed far more disgusting than it used to be.

Siddoh sucked in a breath and gagged. "Shit." He coughed. "So where is everyone? I don't get even a hint of an evil aura." He did a slow circle in the bare, stone entryway. "Where on earth are we, anyway?"

"To be honest, I don't know the answer to that." Anton shook his head slowly. "Never have. I don't even know for sure that we're *on* earth." He laughed dryly. "Mast—my father was careful about controlling certain information." He threw his hand over his shoulder. "There are no windows or doors except the portal out into the woods, which always made me think either we're underground or…"

"Or?"

"…somehow in some kind of alternate dimension."

Siddoh whistled.

Anton didn't respond but wandered slowly, hands open and at his sides. He stepped through a stone archway that opened onto a long hall. Body memory steered him right toward the living area: the eating hall, the Master's private quarters, rooms for the wizards to bunk in. Everything sat empty but waiting, like they'd all just stepped out for a smoke break or something. Nobody anywhere.

He turned back the way he'd come. His footsteps clapped on the floor during his long trek to the ceremony room. This was the only room in the place that didn't look like something out of the Stone Age, but Anton still avoided it whenever possible. The tiled walls and floor, the drain in the center—they were all there for easy cleanup after the sacrificial ceremonies.

It was all he could do to stay standing when he entered.

Two defiled bodies lay side by side on the floor, not yet taken for "disposal." The chests were cut open. Blood everywhere. He swallowed the bile in his throat and brushed off the tears that sprang to his eyes. They were a male and a female. The woman's light green eyes were wide in terror. Frozen that way.

The stench was indescribable.

"Oh hell…"

Anton didn't look up at the sound of Siddoh's voice. He was still stuck on those two matching tattoos. Calla lilies, intertwined with matching halves of the sun and moon, on the back of their wrists.

"They don't usually just leave them like that." He closed his eyes, but the image was just as clear so he opened them again. "The tattoos…"

Siddoh pushed a hand through his hair. "Mating symbols." He gestured vaguely. "You can tell by the style they were done fairly recently. Ink's dark. And the colors and whatnot. For a long time, convention held that they were done with black only. 'Course back in the day, you know, before we had the mechanical needles and everything…" His voice faded and he furrowed his brow, probably wondering just as much as Anton why he was talking about tattoo technology just then.

"Anyway, we'd better get back. Just got word from the boys that there's increased activity in the residential areas. The others have already headed out. Something tells me your wizard brethren got wind of this expedition and used the opportunity of our diverting manpower to bring some damage."

Shit. How? "Siddoh, I didn't know. There's always someone here. My father rarely leaves."

The big vampire rubbed his eyes and turned for the door. "Let's just go."

"What about these two?"

Siddoh hiked his shoulders. "Hate to say it, but taking them out of here is too risky. For all we know, the bodies have been rigged or messed with in some way."

"I just don't understand how they could've known. I swear I haven't been in touch with anybody."

"Doesn't matter how. Just matters that they did."

They stopped short when they reached the portal in the stone entry hall that would take them back outside. The shimmery, dark oval was a narrow space as such things went, and the two men couldn't go through side by side. Nor would Siddoh trust Anton to go through ahead of or behind him. So they went out the way they'd come in.

In the world's most uncomfortable bear hug.

The two rolled apart as soon as they hit solid ground. "Sorry 'bout that, buddy. Not usually too keen on cuddling up with the males my exes are fucking, but I think we have a problem."

Anton was still struggling through rage and despair at seeing the couple in that room. It wasn't like he hadn't grown up with it, hadn't seen the ritual many times—far too many times—before. But still… His eyes burned. Even after living with it, he never got used to the aftermath like that. And the couple, newly mated.

In love.

He sneered at Siddoh and started walking in the direction of where they'd parked the cars. "I don't think you really want to go there."

Siddoh must have invoked his power to go invisible because the air around Anton stirred and the weight of a heavy arm landed over his shoulders, but he couldn't see Siddoh at all. "I think we do need to go there."

"And why is that, exactly?"

"'Cuz whatever went on before with me and Ty, I'm still out to protect her and I want to make sure we're on the same page."

Anton flung off the invisible arm. "I wouldn't be out here with you at all if I didn't intend to protect her."

They pulled up to the car. The vehicle lights flashed and the two got in. "You sure about that?" When the doors were closed and locked, Siddoh reappeared with his face inches from Anton's, eyes narrowed and fangs extended. *Oh shit.* "Because it looks an awful lot like you led us on a wild-goose chase so your posse could lead our civilians into an ambush."

Chapter 15

"Not that I don't appreciate helping others, but what are we doing here again?"

Tyra pulled on a pair of thin plastic gloves and managed to scowl down at Alexia without missing a beat as she stirred a tray of beef-and-cheese macaroni. "Because Thad's not letting me go to try to take down the wizard king, and it has been made clear that there will be consequences if I disobey, yada, yada. You were moping around bored anyway, so why the hell not do something useful with our time?" She pointed across the shelter's kitchen to one of the newer volunteers, a short Hispanic lady whose name Tyra couldn't remember. "Go help her with, uh, something."

Alexia smirked and spun on her heel. Jeez. The little human sure was a gloomy one. According to Isabel, the girl had a sunny side but Tyra had yet to see it. Tyra turned back, however, as the residents began to file into the dining hall through the double doors. She was filled with the warmth from doing this job that gave her such satisfaction.

Her dad had made a good suggestion when he'd prodded her to find a way to connect with her human roots. Tyra was already mourning the day when she'd have to quit, although considering the high staff turnover, it could easily be many years before anyone noticed that she hadn't aged much at all.

On the other hand... Tyra narrowed her eyes at Rolan, the soldier that Thad had sent along to keep an eye on her. Job satisfaction wasn't what it used to be. *If Thad insists on sending muscle every time I come down here, this won't last long. That guy is doing a terrible job of looking inconspicuous.*

"Evening, Miss Tyra. Did you have a good vacation?" Selena, the girl Tyra had developed such a fondness for since she and her mom had become residents at the shelter. Goodness, the girl seemed to have grown inches and inches in just the few days Tyra had missed.

"Selena, look at you."

"Did you have a good vacation, Miss Tyra?" Lisa, Selena's mother, put a protective hand on the girl's shoulder to keep her from getting too far ahead.

Tyra's mind was blank for a moment. Vacation? Right. The night she'd disappeared, she had told everyone she was going on vacation. Yeesh. "Wonderful. Restful. Good as new." Her laugh was nervous, and her smile had to have been fake as hell. Even she could tell it was pasted on weak and crooked, but she prayed it was convincing enough.

"Well," Lisa said. "I have wonderful news. We'll actually be leaving tomorrow after breakfast. I managed to reach an old friend out of state. She runs a small business and could use some administrative help."

Tyra clasped her hands together. "Oh, that's great. Congratulations."

But even as she unjoined her hands to serve some beefy macaroni to the next person in line, something dark and loud and pungent came over her like a deluge. Her gut churned. The entire perimeter of the shelter was fenced in. The wizards hadn't come this close before. And never—

Her cell phone buzzed in her pocket. Thad. *Get back home NOW*. She turned to look at Lexi, who stood wide-eyed and frozen with a massive can of mixed-fruit salad in her small hands. Human or not, the girl had been attacked by a wizard only a few weeks before and knew what she was sensing.

Tyra smiled again at Selena and her mother, and tapped the kindly volunteer next to her. "I'm sorry. I have to go."

She motioned to Lexi, who dropped the can on a nearby counter like it held dynamite. The two squeezed out through the main double doors of the cafeteria. They veered at the line of male residents waiting to get dinner, and Tyra pulled Lexi against the wall, leaning down to whisper.

"Okay, we need to get everybody into the cafeteria. I'm going to announce that the men can go in. Do me a favor, and go in and tell the officers that there's a disturbance. That other officers are taking care of it, but that they need to control things in there. Tell them to put the chains on the doors, and screw the fire hazard for now. And then stay put. Stick close to Rolan, okay?"

Lexi nodded, scared but silent.

Tyra pointed to Rolan. "Stay with Alexia. Make sure she and these other people are safe." She looked around. Her senses had never been strong when it came to wizards. That was a bad thing in this case because the fierceness of the malevolent vibes probably meant they were all the hell over the place. "I think I'm gonna need some backup. You have Thad and Siddoh's numbers in your phone?"

He nodded.

"Good. Tell Thad what's going down. Tell Siddoh I need backup if he can spare it." A deep breath and Tyra's gut churned again. Black spots danced in front of her eyes. "As much as he can spare. Fast."

Rolan went.

Tyra pasted on another fake smile. Her teeth and cheeks were starting to hurt. "Gentlemen, the women and children are still eating, but due to some unforeseen problems, we have to have everyone in the cafeteria at once tonight. We're going to let you all in early, but I'm going to expect everyone to be on their best behavior, okay?"

There were murmurs and nods and shuffles as everyone filed into the cafeteria. When the last man was in, Tyra slammed the heavy door shut and raced down the hall toward the back exit where the inky, repellent evil was strongest. Good thing it was dinnertime and everybody was in one spot.

She reached under her bulky winter sweater to her waist holster. At least she had a gun, and she had fed recently. Was Anton okay? Was this happening because he and the group had failed to kill his father? Or because they'd succeeded? What if Alexia couldn't reach Siddoh?

"Miss Tyra."

The small voice stopped her heart almost as surely as it stopped her footsteps. "No," she whispered. Then louder: "Selena, you need to get back to the cafeteria with your mom, honey." The child's eyes opened wide, and Tyra turned to follow the path of their stare. She moved to place a barrier between the child and the man she was looking at, and nearly lost her breath.

She found the words, just barely, to say again, "Selena, get back to the cafeteria *now*."

Tiny feet scampered behind her, and just when Tyra thought maybe she could relax, boot steps echoed on the linoleum as well. Shit. "Hey, Tyr—" Rolan. She spun. "Oh my God."

The young vampire fell in an ungraceful heap. Unmoving. His chest rose and fell enough to make it apparent that he was still alive at least, but…

"What the hell did you do to him?" Tyra's gaze fixed narrowly on the figure that had appeared at the end of the hall. The man was smiling, an oddly charming smile despite the black voids of his eyes that seemed, even from where she stood, to stretch on and on forever. What was funny was that as close as she stood to him now, she didn't feel the malevolent aura. Indeed everything was strangely calm except for the erratic dance of her heart, which was skipping around like a break-dancer on meth.

How was that possible?

He was covered in a long, black trench coat and his head was shaved, but she'd have known the face any-where. It was an older, seemingly wiser version of the one she'd woken up to from her suspended rest. *The one she'd stared down at while making love…* had it only been hours ago? This had to be Anton's father. The somewhat mythical Master of the wizards.

The man smiled and bowed slightly, as if this were some sort of formal event and not a face-off of enemies. "Miss Tyra. I *am* pleased to finally meet you." He smiled again, more broadly this time. "Now. I would appreciate your coming with me. I've gone to a lot of trouble to get here, and if you don't comply, I assure you it won't take much to raze this entire building and everyone in it, including your incompetent foot soldier and that adorable little girl back there."

—∿∿—

In Alexia's mind, she was dancing. Free. Laser lights flashed and pulsed, voices chattered. Her body whirled and writhed, and sweat rolled off. Smoke burned her nostrils and her legs were on fire, but none of it mattered so long as she kept moving. Her chest thumped and her body vibrated in time to her favorite Max Graham remix of Conjure One's "Sleep," and she could float among the stars. *Free.*

"Ma'am, did you hear me?"

Alexia shivered and looked at the police officer. Well, it was a fun daydream while it lasted. Better than standing out here in the butt-ass freezing cold with the homeless folks, being harassed by the cops. Which, by the way, *did* remind her of a party, but the flashing lights were from all the cop cars, and the chattering and bodies were the folks shivering in the cold and nothing more. The officer in question… well, she wasn't so sure he was a real cop at all. He had that cold, nasty soulless thing going like the wizard who had attacked her in Florida awhile back, and he touched her a little too much. Every time he did, the urge to knee him deep in the balls and run for it was very, very, very strong.

She scanned the crowd. The other police officers. Were they all wizards? Some of them? Just the one talking to her? The flashing red and blue glinted magically off something on the officer's hand as he took her statement. A pinkie ring. Right. Something about that rang a bell. And his head was shaved bald, just like the wizard that attacked her in her and Isabel's apartment in Florida. She looked around. Did any others have that ring?

One… maybe…

"Ma'am?"

She blinked again and looked at the man who loomed over her, a good foot taller at least. Hell, everyone was a good foot taller than she was. He actually looked quite a bit like the prisoner that she'd seen Siddoh manhandling across the grounds. The one Tyra seemed to have a thing with but didn't want to talk about. The face was different, though… she hadn't gotten a good enough look to know for sure. "I'm sorry, what?"

"I'd like you to explain to me again what made you tell the volunteers on duty to chain the cafeteria doors."

"Um." She bit hard on her lip, and tasted her own blood and honey-vanilla lip gloss. Was there a right answer here? This was one of the bad guys. He already knew damn well why Tyra had herded the volunteers into the cafeteria. Was there anything to be gained by making up a story? Maybe if she played dumb they would let her leave.

But just over the wizard's shoulder, barely visible in the shadows, was Lee. God, but she hated how much it lifted her just to lay eyes on him. Okay. She stared, making sure he knew she could see him. Making sure he knew that she knew that he knew. Her pulse picked up speed, because then she had a plan. Probably if she didn't get her ass kicked, then Lee was going to kill her for it. She crooked a finger at the fake wizard officer, who took the bait hook, line, and sinker. They always did. He leaned close.

"Okay, see, how about you tell me where my friend is and what you guys want with her, and I'll answer your questions nicely."

The wizard grinned. Hell, he was actually kind of hot, or would have been without the whole "vampire killer" aspect of his persona. The wicked smile spread across his face slowly as he straightened, putting his little fake notebook into his pocket and folding his hands behind his back. "Ma'am, I think this is a conversation that we need to have at the station."

She smiled a fake smile in return. *What was the deal here?* "Well, why don't you leave me your business card, and I will be happy to contact you during daylight hours."

"Hmm." He pressed his lips together. "You see, that's a problem, ma'am, because you're already in quite a bit of trouble for providing false information to the authorities."

"I didn't provide false information." Her gaze flicked to the shadowy area where Lee had been standing, but he wasn't there anymore. *Shit, where the hell did he go?* "I told the volunteers and the officers that were monitoring the inside of the cafeteria that there were trespassers on the property." She narrowed her eyes pointedly and then raised her eyebrows for effect. "That was totally true."

"Ah, but we were only coming for what was ours," he murmured. "And I'm sorry, ma'am, but you're going to have to come with me." That he said louder.

A large hand with bony knuckles wrapped around

her upper arm and dragged her toward the edge of the crowd. *Ow.* It was going to leave a bruise, but she didn't so much as twitch a face muscle to show the pain.

They were fast approaching what looked to be an unmarked squad car, which, come hell or high water, she refused to get into. She'd seen that safety lesson on *Oprah* enough times. So she did what most women of diminutive stature did in times like these. She went for the kneecaps, and then she went for the jewels.

The Doc Martens she wore weren't only a fashion statement.

Her heel connected with one of the guy's knees with a satisfying crunch, and she crouched low to throw her body weight into slamming her elbow between his legs. The male doubled and howled in pain. She twisted free of his grip but tripped on his big, stupid foot. Then the cuffs were snapped on. Shit.

She thrashed and made noise and kicked, but nothing much was accomplished. *Good lord, I look like one of those desperate people on* Cops. She hated being so small at times like these.

The male got in, sneering at her through the protective barrier. "Nice try, bitch." He was still gloating when he was lifted and shoved over the console into the passenger seat. The wizard's head hit the window, and blood spattered across the glass.

Oh. *Nasty.*

Lee settled into the driver's seat and wiggled a knife out of the wizard's skull. He wiped it on his pant leg and started the car. His blue-green stare pegged her from the rearview mirror. "You. Are going to owe me big time for this." Not another word was said as they peeled out.

Chapter 16

ANTON JERKED FORWARD TO GET IN THE KING'S FACE but didn't make it very far. "I'm telling you, I didn't fucking know." Thad and Siddoh had brought him back to the tiny, cold building with the thick stone walls. This time, no more mister nice king and bodyguard.

This time, they'd decided to use the shackles.

Anton had talked Siddoh down from nearly ripping his throat out before the car trip back, and the bulky vampire now only stared him down in stony silence. Just an angry tic at the large male's temple and the flare of his nostrils separated him from a wax statue in appearance. Thad paced, stopped to growl at Anton, and paced some more.

The king stopped and ran a tongue around his fangs. His blue eyes were icy and unforgiving "Thing is, I want to believe you. Siddoh here says you appeared to be legitimately distraught over what you found at your father's den. But I don't need to tell you what a cluster tonight turned out to be or how it looked real fucking bad for you."

"I cannot help how it looked." Anton jerked again. Metal dug into his wrists. Even in nothing but a black T-shirt and fatigues, his blood boiled at a million degrees. "You have to let me out of here so I can find Tyra."

"I've got guys looking, Anton. No offense, but you've got minimal combat experience, and while your refusal to take part in the wizard power-exchange ritual is commendable, it leaves you ill-equipped for fighting."

Red. Literally, Anton saw red. And black and spots. Pain radiated through his neck and jaw. His wrists. And fuck, he was burning up. "Listen, Thad. It isn't my fault you were dumbass enough to send her out with a shitty guard on her."

He ducked his head just in time to steer clear of Thad's fist. The smart thing might have been to stop antagonizing, but rage coursed through Anton's veins like battery acid. This was about trust, not fighting ability. Anton shook his head and kept going. "I didn't sabotage jack-shit. I have been trying to help your asses. No." He all but spat the words on the floor. "No, I've been helping *her*." He stretched to the length of his restraints, not to threaten but to meet the king eye to eye as best he could. To show the full force of his rage. The truth of his words.

"Shoulda torn you apart when I had the chance," Siddoh muttered again.

"Save it, asshole."

"How about both of you save it," Thad snapped.

Every inhale seared on the way down like he was breathing fire. Anton had to fucking get out. He had to get to Tyra. "Let me the fuck out of here, Thad."

"Look—"

"No, *you* fucking look. They *do* teach us to fight at the evil overlord boot camp, you know."

"You can't go after her alone, man. And no one wants to be your backup."

"The fuck I can't. Thad, come on." Anton stared hard, male to male, into the king's impassive face. "I go in there to get her, I may die. Something happens to her because I didn't, I'm dead anyway. That's what all of this has been about from the very beginning."

Deep inside, a giant, invisible fist squeezed his heart hard and the contents gushed out, hot and heavy, and the tears came without warning. Thad was good enough to pretend like something on the wall was incredibly interesting. Finally, when Thad sighed and relaxed his posture, relief seemed to be just around the corner.

But then Thad dropped the axe on him. "I'm sorry, Anton. I can't in good conscience—"

A horrible sound echoed in Anton's head. It must have been his voice because his throat burned so damned badly, but the sound was oddly distant. His blood burned him from the inside out, and he barely noticed when the metal bracelets fell from his wrists and hung by the wall, twisted and *glowing*.

Oh shit… His body was bright red. As in hot. And very, very naked. The clothes he'd been wearing were burned to ash and long gone. Every bit of him glowed. As in *every* bit.

"What the good goddamn…"

Siddoh's astonished utterance took Anton's attention away from his radiant naughty bits. "I… I…" Thank fuck he started to cool off as his anger subsided, if only mildly. He looked from Thad to Siddoh and back again. "I didn't know I could do that."

For a while neither spoke. "So it seems you participated in the blood ritual after all," Thad said finally.

Anton set his feet wide and lifted his chin high, despite his total lack of clothing. He would not apologize for this. "Never actually said that I didn't. I was against it. I got out of it when I could. But I did what I had to do to survive."

Thad paced slowly. In the back of Anton's mind a clock ticked. *Ticktock, Anton.* Precious moments were slipping by while he was locked in this room. Arguing.

"Thad, I don't know what my father has planned, but I have plenty of guesses and none of them are good. You want to fry me for the vampires I killed, you can do it when Tyra is safe and my father is dead. Christ, I'll lie down naked on the lawn out there, and you can let all the angry villagers fucking have at me if you want to, but *now is not the time for this!*"

Anton's chest heaved and burned. He couldn't delude himself that Tyra returned his feelings. For him, she was the closest thing he would ever get to a true connection with someone. He could go out more than happy, knowing he'd made the world safe for her and her kind before he died. And at her brother's hand? Hell of a lot better than at another wizard's.

Thad glanced at his watch. "Okay. I still don't like it, but at least you might not get your ass handed to you out there. Siddoh, get the man some clothes."

—◦◦◦—

Would telling the wizard leader she'd been expecting somebody taller change her chances of leaving this scenario alive?

Tyra suppressed a shiver in the frigid, stone-walled room. She stood face to face with the "Master" in the austere confines of a small space that reminded her a great deal of the interrogation cells Thad kept on his property. There wasn't much in the way of stuff to focus on in there, other than Anton's father. Boy, she really wished there was.

At first, she hadn't found him terribly intimidating beyond his threat that he might destroy the shelter if she didn't play nice. He hadn't even put out the kind of evil vibes she would have expected from one supposedly so powerful. She'd wondered if he might be a decoy until she'd looked into his eyes again.

And then, then she could admit that she was frightened.

His eyes were… voids. No, not even that. Void implied dead and soulless. This was… she'd noticed it back at the shelter, but she couldn't put a finger on just what it was. There was emotion there all right, but it was a kind of hate she couldn't put a name to. And obsidian burning… Damn, it was just the strangest thing. "I'm glad to finally meet you, my dear."

Her lip curled just a hair. "I'm not your anything."

"You have no idea how wrong you are, my girl." He smiled. Strangely, another rather charming smile. She could see where Anton got his gray eyes and the strong features of his face, and how disturbing was that?

Always a fan of personal space, Tyra longed to take a step or five away, but she refused to be the one to back down, and old Master here clearly didn't mind being a close talker. "So enlighten me."

The wizard picked at what looked like a hangnail. "It isn't all about power, you know. We also need the blood to survive. After childhood we age rapidly without it. Far faster than humans."

Huh. The mental leap wasn't hard to make. They knew that vampire blood affected wizards biologically. It seemed to extend their lifespan and turned their bodies to ash with full exsanguinations. Handy for the vampires when it came to body disposal. That also might explain why Anton looked older than he was. Nevertheless… "You don't have fangs."

"As you know, we've gotten our blood through different means." He leaned a hand against the side of his face. It changed the way he looked to sad and tired.

She hated that even more than she hated him. Feeling even an infinitesimal amount of sympathy toward him was something she could not allow.

"Our race is dying." He leaned forward, resting his elbows on his knees. The wide-eyed expression he wore was practically earnest. "Primarily, we've reproduced over the years by mating with humans. Over the centuries we've diluted the bloodlines. Bound to happen, I suppose." One evil wizard palm rubbed over the other slowly, as if there was dirt or dust he might brush away. "I'd hoped our wizard genes would be strong enough to overcome, but I've been seeing the signs for some time now."

Tyra's body shook inside; she had to get out of there. Why was he telling her this? Did he honestly expect sympathy? "Good. *Good*." Tyra forgot herself and stepped backward. "All the better if your species dies out and stops killing ours. I will *not* feel sorry for you."

"You are entitled to feel however you wish, but this is about vampire survival as well as ours. You may have noticed greater numbers of your vampire kind being killed by my wizards of late."

"No, I—" Could she even be certain? Over a week in torpor to recover from a near-fatal power drain, and before that she'd been focused on her volunteer work at the homeless shelter. She hadn't gone out to fight during the weeks while Thad was searching for his queen, for Isabel. So really, could Tyra even be sure what had gone on out there? Very vaguely, she recalled Siddoh having said he suspected that the wizards were stepping up their efforts.

She shook her head. It wasn't as if she could trust this guy. "That's not a reason for us to help you." If anything, it was a reason to strike back harder. Recruit more fighters, if they could. Now that they knew for sure there was a chink in the armor… Her entire body perked up at the thought. She couldn't wait to tell Thad.

"Of course not." And now his smile was disgustingly indulgent. "But consider this. The more diluted the bloodlines of our later generations, the more difficult to absorb vampire powers and the faster they will age. They're more bloodthirsty with each passing day, you see? Our kind is being compelled to kill yours in greater and greater numbers."

She looked then into those dark gray eyes and longed to touch him. To feel him out for the truth. Then hated herself even more because there was no way in hell she could do it. Not the way she would need to in order to glean his emotions. *Come on, Ty. Yes you can. Don't be weak. Don't be stupid. You can handle just grabbing his arm, can't you?* She took a step.

He stood. "You, though. You have the strength of both species. The ability to absorb powers without having to consume organs or flesh."

What? Oh, no. Noooo. If he was implying what he sure as hell seemed to be implying… hell, motherfucking, no. "My mother was human."

He pursed his lips. "I can see why you would have thought that. I can assure you she wasn't. And I can assure you that your father knew. He tried to kill me four months ago. I suppose he thought it would keep us from having this very encounter."

Instinctively, she reached for a weapon she no longer had. Shit, she was going to kill this bastard. Her palm heated with the beginning of a fireball.

"I know what you're thinking. I didn't kill your father." He turned to offer his back and bowed his head. "And since we're sharing information just now, I'll trust you not to attack while my back is turned. I hadn't planned on killing you either, but plans can change. Look closely at the birthmark, right at the top."

She did. It was the shape of a perfect heart. "Okay. So?"

"You have one just like it in the same spot."

"So what? I have birthmarks all over." Hers wasn't really like that. Was it? Who gave more than passing attention to all the random spots on their bodies?

"I mark all of my own kind with them. Every wizard offspring is born with one." He turned and looked at her again. Now his grin was sinister.

She stared. At the eyes. At the smile. She didn't respond. There wasn't anything she could think of to say.

Without warning he clasped hands with hers. Her nerves and veins lit up like the Beltway at nighttime. A rush of power flew through her bloodstream. Similar to what she experienced just after drinking blood but stronger. Louder. The buzz in her ears was fulminating and lovely. Her heart nearly flew from its confines in her chest cavity. "My God."

"Use one of your powers. Any one. Go ahead."

This had to be some kind of trick.

He stepped back and raised his arms, palms facing the ceiling. "No tricks. I only want to show you the possibilities that are open to you. Try to. Go ahead."

"I—" Curiosity got the better of her. Like she had the morning she'd been examined by Dr. Brayden, she focused on the intent of making flame engulf her hand. Not only did it take barely any focus, but there was a wall of fire between them in a matter of seconds. Holy shit.

Holy *shit*.

On the inside, Tyra cringed. She wasn't one of these assholes. She wasn't. Her hand dropped to her side and the fire died out, as did the heady buzzing in her system.

"I hadn't realized until just recently that the females can absorb powers without the ritual." He continued. "Or maybe it's only you who can because of your vampire blood. Obviously, the first step is to find the female wizard offspring. We can't breed with them; we gave up on that long ago. But they'll die if they're not brought into the fold."

He rubbed the back of his neck. "I'm not foolish enough to think that our two species can simply broker peace after so many centuries. I only want to study your power. If we can acquire powers without killing, perhaps wizards and vampires can one day have a new relationship. I'm after survival here."

She snorted and folded her arms over her chest. "Like as in mate together? You're kidding. We're not going to help your race, not after everything you've done."

He mimicked her stance. With an inclined head, he gestured toward her. "That felt good, didn't it? The power I just transferred to you?"

Already the intense hum was dissipating, but a gentle pulse remained and she couldn't deny the rush had been pleasurable. Damned if she'd say so, but the smug smile on his face told her that she didn't have to.

"There's more where that came from, if you help me."

He thought she was that easy? Anger accelerated the *dum-dum-dum* of her heart. It wouldn't work, would it? No. *Don't even think it, Ty. Don't even think he might really stop killing your kind.*

Not even to save his own race?

Her own race?

Tyra blinked. All at once she was light-headed and sick to her stomach. Last thing she wanted was to lose face by puking on the Master's boots.

This time when Master grinned, it wasn't charming. It was back to befitting of the evil that she knew him to be, and that anchored her. *The many faces of evil.* So much of what he'd just told her had turned her world upside down and inside out. She could face this monster. She knew monsters.

He leaned far too casually against the far wall of the room. "Think it over," he said. "You'll be back. I have no doubt." His feral grin widened. "After a taste of what I just gave you? It won't be enough. Trust me."

Chapter 17

ALEXIA HAD NO IDEA HOW FAST THEY WERE GOING. Fast. The dead wizard up front was flopping around and smearing blood like something out of a bad horror movie. Hell, it *was* a bad horror movie. She held on in the backseat and tried to breathe.

"I hope you're happy with yourself for that sassy little production of yours, Lex." Lee's square jaw and sharp fangs were menacing from her view of his profile, and his eyes glowed from the light of all the instruments and dials and whatnot up front in the car when he turned back to growl at her. "On the upside, you helped to confirm our suspicions that we've got wizards hiding in the local public sector. Pretty sure we could have found a way to do that, though, that didn't involve me ditching a body and a cop car in the woods off Route 9 on the way back to the estate."

How had she not foreseen how that would play out? In a way they'd been lucky. *She* had been lucky. The wizard had been no match for Lee, and the kill had been quick. Except for speeding away in a cop car, which had probably raised a few eyebrows, they'd gotten away easily enough. "I thought maybe I could get him to tell me where Tyra was. I was trying to help," she muttered. Honestly, she hadn't really considered that Lee would kill the guy. Sometimes it was easy to forget what he was capable of.

She wouldn't forget again.

And now, as they sped along the back roads, it was so late that no cars were on these winding turns. Most of the folks around here were farmers who went to bed at the appropriate times. She held back the urge to suggest maybe he should keep his eyes on the road, given how fast he was going.

He didn't seem interested in her opinion just now.

When they reached an isolated stretch of road, he pulled the car off into a wooded area. "Where are we?" she asked. They seemed to be near the estate; the area struck her as familiar. But jeez. This time of night, everything around the area looked the same. Trees. Road. More trees. For someone like Alexia who was used to navigating by visual landmarks, it was hellishly easy to get lost.

Up front, Lee grumbled but didn't answer. Something in Lexi's chest tightened. She hated—*hated*—knowing someone was angry with her. Okay, she'd fucked up and she deserved this one, so she'd take whatever lumps she had to. And hell, maybe having Lee mad at her wasn't such a huge loss anyway. It wasn't as if they *were* anything to each other. Really, they hardly knew each other.

Still, she couldn't stop herself from apologizing. "Lee, I'm sorry. I knew what he was, and he could tell that I knew, and he was asking all these questions. I wasn't sure what to say. I'm sorry I said the wrong thing."

Small trees bumped and cracked and gave way under the vehicle's weight. He killed the headlights and they bounced along in darkness, probably aided by the sharpness of his acute night vision. At least she sure hoped so. Lexi couldn't see where they were going at all.

"Lee, I really am sorry."

Her voice, usually full of bitch and defiance, had just the tiniest crack in it. She pressed her lips together. Damn being a woman with emotions. He was sitting there judging her for it right now; she just knew it. Thinking she was stupid. Thinking she was weak and inferior. Too *human*. Well, she couldn't go back in time. For damn sure, she couldn't do a thing about her place in the evolutionary food chain. If apologizing wasn't good enough, he could go fuck himself.

Fury at his constant superiority roiled in her gut and helped her to get a handle on things. She breathed long and loud and a bit shakily, but she said nothing more after that. Probably better that way. Nothing good happened when they talked to each other.

As soon as he threw the car into park, he was in some kind of weird, robotic disposal mode. Body on the ground. Slice. Slice. Slice. Kick. "Bye, asshole." It might have been disgusting if it hadn't been so damned fascinating. She could have sworn the wizard's body was shriveling up right there on the spot. Lee came around to the back door, on the opposite side so Lexi wouldn't have to step past the gore. "Come on."

She scooted toward the door but stopped when he reached to grab her arm. "I can get out myself."

He took hold of her arm anyway. She hadn't realized she still was wearing a cuff until he helped remove it. "Yeah, well I'm sorry to tell you this but we're gonna have to get out of here fast. I can move a hell of a lot quicker than you."

Next thing she knew, she was being slung over a very large shoulder. "Lee. Are you out of your freaking mind? Put me the hell down, you son of a bitch. I'm going to tell Thad about this."

"Excellent. I hope you do." Dead leaves and dirt and branches flew beneath her as they sped along what was probably the tree line parallel to Route 9. Alexia expressed her displeasure by pounding Lee on the back with her fists. He'd get tired of it and put her down eventually.

Or maybe he wouldn't. They'd made it back to the vampire estate, and she was still calling him every name in the book and had resorted to biting him on the shoulder. Which didn't have one fricking ounce of fat on it. Still no dice on getting out of the sack-of-potatoes gig.

Finally he stopped to set her down on a fallen log, which allowed them to be at eye level. Tears streamed down her face, and if looks could kill, she hoped he'd be fucking on fire by now. She pulled up the edge of her shirt to wipe the tears away, for what little good that did. They kept coming.

"Do you have any idea how close you came to dying tonight?"

She hiccupped and swiped a hand over her face. She struggled to keep her voice even. "I guess I didn't, at first," she admitted.

Lee flexed his fingers and reached forward like he was about to make a grab, but he stopped and pulled back. "I am so fucking mad at you."

Grr. Alexia's toes curled up inside her Doc Martens. "I'm pretty fucking mad at you too." Little did he know that it had nothing to do with the dead wizard.

She shivered and her foot slipped on some loose tree bark, which tossed her right into his arms. He was aroused. Holy crap, was he ever. The hard length of him pressed against her, and his grip, awkward at first, tightened. The fingers of his large hands spread across her back into something more intimate and familiar. She tilted her face up to look into those aqua-colored eyes, which glowed in the moonlight, dilated with desire she would've given almost anything to see a week or two ago. A few hours ago, even.

Before he threw her over his shoulder and humiliated her.

"Lee…" His nose brushed against hers, and her body tensed. She pushed against his chest, but fear took away her words. Without another second of thought, her knee made contact with his family jewels.

"Fuck. Alexia…"

His hold loosened and she ran, not looking back to check on him or apologize. He was a badass vampire; it wasn't like he needed her to wait for him. He'd be fine.

Chapter 18

"ANTON."

Anton spun toward the sound of Tyra's voice. They had nearly gotten to where the portal ought to be when she torpedoed out of the woods like a heat-seeking missile.

Anton sucked in a breath. Without thought, his hands went to either side of her face, his lips on hers. The kiss was hard and intense, like somehow he could bond their souls together with their lips. For those few seconds, nothing else mattered. He gathered her into his arms, and nothing had ever been more amazing. The solid warmth of her body and the softness of her curly hair were even better than before.

The smell of her, though, was like stale smoke and staler blood. He knew that smell. "You've seen my father."

She nodded into his shoulder.

"Tyra?" Behind them, the three males who had accompanied Anton shifted and shuffled uncomfortably, and he couldn't have cared less. Tyra was in his arms, and he didn't want to let go. He patted her back. "What happened? How did you get away?"

"He let me go. Just… let me go. He said I'd come back on my own." She hugged herself as if to ward off the chill. From the expression on her face, it was clear that she was haunted by the encounter. He couldn't blame her. Over his dead fucking body would Tyra come back here on her own.

Someone cleared his throat and approached. The one named Xander, who apparently had been out of commission until recently… something about losing his mate. Anton remembered the bodies with the tattoos he'd seen in the ceremony room, and a hard pang hit his chest. His father and the evil of their clan had done so much damage.

"Listen, guys, I hate to piss in everybody's Cheerios here, but this is so clearly a trick." The male looked around. "The leader of the wizards, who none of us but this guy"—he jerked a thumb toward Anton—"has actually seen, kidnaps Tyra and then just lets her go, no strings attached. No wizard idiots lurking in the bushes to attack. What about him?" He gestured again toward Anton. "How do we know he's not setting us up or something?"

Ah, yes, because Xander had not been present for that first go-round through the portal. And what a shame.

Cold from the night air and the chill of the angry male's words had Anton aching to grab Tyra to pull her close again. *Aching* to. He held off out of respect for her. She fought with these men, and it wouldn't do to make it look as if he needed to hold on to her. Besides that, he didn't want this vampire to think Anton would use Tyra as some kind of shield against his ire.

While he worked to choose his response, biting wind swirled in Anton's nose. It was almost metallic in scent, wind and pine, and it reminded him of that first night that Tyra had drunk from him. He closed his eyes for a beat to take in the memory. When he opened them again, Xander had stepped closer, fists clenched in angry-vampire mode. Not for the first time, Anton's eyes lit on the mating tattoo on the male's left wrist.

A hummingbird drinking from a flower. Very attractive. Very familiar.

Something had nagged at the back of his brain since first seeing that tattoo. He remembered. His gut twisted and the words tumbled out before he was entirely aware of what he was saying. "Your mate. I'm so sorry. She was unconscious when they brought her in. Sometimes they aren't. She didn't suffer. I hope that helps, at least a little."

Anton saw the whole thing coming before it began, saw the vampire's face contort as understanding dawned, saw the knuckles come flying, and the blood spray. He brought his arms up to guard against the blows, but he let the male have his rage and his hurt. It was what they both deserved. He hadn't killed this vampire's mate, but it was atonement just the same. Anton *had* killed in the past, after all.

Somewhere in the distance there was shouting. Tyra. That was good. She was safe, probably. Although, God… what had his father done? Why had he taken her, and why had he let her go? It had to be some kind of a trick, and fuck if he knew what the old bastard had planned.

He couldn't let this vampire kill him; he wasn't sure yet that Tyra was out of harm's way. That look on her face… something had happened. Anton had to find out what that sick fuck had done to her, and he had to make it right. With a primal yell through swollen lips, he exploded upward, catching the angry vampire under the chin.

"I said stop." Tyra caught him around the middle.

Siddoh and the other vampire grabbed Xander, who was wild-eyed and staring at Anton the way a hungry lion eyed wounded prey. No question, the male was desperate to go back in for the kill.

"Anton, are you okay?"

Her hand cradled his swollen face gently. He'd never been any prize in the looks department, but this sure as hell wasn't going to help him. "It wasn't me," he murmured. "His mate. I saw her, but I didn't take part in her ceremony. I should have tried to stop it. I should have tried to stop so many of them…"

"Shh, I know."

But she didn't know the whole story. Not yet. They hadn't had the chance to talk about it properly. And no sooner had the thought formed in Anton's head than a warm, soothing sensation formed just where Tyra's hand touched his face. The pain abated even as Anton's heart shriveled and dropped into his gut.

Tyra was healing him. Now she did know. She'd absorbed his power by drinking his blood.

———⁓———

"Anton."

He didn't answer. In fact, nobody said a word. Even Xander, who had been snarling and flailing against Flay and Siddoh for another chance to tear Anton apart, was suddenly still. Tyra's hand glowed faintly like a feat of magic, warm amber against the swollen, bloody mess on Anton's cheek. As if he'd just guzzled a pint of her blood, a split on his lip began to seal. First the blood seeping out of it dried up, and then the skin knit together, leaving the lip a little chapped but otherwise no worse for the wear. Well lit from the three-quarter moon, the swelling and bruising of his cheek receded underneath Tyra's fingers.

Part of her—the part that was horrified by the implications of what was going on—wanted to pull away. To run. To slap him in the face, hold him down, and let Xander finish what he'd started or, hell, even beat the shit out of him herself. Part of her was... fascinated.

What did it mean that she'd absorbed a power from Anton, but that she had never sensed evil from him? Then again...

You could be the key to returning the balance. You and the other female wizards.

Tyra dropped her hand, and the light on her palm faded and winked out. Anton seemed to brace himself for what she'd do next.

She'd always had poor radar for the malevolent aura that wizards radiated. Siddoh's was the best; he could smell them miles away. Tyra... she'd always assumed that being half human made it tough for her to detect the wizard evil. But what if Anton's father spoke the truth? What if she'd never detected the evil very easily because she, herself, was part of that evil?

"Tyra..." Anton's breath sawed in and out.

She held up a hand. "I can heal, Anton."

He frowned through the cuts and bruises that remained on his face. "I can see that."

"Explain this to me."

Not that she needed him to. She already knew. Hell, everybody standing in that forest knew. It wasn't rocket science. One of the reasons she'd been choosy about mates over the years was that she'd absorb the power of any mate she both slept with and fed from. It had happened with Siddoh. It had happened with *Anton*.

That meant that Anton had participated in the

disgusting ritual that the wizards used to acquire vampire powers. A quick glance around at the rest of the team showed a mix of expressions ranging from anger to concern, but not one of them appeared to be surprised. Not one. So she had been the last to know, apparently.

Nice.

Should've been more choosy, Ty. "Huh." She laughed. "I can't believe it." Though whether she couldn't believe Anton or herself was tough to say. Somehow she had come to trust him more than she realized, and this… this cut deep. Wow, did it ever.

"Tyra, I didn't know how to tell you." His fingers wrapped around hers.

Tyra broke contact, and she laughed again. Admittedly, a little more hysterically this time. "Gosh, you're right, Anton. It certainly is a tough call. Not exactly first-date material. But maybe knowing before we fucked would have been useful."

The other males mumbled and shuffled uncomfortably off to the side.

"Tyra, I'm sorry."

"Sorry?"

His face reddened. Angry, was he? Good. So was she. "Yes, goddammit, I am sorry." He looked over at Xander, still held by Flay and Siddoh but no longer struggling. "And I did not kill your mate, but I am sorry to you as well." Back to Tyra. "Look, I was trying to survive. I did everything I could to avoid involving myself in the ritual, but I was living among sociopaths and murderers. I was trying to survive. I did what I had to, yes. And how the hell was I supposed to just come out and tell you that when we were about to make love?

Or immediately after, when your brother was beating down your door and I had just realized that you were half wizard."

The red in his face blossomed and expanded, everything glowing like a banked fire. Shit, another power. Another one? And he knew that she was part wizard. Judging from the look on Siddoh's face, so did he. Was this news a surprise to nobody but her?

"How many, Anton? Can you be honest with me about that, at least? How many times *did* you participate in that disgusting ritual?"

He cleared his throat. The ember glow died down. "Twice. Only twice."

Tyra's head swam. She couldn't think and couldn't breathe… what was she supposed to do with this? What else might he have kept from her? Oh Jesus—what if this whole thing between them really *had* been a lie? "I'm so stupid."

For all of her hundred-plus years on the planet, she could still be really naive sometimes. What if this whole thing had been a trick all along? For all she knew, Anton and his father were in this together, trying to muddle her head and get Anton close enough to verify her powers so that they could recruit her. Or worse, claim all of her powers for their own. Oh. God. Why hadn't she thought of that?

Her heart jackhammered in her chest. "I shouldn't have trusted you."

Anton started toward her. "Tyra, don't say that. I love—"

"Don't you dare say that to me, asshole." Almost without thought, she sent a fireball shooting from her hand and barely missed him. There was a scuffle and some shouting, but she didn't stick around to see what the final outcome was.

She turned and stormed through the trees, unsure of her destination.

Chapter 19

XANDER FLOATED A SHORT DISTANCE FROM THE FRAY. Or what had been the fray only moments ago. What remained were a couple of sad, disgusting excuses for defenders of their race. And then there was Anton, looking very much like his soul had been ripped out. Though Xander's own arms remained held by Flay and Siddoh, it was unnecessary. Xander could do nothing but stare at the broken wizard, while the *glub, glub, glub* of Xander's own heart floundered in his ears.

He closed his eyes and was immediately sucked back into his skin. *Well. How disappointing*.

Tam's death was as fresh as if it had happened yesterday. The moment she was gone, her death had resonated to his very core. Her life force, the invisible heart that had always beat so swiftly alongside his own, was gone. Just gone. And in its place, to this day, was a gaping, open void that nothing in the world could ever fill.

He carried the ache every day, the burn and strain of a supernaturally powerful heart that insisted on beating continuously despite the fact that Xander would have much preferred for it not to. It still seemed so improbable that he could haul around two hundred pounds of muscle and bone and somehow get from point A to point B for as long as he did without just collapsing into the dust. There was, after all, nothing that made him want to go on. Nothing that made him feel peace.

Nothing that ever would.

Not even killing the wizard in front of him who had seen her die.

Who had… Xander's eyes burned as he stared at the wizard named Anton. Who had tried, it would seem, to do Xander a kindness of sorts by letting him know that Tam had not suffered. At least not as much as she might have. It wasn't much, but it was something.

There were questions, clearly, about the wizard's allegiance. Of course there would be. One didn't just waltz in off the street claiming to be a defected wizard, and frankly, Thad had given the man liberties that surprised Xander. Still, there were questions. Rumors that he'd orchestrated a fight that occurred downtown earlier. That he'd made it possible for Tyra to be taken. There were a lot of problems here.

But looking at Anton now, Xander was fairly sure this guy was no traitor. Not to the vampires, anyway. Not to Tyra. Not judging by the look on this guy's face.

Xander approached Flay and Siddoh, and brought a hand to each of Anton's shoulders, pushing at the grip of his superior officers. "I won't hurt him. You can let go." The resistance with which the two older males complied was understandable, but he spoke the truth.

Remarkably, for the first time since Tam's death— even after all these months of guarding Theresa and now her baby—Xander was looking into a mirror. A man who was gripped by a torture worse than death and yet somehow remained standing.

Xander offered his palm, which Anton stared at in confusion with his brow creased, as if Xander had asked him to solve a riddle.

"Come on." He jerked his head in the direction Tyra had run. "Let's get a move on. I still hear her going through the woods."

Anton cleared his throat. "It's disgusting, you know. I never wanted to be a part of… any of it."

"I know." And Xander did know. He wouldn't have claimed to even five minutes before. But the total devastation on Anton's face when he'd realized that Tyra was lost to him forever? Every light had gone out in that male's soul. And she *would* be gone now. Anyone could see that. It was enough to make Xander believe the conviction of the wizard's words. "But seriously, we have to get moving. She's a danger to herself, and she's not thinking clearly or she would've teleported somewhere by now."

He inclined his head toward Flay and Siddoh. "You guys should report in with Thad. She's pissed off, and we don't know what Dr. Evil said to her, but we know it couldn't have been good. You should at least prepare him for bad news."

Flay jabbed an accusatory finger. "Don't kill him."

Anton had managed to find his get-up-and-go, and Xander followed after flipping Flay the one-finger salute. *Jeez.* Flay and Siddoh tossed dubious glares over their shoulders before speeding off into the woods in the other direction.

Truly, though, as Xander thought about it, he couldn't imagine what being born on the other side of that fence would be like. They had always assumed that the wizards were all just… soulless. That they killed because they liked to kill. They wanted to claim vampire powers for the sake of having power, and that was that.

This one clearly hadn't wanted to but hadn't had a choice. Had been forced to kill vampires who had done nothing wrong because it was either that or be killed himself. Xander could not forgive necessarily, but he could appreciate on some level that the man had lived in his own kind of hell.

The sound of arguing and a scuffle made Xander pick up speed, but when he reached the source, he found Anton on his ass in the middle of a frozen patch of ground. "She's not interested in discussing things further," Anton said. "You want to go ahead and beat the shit out of me some more while I'm down here?"

Xander rolled his neck and looked down at the wizard, who was still bruised and a little bloody, though already showing signs of healing. Interesting.

Xander punched Anton on the arm but then helped pull him to standing. "Don't tell me you're going to let her just push you around like that. Come on, we've stayed here far too long. God knows what your leader has planned. And now that you've given me permission to give you a beat-down, it's taken all the fun out of it for me."

───✧───

Lord knew how long she had crashed through the woods before Anton had caught up with her and she realized she was being a total idiot. She was visible. She was making too much noise. She was on foot when she should have teleported. What she was *not* doing was thinking clearly.

"Okay, Ty, get a grip on yourself here." She stopped against a storm-damaged evergreen. A broken branch jabbed into her back and gave her a refreshing wake-up call while she got her bearings. This thing with Anton? No, she couldn't get her head around that just yet. She was too… God, she just couldn't think when it came to him. Cold ice filled her chest. Panic and fear and a whole lot of oh-what-the-fuck-have-I-done? Because how stupid—stupid and disgustingly naive—she had been to let him into the estate, to let him near her brother. Into her bed, into her heart.

And this thing with his father… That would be a *hell* no. She had accepted her human side a long time ago, and because she was stronger than most vampires, she'd managed to make peace with it.

Because she was more powerful than most vampires. In more than a hundred years, nobody ever thought that was odd. "Oh my God, why didn't I realize?" So few of their kind bred with humans, but the ones who did usually produced physically weaker offspring. It was a big reason for that whole "human-vampire interaction" law that the Elders' Council had brought to the table recently. It had been so easy for her to ignore the obvious.

Tree bark scattered by her head. Someone was shooting at her. She crouched low behind the tree and pulled out her gun.

"Tyra."

Anton. What the hell was he doing? That idiot was going to get himself killed running through the woods calling to her like that. And just as quickly as they'd started, the sounds of him running stopped. Shit, what had happened?

Was he okay?

How badly she wanted him to be all right almost knocked her over. She slithered along the ground in the direction she'd heard his voice come from. Fiery pain bit her in the shoulder, but she ignored it as best she could and pushed forward. She'd fed not too long ago; her body could handle it just fine.

Sure enough, even as Tyra rolled to return fire, her body's superior healing properties started to expel the metal from her body. Key word: started. "Damn," she muttered. She didn't have time for this. Fingernails dug and pulled. Her fangs sank into her lips and she tasted her own blood, but it was far better than crying out against the pain.

Something moved in the trees. A slow, tentative sweep of pine needles from across the way, like someone pushed a branch aside. Was that where Anton had been shouting from? Shit, she couldn't tell what was what. Her night vision wasn't as sharp as a pure-blooded vampire's, and everything was just far enough into the shadows that she couldn't see clearly. She could throw a fireball to light things up, but what if she aimed wrong and hit Anton?

"Dammit, Tyra, this is ridiculous," she muttered. "You never had this kind of trouble fighting alongside Siddoh all those years."

Okay, slow it down. You're overthinking everything.

A twig snapped ahead and to her right. Then, silence closed in from all other angles. She took a chance and scooted back under the cover of an evergreen. Her hand warmed, and she focused her energy on charging the fireball that gathered there. She waited. She sure as hell hoped that Anton was all right, and that if he was, he was smart enough to stay put. Because the first thing that came out of those trees was going to burn.

She was seated comfortably, and the flame she cradled in her hand was fairly small. Her heart was hammering a mile a minute, but that was another story altogether. In theory, she could wait this out for a while. She tried to get Zen about it, like Lee had taught her years ago, and focused on the in and out of her breath, the movement of her abdomen, and the flicker of the fire in her hand. But she kept looking through the trees for Anton.

Maybe she was still afraid to trust him, but she wanted him to be okay. She cared for him. Deeply. But she had spoken an important truth that first night when they had come looking for his father together. *She couldn't afford to be wrong*. And now, knowing that they came from the same blood, so to speak? It changed everything.

A rustle and snap came from across the way. Footsteps approached. Tyra took aim and let her fireball fly.

Chapter 20

ANTON JERKED WHEN A HEAVY HAND LANDED ON HIS shoulder. Another hand held a jacket in front of him.

"Here," Xander whispered. "You left it. Back there. You should put it on."

Anton glanced over his shoulder. "I did?"

The vampire—Xander—crouched and met him eye to eye. Why was he on his knees here in the dirt? Why was it difficult to breathe? Anton had a moment of flashback to the morning when he'd woken in woods just like these after his father had tried to kill him. For all he knew, it had been these very woods. Then it had hurt to breathe because of injury. Because of bloody gashes and a punctured lung and fuck knew what else.

Now?

Tyra had shoved him away when he'd tried to explain. Twice. And now she was under attack, and this Xander had just stopped Anton from going after her because of his fucking jacket?

But light exploded from nearby and Xander pulled on Anton's arm. "Looks like she's hit one. Come on."

Of course she had. After all, she was powerful, a perfectly competent fighter. She didn't need Anton to defend her. They'd been clear on that, hadn't they? Added to that, what little trust she'd had in him had been shattered the moment she realized what he'd been keeping from her. That he'd already known she was part wizard. Not that she'd stopped to ask how he knew. Not that he'd said.

How should that have gone down, exactly? Would it have been better to blurt it out, right there in front of her fellow vampires, one of whom she'd been previously intimate with? *No, you see, baby, I really have cared for you all along. I didn't realize you had wizard blood until I saw the birthmark on your naked body after we did it. You know, after I drank your blood and stuff? Boy, that was surprisingly hot. But I guess you're not gonna let me do that again, on account of now you think I want to cut your chest open and eat your heart. I have to tell you that is the most disgusting thing I've ever done. Thanks a fucking lot.*

He guessed he couldn't blame her.

Maybe it was foolish to think they'd connected back there when they made love. Maybe... was sex always like that? He guessed he needed to be with another female to make a true comparison.

He'd rather eat a vampire heart.

Wind blew. A tree branch slapped him in the face, and he laughed at the ridiculous direction of his thoughts. Once the sound bubbled up and out of his mouth, it gained in speed and volume, and the release was amazing, not unlike the killer orgasm he'd had when he'd made love to Tyra. Not quite as satisfying but almost as necessary. The anger and frustration and all that sheer cluelessness over which way to turn next.

He had to get it out.

A hand landed over his mouth. "Buddy."

Anton laughed more. His breath clouded around the fingers covering his mouth.

Someone shook his shoulder. "Buddy."

Anton coughed and sobered up. They'd come out just to the right of a tree behind where Tyra was fighting a wizard. His pulse spiked, but then he realized that one already lay dead on the ground and the other was probably not long for this world. She'd just kicked him against a tree and set him aflame. That fire thing of hers was a cool power, no question. His heat power didn't seem to work like that.

Look at her. No, Tyra really hadn't needed either of them to help. Meanwhile here was Anton, laughing in the woods like a lunatic when everything was going to shit around them. No wonder she didn't want him.

"So, this is what it looks like from the outside, huh?"

"What?"

Xander's smile was genuine but sad at the same time. Anton noticed that he had long, very sharp fangs. Tyra's were less prominent, more blunt in appearance unless extended for feeding. Maybe because she wasn't a full-blooded vampire? He flinched when across the way Tyra shoved the wizard's head against a tree trunk. Anton hated to even think about it.

"It's the crazies, ya know?" The vampire scratched the back of his neck and shifted uncomfortably. "When I lost my Tam, I felt it in here." He thumped his chest with a fat thumb. Anton glanced back at Tyra when Xander's eyes got watery. "And you know, for a long time I was off the deep end. But that part at the beginning, it's the worst. When you're denying and then you're flipping out and then…" Alexander met Anton's stare. Strong enough, apparently, to face him even with a drop of moisture sliding out of one eye. "And then you think maybe you're gonna just die right then and there because you don't have the other half of your heart anymore."

Anton's gut burned and twisted. He wanted to curl into a ball like one of those stupid pill bugs some of the other wizards used to take matches to when they were children. Wait until the world and everything awful went away. Tears stung behind his own eyes, but out here in the woods with enemies attacking was not the time for some kind of manly pity fest. "I'm sorry. I swear. If I had been able to save her—"

"No." Xander grabbed Anton's arm as if he, too, had reached the conclusion that it was time for them to move. "I know. Look." Xander pointed to where Tyra had the wizard facing a tree, with a knife out ready to land the deathblow. "Tyra's still alive, okay? I just think you need to keep sight of that." Xander swallowed hard and pressed the again-forgotten jacket into Anton's hands. Funny, it wasn't until Anton put the thing on that he really felt the cold.

"I know."

"Of course you do." Xander clapped him on the back, then jabbed him hard with a finger to the chest. "So you don't waste that, you know? I saw you give up back there, and what I'm trying to tell you, my friend, is as long as that heart of hers is still beating inside her chest, you don't fucking waste that."

Anton sucked in a deep breath. Xander was absolutely right. He needed to find a way to make things right with Tyra, and he needed to prove himself. A few feet away, she dropped the body to the ground and turned to him. She smiled. *Actually* smiled.

Anton smiled back. His chest flew wide open and all

the fear escaped, thanks to the way she looked at him then. He wasn't sure what had changed her mind, but he could believe that everything was all right when she smiled at him that way.

He had just taken a step toward her when a sphere of light blasted through the trees and hit Xander in the back of the head.

—*w*—

"That face of yours is pissing me off, rabbit."

Thad squinted in the dimly lit kitchen and growled at the goofy, cheerful countenance of a cartoon bunny on the container of strawberry powder in his hand. Isabel was supposed to have gone to bed early, but forty goddamned minutes later she'd woken up to go to the bathroom and decided she needed strawberry milk to get back to sleep.

Of course she did.

He leaned against the granite countertop. "Baby's as big as a key lime. Already she's peeing like it was one of her new assigned duties as queen," he said to the rabbit's silly grin. "Soon we'll need to move a mattress into the bathroom."

He dug for a long iced-tea spoon in one of the drawers. "Sister's missing. Another Elder Council meeting is in a few days. No speech prepared for that. Busy making flavored milk. Fucking first-world vampire problems." An open honey-maple cabinet of glasses gave him pause.

"Something wrong, buddy?"

Thad threw a look over his shoulder at Siddoh and Flay standing in the doorway to the hall before returning to the issue at hand. "If I get too small of a glass and she's still thirsty, she'll send me back for more. Too big, and she'll be up another ten times during the day."

Siddoh grinned. "Either way you don't sleep."

Thad dropped his chin to his chest. He sighed and grabbed a stray Redskins souvenir cup someone had shoved alongside the drinking glasses and filled it with milk. "This way I get points for effort, and maybe if I'm lucky she won't wake me up the next time she has to go to the bathroom." He sat at the kitchen's small bistro table with the long spoon and the strawberry powder. "So what's up, guys?"

Siddoh looked impossibly large when he perched on one of the bistro chairs. Thad didn't look that ridiculous when he sat on those things, did he? They needed to rethink the furniture in here, too. "Things went nuts out in the woods. Good news is, Tyra's okay. Wizards had her, but they let her go."

Thad let go of the spoon. It kept spinning on its own in the glass, carried around in circles by the force of the milk. Relief took the tension out of his body, but it rebounded again when he weighed Siddoh's words. "What do you mean 'let her go'? They don't do that." He looked from Siddoh to Flay. The blond-haired vampire nodded confirmation.

"We don't know exactly what went down except that he dropped the bomb about her wizard blood, and she went off half-cocked when she realized she was the last to know."

"And that her wizard friend had stolen some vampire powers," Flay interjected.

Thad cursed. And cursed some more when he slid

off the seat and milk sloshed onto his hand from the overfull cup. "Okay, so what are you two clowns doing back here?"

Siddoh pushed back his chair as well. "Xander and Anton are cleaning things up with Ty. We wanted to fill you in."

Thad sipped the milk. Tasted okay. Fingers crossed, he rinsed the spoon and put it in the dish drainer by the sink. "All right. Listen—" From the corner of his eye, he caught Flay's tired lean in the doorway. "Flay, report in at the barracks, would you? I need to have a talk with Siddoh."

Cup in hand, Thad stepped close to Siddoh once they were alone. The estate was mostly dead at this time of day, but it paid to be sure nobody would overhear. "How much do you know about Lee's history? The way-back stuff, I mean." Siddoh, at almost four hundred years old, was the closest in age to Lee of Thad's inner circle.

Siddoh rubbed his chin thoughtfully. "Aside from the shit with Agnessa, not a whole lot. Parents both died early, mother in birth or soon after, as I understand it. Father…" Siddoh frowned thoughtfully. "He came over from the mountain areas when your father did, I think. I've gleaned they didn't have a good relationship, mostly because Lee won't talk about him. Then again, Lee doesn't talk about much of anything." He glanced over his shoulder and moved even closer to Thad in the kitchen. "What's this about?"

I wish I knew. "Maybe nothing." Thad shook his head. "Council elders wanted to reopen the issue on human interaction. And they want to lower the soldier retirement age to eight hundred. Lee didn't take it so well."

As if on cue, there were footsteps in the hall. Ivy, his house manager, headed toward them with her long, dark hair pulled up in a ponytail. She was too busy sorting a stack of mail to notice them.

Thad jerked his head. "It was Ivy's father who was so hell-bent."

Siddoh stepped back, stuffing his hands into his pockets. "Honestly? It could be nothing. It could be as simple as he doesn't want to have to retire in a hundred years, 'cuz hell, I'd like to think I'll still be in prime fighting shape when I'm that age, too. Realistically? Lee's a little cagey, and he can be wound pretty tight. They do some sort of a background check or something before induction, right? Maybe something he doesn't want found."

Thad took another sip of strawberry milk, and his stomach turned. "That's what I was wondering."

"Dunno, man. This sort of thing is why I'm glad not to be in your shoes. Listen, you're in charge, though. You can smack this shit down, right? Or maybe compromise. Give a little on the human interaction stuff in exchange for the other thing."

Thad had already given serious consideration to that option. His primary resistance to the human-vampire interaction bill had been that it would make the existence of half-human vampires illegal. It would have affected his own sister. Only now, it didn't affect her, did it? Still, it was a slippery slope. If they started regulating these things by law, where did it end?

"I'd better get Isabel her milk," he said.

Siddoh nodded and took another step toward the door, stroking his chin. "Look. No love lost between me and Lee, you know that. But the way I figure it? He's always been a good fighter. He's always been loyal. Some things are better left buried."

Chapter 21

"CAREFUL WITH HIM."

"I'm trying."

Anton grunted and repositioned Xander's body. Turned out two-hundred-plus pounds of vampire deadweight slumped against one's shoulder was a lot of fucking vampire deadweight. He did his best to let his new, tentative, unlikely almost-friend to the ground gently, but it was a little like dropping a car to the ground gently—there wasn't much choice.

Especially not when enemies and projectiles were coming through the trees. One of them whizzed uncomfortably close to Anton's ear. As Anton dropped the lifeless body, his fingers met the solid comfort of a gun holster. He managed to pull the thing free and fire back in the direction of the oncoming offensive.

"You're sure you know how to use that?"

He shot Tyra a look. Embarrassingly, she was right about Anton's lack of weapons training. He didn't know his way around a gun the way she did. They'd gone over this before. But he could hold his own. Loading and unloading a weapon wasn't his strong suit, but he could point and fire, dammit. So he did. And was rewarded with a muttered curse and a thump. One of their assailants was down.

Too bad there wasn't just one.

Gratified by the groan and quiet whoosh of air from

Xander's lungs when Anton crouched to roll his body against a log as best he could, Anton grabbed Tyra, plastered both their backs against the largest tree trunk he could find, and listened.

"So you've forgiven me already," he whispered.

Tree bark crackled behind her head when she shook it. "We have bigger problems right now."

To the clearing in front of him, he projected, "All right, guys, we're waiting."

Three wizards stepped into view. He didn't recall their names, but he knew them. Of course he knew them.

"Gone to the dark side, Anton?" a skinny one with pasty skin and a hook nose sneered. One of his father's lapdogs. Not that most of them weren't. Few of the wizards seemed to be freethinkers in any respect, which was of course what the Master wanted, but some… some really aimed only to please Anton's father in a particularly disturbing way.

Anton laughed. His side burned. Either something had hit him, or his earlier wound had torn back open. He cocked Xander's gun again. How many times had he fired? How many rounds did the clip have? This was where better weapons knowledge would come in handy. "Hardly the dark side." *Uh… whatever your name is*.

The taller wizard next to Hook Nose crossed his arms over his chest. "The vampires are our enemies."

Anton wanted very much right then to step in front of Tyra and block her from their view. Not that he'd try; she'd kick his ass for that. But these guys were too sleazy and filthy to look at her and think the things they were probably thinking.

Hook Nose pointed to Tyra. "This one's really hot.

This why you defected, Anton? Taking a walk on the wild side?"

Definitely too sleazy and filthy to be looking at her.

Tyra harrumphed quietly beside Anton. It was the only warning Hook Nose got before she set him on fire and then turned invisible. She must have rushed him. There was some grappling; Hook Nose was strong. From the sounds of things, Tyra was struggling but she had him on the ground, and with his robes on fire, it was probably only a matter of time.

And there was another wizard to be dealt with.

Despite the winter chill and the thirty-degree weather, Anton's body got hot. His power. He didn't understand how to wield it, but there was no time like the present to try. He smiled flatly at the other wizard. "You know, you all stood by and watched while my own father nearly killed me. So that makes *you* my enemy."

He turned to fire on the third wizard, who had been silent but creeping toward Anton and Tyra from the periphery, dropping that one first. "Thought I wasn't watching, didn't you, asshole?"

"Nice one," Tyra called, visible now from her position a few feet away. One steel-toed boot kicked at Hook Nose without mercy. The power practically rolled off her in waves.

Anton had to admit a sense of pride that welled up at her approval, but he had to tamp it down. Anger seemed to help the power get stronger. He tried to shoot the gun again, but it jammed or something and he didn't stop to discern the reason before dropping the weapon into his jacket pocket and running for the tall, skinny guy.

Anton did have a decent level of hand-to-hand

training, and said hands were glowing an eerie orange. He and his brother had sparred together quite a bit, though really Anton had never been sure if his brother wasn't actually trying to kill him that whole time.

"Holy shit." Tall Man, the weasely little shit, started running when Anton's glowing hand came after him.

"Yeah, you better run." Anton's arms and legs were longer. He had the guy's ankle without even having to stretch far. His anger and loss all channeled into the glowing hand. The glow flowed from Anton's body into the wizard's, and the wizard screamed. Writhed. It was awful enough that for a moment Anton wanted very much to let go.

He held firm.

This guy would kill him if given the chance. Kill Tyra. And if he let the wizard go, he would run screaming back to Anton's father to rat him out in no time. This was kill or be killed, just like it had been growing up. If anything, the reason was far more just.

The veins on the enemy male's head stood out in relief. A slow, dull throb echoed inside Anton's head. The *glub, glub, glub* sounded slower and slower. The wizard's eyes bugged out, screaming disbelief. For a moment there was recognition there, scrabbling and clawing on the wizard's side and grim determination on Anton's, when they both knew that the young wizard was about to die.

Anton's gut churned, and it was all he could do to hold down the bile when the kicking stopped and the glow dissipated. And there was no time to think about what he had just done, because Xander still lay tucked against a tree trunk, seriously injured if not dead.

"Anton, are you okay?"

Everything swam in front of Anton's face for a moment, but he forced himself to his feet. He could manage this. He'd managed eating those vampire hearts. Somehow, he lived with himself after doing those hideous things. Living with himself after killing an enemy should have been no contest. Why was it just as horrifying? But he wouldn't be weak in front of her.

He managed a nod.

"It's not me that I'm worried about." Shaky and confused, he knelt by Xander's crumpled form. Sticky, damp blood matted the vampire's hair. The breath and heartbeat were weak. Anton worked to calm his body and his mind. Prayed he could listen for attack with one ear while he worked to heal the vampire. Prayed there was enough energy left in his body to heal Xander after using his other power to kill that wizard. Just... prayed.

For someone who didn't believe in God, he'd certainly been doing a lot of that lately.

Something else was wrong, and while Anton focused on bringing the tawny glow of his healing power to the forefront, it remained out of reach in his consciousness. But with Xander's head cradled in his hand, he glanced at the sky and the answer became clear: dawn would be coming soon.

—ᴡ—

For the first time since this whole mess between her and Anton had started, Tyra saw a problem she knew how to solve. Her shoulder rubbed against Anton's when she knelt in the dirt at Xander's head. "It would be good if we could get him away from this log and flat against the ground instead. Then I'm going to put my hands underneath yours, okay?"

Anton moved and together they shifted the unconscious male's body onto his back. It was clear to Tyra that he handled Xander with care. Thoughtfully. "Okay."

She guided Anton's hands and covered them with her own. There was an oozing wound but Xander was breathing evenly. "Well, I'm not a doctor but it looks to me like the damage is mostly only to his neck and scalp. We can hope, anyway." She shook her head. "Poor guy, first time out in the field after his mate dies, too."

A familiar cold slush washed through Tyra. Anton's sadness. Pain. Okay, this wouldn't do at all. *Think, Ty.* She needed him to be able to flex his power. She needed to get him a little angry.

"So obviously you've figured out how I absorb powers," she said quietly.

"I have." His chest moved in and out. "Had a nice talk with Siddoh. Friendly guy. You've gotten one from each of your lovers, seems like." He didn't look at her but stayed focused on Xander. Already though, energy was starting to build in his hands and pass to hers.

"Uh-huh." Now, she just needed to get off the jealousy button before she mashed it to death. "Now. Take a deep breath for me."

He did.

"Feel how your hands kind of pulse, and tingle? Mine are."

"Huh. Yeah."

"Right. Good. Breathe into it. Like bellows on a banked fire or something, right? I know we're new at it, but I figure we've both got this healing power so we ought to be able to work together to magnify it."

His stubble scratched against her cheek when he moved. It was comforting on a very basic level to be close to him. Amazingly, surprisingly, disturbingly so.

So they breathed together in the early morning dark, and an awe filled her when energetic vibrations passed back and forth between their fingers and into Xander, growing in intensity like nothing she'd felt before. The pulse got stronger. Their hands glowed, the light concentrating around the wound in the back of Xander's head.

"That's amazing," Anton murmured.

"Yeah." It was. She could admit to herself that whatever supernatural power jolt she'd gotten from Anton's father, there had been temptation there. *Now* she could admit it, because this power exchange with Anton was far more gratifying.

Darkness lingered, but morning wasn't too far off. There were sounds in the distance of people starting their day. A loud truck rumbled past on what was probably nearby Route 9 and Anton jerked. For a moment, the heat in their hands faded.

"I'm listening. You just focus on our hands." Anton might not be used to keeping an ear out for trouble in the woods, but this she could do. It was funny, actually, how usually she had to be so careful not to drain her energy while using her abilities. But right now, breathing through this healing thing with Anton? It might have been almost relaxing if Xander's well-being hadn't been on the line.

Anton shifted closer. "Got it."

Xander groaned on the hard ground beneath them. "Good. This is good. Let's keep going, though, if you feel up to it." Their fingers were laced together; she wasn't sure which of them had done it or when it had happened.

They focused for a minute more, until Xander struggled and tried to sit. Anton helped prop Xander against the fallen tree but held a hand to his shoulder to prevent him from standing. "Hang on there, big guy."

Tyra nodded her agreement. "You got whacked pretty good back there." She grabbed Xander's arm when he went to touch the back of his head. "I wouldn't go poking at it. How do you feel?"

Xander grunted. "Like ass. What about you? Everything okay with you two after meeting the in-laws?"

That was a good question. There was so much to discuss, and there wasn't time now. She gripped Anton's shoulder. "When he came to the shelter, your father threatened to destroy the place and everyone in it unless I came with him. And then he just let me go without any argument at all. He said I'd come back willingly on my own. Doesn't that sound weird to you? I just realized, I don't know what happened down there after I left."

Anton licked his lips. His breath puffed white in the predawn cold. Had he managed to forget about that? "That sounds extremely weird to me."

Panic set in. "He specifically mentioned that little girl. Selena. He said she was 'one of his.' What if he does something to hurt her?"

He put a hand on her arm. "Call. It can't hurt to check in."

The phone in the shelter's main office almost rang through to voice mail. She sagged with relief when she heard Beverly's voice pick up on the other end. "Ash Falls Inter—aith." Lord, there was a crazy amount of static on the line.

"Bev?" She put a finger in her ear but it didn't help much. "It's Tyra. Just checking in. Everything okay down there?"

"Ty—a? My God, some kinda *kkkttt kkkttt* going on down here. Bunch of *kkkttt* impers—ing cops and busting down doors—"

"Beverly! Shit." The line had gone dead. Tyra met Anton's questioning stare. "I could hardly understand anything, but something's wrong down there."

"Tyra." Xander held up a hand. "I can walk. It's not that far back to the estate grounds. You guys go check it out."

"Mmm-mm." She grabbed Anton's shoulders. "Stay with Xander. It looks to me like we've only got an hour or so before daylight, and he shouldn't be left alone in his condition." She planted a quick, firm kiss on Anton's lips. "I'll call for backup immediately if there's a problem. I promise."

"Tyra, wait."

Anton threw a hand out, but she wrapped her arms around herself and disappeared, reforming moments later in her darkened office. She needed to check on Selena. The sounds of chaos and the inky black evil presence immediately told her what she needed to know, and they were *not* good things.

She'd fed recently. Minor bullet wound aside, her powers were well charged. Still, from the sounds of things, she was going to need help. And it stung to call for backup, given the ludicrous girly-girl way she'd run off back in the woods. But sometimes you had to suck it up.

But she blasted the team with a text instead of calling.

Then she took a deep breath, faded to invisible, and stepped carefully out the office door. "Oh, hell," she muttered to herself.

Wizards masquerading as police officers were roughing up groggy, tired residents. Their focus, it seemed, was the women's wing. Or rather, the children.

"Turn around," one officer barked at a frightened little girl with wide, blue eyes.

A quick look at the child's neck and the officer moved on. Tyra's hand went to the back of her neck. They were looking for that birthmark. The females. Anton's father had said he'd ignored the females before now, and Siddoh had once voiced a suspicion that the wizards recruited their offspring very young. Until now, she hadn't realized exactly what that might mean.

She had to get these guys out of there.

Not really bothering with whether or not she bumped into a fake police officer, she ran the gauntlet of the women's hall until she reached the exit at the far end of the hall. There was a playground just outside the door for use during the day, though at night the door was kept closed and there was an alarm set.

When she reached the door, Tyra uncloaked herself and let out a shrill whistle guaranteed to draw the attention of every person in the place. "Down here, boys."

Sure enough, almost every wizard looked up from their harassment duties, startled to see her in their midst. And anyone who might have missed the whistle looked up when she backed against the push bar for the exit doors and a piercing bell sounded. "Yep. Vampire alert, guys. Everyone out to the playground who wants to fight me." At first, only a few of the troglodytes stepped forward, so she added, "What, afraid to fight a girl?"

That did it. That *always* did it.

No sooner had she hit the pavement of the basketball court than a dozen or so poorly trained wizard ninjas in even worse-fitting cop uniforms were filing out of the building like lemmings on their way to jump off the cliff. And she was ready; fireballs charged and standing by. She could hold them off until backup arrived, no problem.

A child's scream came from across the playground.

The split second of inattention cost Tyra dearly, and next thing she knew the swarm was too close for comfort. And the source of the scream was clear. On the far end of the blacktop, next to the swing set, was little Selena. Who was still screaming. Lisa, her mother, lay on the ground. Clearly the woman wouldn't be getting up soon.

"Oh no." Tyra started toward Selena, but someone— one of the larger Cro-Magnon wizards—landed a punch right under her eye.

Chapter 22

Tyra had a lot of fighting experience, but there were too many enemies on the shelter playground to handle easily. She spun on the blacktop but the hit she'd taken had landed on that special spot right on her cheekbone. Her head swam. Pain exploded behind her eye, and the swelling obscured her vision immediately.

It wasn't a big deal. As soon as she could feed, that would heal. A wave of sadness washed over her even as she cracked two wizards in the kneecaps. Where did things stand with Anton?

One problem at a time, Ty.

A wizard grabbed from behind, and she held tight to his arms as she walked up the front of another wizard who had approached from the front. She smashed her size-ten boots in the second wizard's face before flipping back over the first one and kicking him between the legs. He went down hard on a faded hopscotch design, red faced and sputtering, "Bitch."

Sure. They were trying to *kill* her, but she was the bitch.

"Miss Tyra!"

She *had* to get to Selena, who was still crouched on the far end of the playground by her mother's body. "Selena, stay right there. Do you hear me?"

Tyra couldn't hear an answer and could only pray that the little girl did indeed get the message. And shit, the shouting from the girl had gotten one of the wizard's attention. One of the smarter ones had broken from the pack. Tyra stopped fighting back and stood still. "Okay, fine, guys. You win."

Hardly any of them were smart enough to stop and wonder why she'd done that. As soon as they closed in, she went invisible and teleported outside of the cluster, dropping a bundle of fireballs in her wake. There was a lot of screaming and rolling around and "what the fucks" as they tried to put each other out. That'd keep 'em busy for a while.

Poor Selena. The girl was terrified and gripping her mother's limp arm for dear life. Tears stung Tyra's eyes. She was within arm's reach of the girl when the frigid wind stirred, and there was Anton's father. The Master. He appeared behind Selena too quickly for Tyra to react, and while his stance was casual, his grip on those small shoulders was firm and unyielding.

His previously charming smile was one hundred percent sinister. "It's time to go, Miss Tyra. I doubt you'll want little Selena here to leave without you."

Selena's eyes were wide and questioning. Tyra glanced around, looking down at Selena's mother, who was clearly in poor shape, and then back to the wizard's grip on Selena. There was no option here, and Tyra knew that.

She reached forward and took hold of the girl's hand. "I'm so sorry, sweetheart," she said.

—◇◇◇—

They were a sad pair, but working together, Anton and Xander managed to stagger in the direction of the main road.

"I appreciate the help. I think we need to get the hell outta here before I get a nasty sunburn."

Anton shrugged out of his leather jacket and handed it to Xander. "Here, throw this over your head."

The vampire snorted. "That's awfully undignified."

"Huh. Well…" He pressed a finger to the back of Xander's forearm; it left a white spot on his skin that was already turning pink. "Would you rather be undignified, or would you rather go up in flames?"

"Shit." Xander searched his pockets and located a pair of gloves. "Alright, let's hurry. This'll only work for so long."

The sky was getting lighter, and neither of them was exactly in peak physical condition. Xander's phone buzzed insistently from Anton's pocket. He'd borrowed it to call Thad and let him know what was going on. Sure enough, it was Thad again.

"What's the status?"

"We're traveling along Route 9 as fast as we can, but Xander is already starting to burn, I'm afraid."

"Where are you along Route 9? Do you see any signs?"

Anton scanned through the trees. "I see a gas station less than a quarter mile up the road and a sign for Route 29, I think."

"Jimmy's Shell station. Get there. Fast." Thad ended the call.

"Shit, okay. Not much of a talker, that king of yours." Anton hooked an arm under Xander to help steady the big, drooping, near-deadweight. "Let's move, my friend. We've been given orders."

Xander groaned. Anton wasn't sure exactly what sun exposure did to a vampire, but it was clearly already happening. That Xander had recently been blasted in the head couldn't have helped matters.

"Okay, Xander, the gas station with the yellow signs up there. There's an overhang with shade, and I'm guessing Thad has some sort of plan for getting us back to your home. So just focus on that sign and go as fast as you can. You hear me?"

"Right," Xander mumbled. "I hear ya." The vampire was sweating, and they were going to have to cross the road where there were no trees for cover.

"Let's go," Anton said. He shouldered Xander's weight and pushed him as fast as he could. The sooner they got there, the better.

Chapter 23

"I SWEAR, YOU HAD BETTER NOT HURT THAT GIRL."
Tyra shook with rage.

They were back in the strange, dank sanctum where Anton's father had brought Tyra before. Cold room, stone walls. Cement floor. Was this honestly where Anton had grown up? The thought only made her angrier.

"I would like to see you try. I'll grant you, it would be a good fight and I have been at a loss all these years for a worthy adversary. But as I have explained, I am of your father's generation and have amassed powers over the centuries that you cannot imagine. The chances are slim that you would be able to beat me."

She smirked and crossed her arms over her chest. "I'd bet your skills are rusty, though. As far as I know, this is the first time in a while that any vampire has seen you. I guess I should feel special."

He laughed heartily, and the sound bounced around the walls of the large stone room. "Ah, and you are. I have explained this to you. So, I suspect, is she." He inclined his chin toward Selena, who was curled asleep in a corner.

Children had amazing coping skills that way. When they had too much to handle, they simply shut down. Tyra prayed that Selena's mother was okay, but she hadn't looked good.

The wizard stood close to her now. Close enough to

reach out and grab. To do a leg sweep and knock him off balance.

"Let me put it to you this way, Tyra. I've figured out something that I should have figured out long ago. And I am a smart enough man to admit when I have made a mistake. All these centuries, I assumed the males were stronger. The female offspring were ignored and eventually perished on their own, or... they were cast off."

Horrible.

"And because of me you've decided otherwise?"

He smiled again. "Exactly so. It turns out, there aren't many females for the reasons I've explained, but when your..." he looked Tyra up and down in a way that made her suppress a shiver, "impressive roster of talents came to my attention and when I realized that you carried wizard blood, I knew that you and the other female wizard children might indeed be the key."

"And you already know where my allegiance lies." She leaned in close enough that she could smell a stale smokiness on his breath. She reached for a knife, but damn, she must have lost it in the fight on a playground. "So what's your master plan, Master?"

"Ah." Neither of them backed down. She sure as hell wasn't going to. "Simple enough." Silence.

She waited, almost certain she could hear the *Jeopardy* theme music playing in her head. He wanted her to ask, and she was just as determined not to. Still, something dangerous lay on the periphery of her senses. Something more than the "mere" fact that she and Selena were in a viper's den with no clear means of escape. Because she would lay good money that letting her go willingly wouldn't happen this time. The first time more than likely had only been some sort of illusory head game. The seconds stretched out, and finally she gave in.

"Okay. What's your simple plan?"

"I thought you'd never ask." This time, she did roll her eyes. Evil asshole be damned.

"I want you to join me."

"You've already said that. And I've already told you I won't."

He continued as if he hadn't heard her. "And if you refuse, I will take your powers by force."

"Over my dead body."

"That's the idea, yes." He nodded toward Selena. "And I will raise her and the others as my own and train them in our ways."

Tyra clenched her fist. "She's a child."

"Yes. Yes, exactly. Just a little older than Anton was when I took him from the foster home. Didn't work so well with him, but with most of the others, the conditioning has taken beautifully. And she's clearly an intelligent little girl. I have no doubt she will serve me very well. Particularly if it turns out she can absorb powers just as you are able to."

The oily voice, the awful implications, hearing Anton's name—Tyra snapped. Everything in front of her was red, and the echoed screams seemed to come from her own mouth. She struck blindly and met with air.

Amused laughter met her ears. "Maybe you won't be such a worthy adversary after all, Tyra. Is that the best you can do?" She whirled in the direction of the voice, but nobody was there.

Okay, so this guy could do invisible too. But she

knew how to work that. She and Siddoh had fought
together enough times. She focused, waited for her vision to grow accustomed to the dim light, and listened.
There it was. The subtlest ripple of the shadows to her
right. She aimed her gaze left, as if confused about
where he was.

"Maybe you're right," she said. The fireball in her
left hand was hidden by her body. "Maybe I should just
give up now." She released the fireball and was gratified
by a grunt of pain and a flare of fire as the Master's
robes caught.

———&———

Thankfully, the gas station was still closed. Anton had
just hauled Xander into the shade of an overhang around
the back of a long-overdue-to-be-cleaned Dumpster
when the SUV pulled into the station.

"Careened" was probably a more appropriate word.

The cloud of dust that kicked up and the wild skid of
the vehicle weren't half as alarming as the tiny blonde
girl who jumped out of the driver's seat, waving a thick
wool blanket.

"Here. Throw this over him, and then shove him the
hell back there as fast as you can."

Smart enough to have a better knowledge of physics
than Anton did, the girl had placed another blanket on
the seat and used that to help slide Xander's body across
to the other side. Xander was still conscious but clearly
physically weak. His skin was red and peeling.

The girl jumped in, pulled the world's fastest three-
point turn, and barreled down Route 9 like their lives
depended on it. Which, of course, they actually did.

Xander groaned, and Anton placed a hand on his blanked-covered body. "Try not to move, buddy. You need to conserve your strength."

Buddy. Anton couldn't help but wonder whether any of these vampires would really be his friend by the time the fallout from this situation had taken place. For that matter, would he even have his life? Would he have Tyra? And if he was still alive but without Tyra, would he have much of a life at all?

He stared for a moment at the gentle rise and fall of the blue wool blanket under which Xander lay. Xander *was* still alive, wasn't he?

The blonde glanced into the backseat. "Hi, I guess you're Anton. Very famous around the estate, for obvious reasons. I'm Alexia. You can call me Lexi, or Lex, or I sometimes even answer to 'hey you.' I'm kind of the resident human, I guess. Anyway, I can't believe Thad actually let me come and get you, but it's a damn good thing he did. Oh. Shit."

A robed wizard had stepped from the tree line on the edge of the road and had a handgun aimed squarely at their vehicle.

"Shit is right," Anton murmured. The fucker actually had a gun? Anton had rarely fired a gun growing up. Master had focused primarily on training them to use their supernatural abilities. This was different.

"Bad guy, right?"

"Definitely a bad guy," Anton confirmed.

"Okay, Anton," Alexia breathed. "Might wanna keep your head down." And the little blonde human, bless her soul, actually sped up. "OhGodohGodohGod ohGodohGodohGod."

The wizard hit the hood with a loud thunk, and a giant spiderweb cracked across the window of the SUV. Anton looked out the back window. The wizard was down for the count, but he didn't think it was wise to tell the girl that. "Well, he's hurt, but I don't think you did enough damage to kill him."

"Oh, thank God." Her forehead nearly hit the steering wheel before she seemed to recall that she was still driving a car—at what looked from Anton's vantage point to be a significant jump over the speed limit—down the winding country road. "I'm sorry. You probably think that's really lame. I know he probably would've killed us."

"Not lame at all," Anton murmured. He could still feel the hot skin and bulging veins of that dying wizard beneath his hands, and the memory turned his stomach. "But he absolutely would have. Sometimes you have to do what you have to do. That doesn't make it easy."

She didn't respond to that one, other than to nod her head silently.

They turned down a narrow access road, one that Anton would have missed entirely if he hadn't known it was there. After several hundred feet they turned again, this time down a single-lane gravel road that ended at… a stone-walled building of some kind. Some kind of dilapidated structure. What had probably once been a storage building for farm equipment, if he were throwing out guesses. It wasn't very barnlike. He wasn't sure what else it would be. Whatever it was, she was heading right toward it and going way, way too fast.

"Okay, I know what this looks like…" Her voice was shaky now. Nerves, probably. From hitting that wizard, or from the fact that they were about to ram a building at seventy miles per hour. "But I swear to God, it's all an illusion." She giggled but didn't sound sure of herself. "Vampire magic, you know?"

No, he didn't know. He hoped to hell she was right. The building loomed closer.

Anton could make out the individual cinder blocks.

And the cracks in them.

"Oh, holy shit—"

He braced for impact.

The bright flash of light reached him even through his tightly shut eyes, but there was no crash. Amazingly, impossibly, unbelievably, there was no crash.

The vehicle coasted to a stop in front of a large barn. "See, I told you."

He managed to pry his eyes all the way open. "You did tell me."

"I know." She tried to make her laugh sound off-handed, but it bordered on hysterical. "I wouldn't have believed me, either. It's a little trippy at first."

"That's putting it mildly." He could have sworn he was about to have a stroke.

She laughed again, eased the car into the barn, and jumped out, dialing her cell at the same time. "Hey there, we're back. Anton's getting him into the tunnel now." She motioned to Anton and then gestured to a door cut into the floor next to the car. "Yeah. I'll tell him." Once the vehicle was inside the barn, the click of a remote had closed the door.

She flipped the phone closed and sat on a nearby wooden bench. "Thad wants to talk to you for a sec. Tyra texted for backup from the shelter and then disappeared before anyone got there. Can you handle getting Xander down the stairs? Someone'll meet you at the bottom."

Anton nodded. "You okay?"

She squinted. Her body was still. Oddly so, given the emotional roller coaster she must surely be feeling just now. She'd just run over a wizard, poor girl. Even he would have been a little freaked. "I will be."

Something told Anton that was her answer for a lot of things, but there was no time to stick around to be sure. It was a sad statement that her having just run over a wizard on purpose—undoubtedly the first time she'd ever done such a thing—was too low on the list of immediate priorities for Anton to be able to help.

Chapter 24

TYRA'S TRIUMPH WAS SHORT-LIVED.

No sooner had she sunk into an attack stance than an arm came down, crushing with surprising force against her windpipe. All traces of the charismatic, convivial Master from before were gone when he spoke. "It turns out that after eight hundred years I do have a trick or two up my sleeve. I told you that I would not be so easy to defeat, did I not?"

It was probably a rhetorical question. Not like she could answer, what with him cutting off her airflow and all.

Her fingers dug into skin that was hide tough. Eyes watered. There was nothing nearby for her to use to grab a toehold, nothing to gain leverage from. She focused on flexing the new power she had absorbed from Anton, heating her body from the inside out so that she could in turn heat the wizard's, but in the panic of the moment nothing was happening.

"Miss Tyra." And to add to the entire snafu, Selena was awake.

Tyra opened her mouth to reassure the girl, but nothing came out other than a garble and a gasp. So she did the only other thing she could think of. She tucked her chin, bit the Master's arm as hard as she could, and while sinking her fangs into it, tried very hard not to think about where that arm might have been.

"Ow." Tyra got the knee-jerk reaction she had hoped for, and she sank in harder, focusing more on using her blunt back teeth to increase the Master's discomfort. It was both gratifying and horrid when he wrenched his arm free and the flesh ripped under her teeth.

Immediately Tyra spun. He'd gone invisible again, but the blood trail had not. And she was, after all, still part vampire. The hungry, bloodthirsty, primal part of her scented the fresh blood, and her fangs crowded her mouth as her adrenaline surged. She glanced at Selena, who stood near the corner, poised but uncertain, with clenched fists. Poor girl had gotten so much more than she bargained for tonight.

"Selena, honey, I need you to get in the corner and put your head down. You got that?"

A small nod.

"Okay. I'm going to do my best to see that you get back to your mom, but I can only do that if you stay out of the way. If you don't watch, that's even better."

She didn't wait for an answer. Couldn't, because in the next moment one of the drips of blood swung with movement. The wizard was taking advantage of her distraction. She crouched low, pulling a knife from her ankle strap when she did. She rushed forward at the same time and was rewarded with a groan of pain when the knife sank into flesh. It wasn't clear where she'd hit, but she'd definitely hit something, and a quiet uneven shuffle could be heard in the far corner of the room. He was retreating to regroup, and he was hurt. Good.

Another fireball formed in the palm of her hand. It was her favorite power. Her first, the one she'd inherited from her father. Probably that was why she loved it best to use in battle. She was most confident with it, and it made her feel closest to her vampire side. And setting the enemy on fire was so cool. She shot a small orb in the direction of the blood trail.

Nothing.

A larger ball, in case the first had misaimed, but still nothing.

Remembering the surprise attack from behind, Tyra started inching backward, constantly sweeping her gaze across the room until her back met the cold stone of the wall. Selena was to her left, curled into a tight, self-protective ball. Good girl.

Tyra got quiet and stretched her senses. She was willing to bet any amount of money he was still in the room. She could feel him. But his presence was nebulous and scattered, like a thick fog rather than something solid. After a few deep breaths, she arrived at a decision. It was risky, but it had to work.

He was in here somewhere; she was sure of it. *Absolutely* sure of it.

Tyra breathed deeply again, all the way to her toes, drawing up every bit of power she could, and then went for it. She backed into the corner where Selena was curled to make sure the girl was protected and then proceeded to fill the remainder of the room with fireballs. Every. Effing. Inch.

If the Master was in there, she would smoke him out, or at the very least, she might get him to drop his cloak of invisibility.

Seconds passed… a minute…

Nothing.

Tyra inhaled, waiting… The drain from using her

powers, especially that last burst of fire, was coming fast. He was in here, dammit. He was in here somewh—

An unseen force yanked Tyra's arm, and she half flew, half flopped against the wall like a rag doll. Perfect. Just perfect. A fist, still unseen, connected solidly with her jaw. Blood and spittle flew.

The fighter in Tyra wanted to fight back, but against whom? Or at least, where? A long cut appeared on her arm and blood welled from it. She thought of that scar on Anton's collarbone.

Anton. She could see now what he had been up against. It would be good to have him to fight alongside her now, like she had earlier. It would be good to have him here at all.

Another invisible fist struck her already tender cheek, but she couldn't connect it with any kind of body. Nobody seemed to be standing over her. She raised a hand and flailed a little, but she didn't manage to touch anything.

Laughter. Wicked, evil, villainous laughter came from nowhere. *No. This can't happen…*

"I did tell you that I would win, Tyra."

Xander woke in a darkened room. His body was incredibly heavy, and holy hell, was he ever tired. If he allowed himself, he probably could have gone back to sleep for hours.

Except… where was he?

He breathed in a familiar scent. "Theresa?"

"Right here."

He turned his head to the side and there she was.

Looking worn and tired, but no less lovely. "What am I doing in your bed? And where is the baby?"

She smiled and ran a protective hand over his forehead. Xander was surprised as much by the gesture as by the comfort he took in it. "Sleeping. They do a lot of that at the beginning. And you're here because this bed is more comfortable than the guest room." She pressed gently on the mattress. "Memory foam. I figured you would be sore. From the sunburn."

He closed his eyes, and as he exhaled, it seemed indeed that he could sink right into the mattress. Through it would have been even better. "Tell me you didn't give me more blood."

"Only a little." Her voice was soft. "You didn't need much. The wizard or… whoever he is. Anton? He had some kind of healing power. It worked on you fairly well, as it turns out."

"Damn." Xander exhaled and shook his head slightly. Turned out too much movement made his head throb. "I never thought I'd see the day when I would find myself grateful to a wizard for anything."

"He seems like a nice man."

"He does. Hard to believe, isn't it?"

Theresa smiled in the semi-dark. All of this was very odd. Their conversations hadn't extended very far beyond day-to-day small talk. And being here in her bed. He wasn't much of a traditionalist, but it was unseemly to him, being in the bed of a recently widowed female.

Xander moved to sit up. "I should go check in with Thad."

Her hand landed on top of his. There was no pushing or forcing, just a hand. Her fingers wrapped gently around his. Somehow, that small gesture was enough to stop him cold.

"I wish you wouldn't go just yet."

"Theresa, I…" He what? He couldn't explain exactly why he felt like he shouldn't be here, only that it was the worst kind of wrong to drink her blood, not once but twice, and lie in the bed she had shared with Eamon.

"Alexander, lie down please. You need more time to rest."

Hardly anybody ever called him that. He must be really exhausted because it was enough to make him comply with her request. "Theresa, I just don't think I should be here."

"I got new sheets, you know."

What? "I'm not sure what… okay."

There were a lot of lines around her eyes when she smiled. "Before the baby, I went a little crazy wanting to get all these new things. It's so bizarre in retrospect, but at the time I was convinced I needed brand-new sheets for the bed in case the baby slept in bed with me. For some reason, the ones I already had weren't good enough. I wanted the best, softest sheets I could find. Fifteen hundred thread count." She ran a hand along the edge of the mattress next to Xander's hand. "Nice and soft, huh?"

Xander had to agree; they were comfortable sheets. Even though he didn't entirely understand where the hell she was going with this. "Uh. Very soft, yes."

"Eamon thought it was crazy. That I'd spent way too much money on something that the baby was only going to spit up on, you know? He was so angry he ordered me to send them back." A delicate fang sank into her lower lip, and a tear slid down her cheek. "But I didn't want to. So I hid them. I never used them until after the baby was born."

Something significant was in that statement, and Xander couldn't... quite... grasp it. Clearly, he was supposed to, though. Shit.

"The mattress and pillows too. You remember?"

He closed his eyes and let his head sink for a moment into the aforementioned pillow. Yes, Xander remembered. Just before the birth Theresa had begun to complain of back pain, and then her water had broken while she was in bed, destroying the mattress on which she slept. The one on which Xander now lay was brand new.

"Yes," he said quietly, "I remember that."

She patted his hand. "Sometimes it's okay to make a new start, Xander."

Ah. That was the message, then?

"I believe this wizard's intentions are good, and I think you already know it's okay to be his friend. And being here... taking my blood..." She ran her hand over the sheet again. "I would return these sheets in a second, if I could, for another day with Eamon in my arms. I would give *anything* in the world to have him back. I know you feel the same about Tam. We can love them and miss them and still survive. A new start is okay, sometimes. Sometimes it's good and necessary, and I believe that they would want that for us. Don't you?"

Her golden eyes glittered with tears in the light of the bedside lamp. His fingers traced over Theresa's brand-new soft sheet, and he wondered if perhaps he didn't need to agree as much for her benefit as his own. "I'm sure you're right."

She leaned down and placed a kiss on his temple. "You rest, okay, Xander? We just got you healthy again, and I'm not ready to lose you just yet."

With that, the lamp by the bed winked out and she left him alone.

Chapter 25

THIS TIME, ANTON HADN'T GIVEN THAD A CHOICE about going back after Tyra alone. He was dead certain that his father had her, and there was no way he was waiting for nightfall. It would be long past too late.

What he saw when he tore through the portal terrified the shit out of him. Tyra was backed to a wall, held by an unseen force, while Anton's father came toward her with a sternal saw. The wizards used them to cut open vampires. To retrieve the heart.

"Nice that you could join us, Son."

The second the buzz of the sternal saw sounded, Anton flew. Blood thundered in his ears. He dropped the gun in his hand without thinking, and the next thing he knew, the saw was against the stone wall in a scatter of pieces. His father's throat was solid and satisfying under his fingers.

Damned satisfying.

As chokes and sputters came from his father's throat, the man's skin burned a bright lobster red in mere seconds. Far faster than the wizard from before. Anger definitely was the trigger. And right now Anton overflowed with rage.

You were always the smart one, you know. Smarter than your brother, Petros. Don't you know I wanted it to be you at my right hand?

His father's eyes were dark gray like Anton's own.

Even as his father's skin reddened and the veins of his head bulged, Anton could see himself in that face, and the plea there tugged at his heart. Some part of Anton was still human—perhaps a far greater part than should have been.

It wasn't in him to kill.

The hesitation cost him. Anton found himself with his back to the wall and his father's hands around his throat. He choked and struggled against the bruising grip. His feet didn't touch the floor, and he couldn't quite manage a grip on his father. He kicked. Couldn't breathe.

And then the Master dropped him. Anton's knee struck the stone floor painfully. He gagged a little when the pressure let up on his throat. The Master's robes were burning.

"Tyra?" Anton's gaze swept the room. She wasn't anywhere.

Something thumped the old monster on the side. *There* she was. Anton shook his head. He'd forgotten she could go invisible too. He was going to need a list at some point. Anton's chest swelled with pride when Tyra's invisible form got another hit in, causing the Master to double over in pain. But that didn't last long.

Tyra's softly grunted "Ow, fuck," and a hard smack against the adjacent wall made Anton go cold. He knew that sound; his body had made that sound hitting that same wall.

The Master had many powers. He'd had many centuries on earth, and heaven knew how much vampire blood he'd consumed. Anton could only guess at some of his father's powers. When Tyra's cloak of invisibility faded, Anton knew they had a real problem.

It wasn't simply that she had hit the wall. Her eyes were still open, but she wasn't moving. Worse, one glance at the fierce clutch of her hands and the tension in her body… she was in pain. He could just tell. Anton had fought alongside Tyra not long ago so he knew she ought to be sturdy enough able to take a hit and keep going.

There wasn't time to figure it out. Anton dropped to the concrete floor and grabbed his father's foot, upending the old wizard before he could deal a final blow to Tyra's head. Anton tackled with all the force he could manage. All the hurt. All the rage. Every evil thing he'd experienced growing up.

Everything he wanted to be for Tyra and couldn't.

Tears flowed down Anton's face. The night his father had first tried to end his life, Anton had told the Master that it was not in him to kill. That certainly was still true.

It was *not* in him to kill.

He did *not* want to kill his father.

Anton, don't do this… I gave life to you.

But there was want, and there was need. He *needed* to guarantee Tyra's safety. Anton gritted his teeth and pressed harder. He envisioned the Master's blood boiling, like a volcanic lava flow. "And you would have taken it away without thought, too."

His father gasped. Sweat rolled off Anton's body. His father practically glowed. Hands clawed and feet kicked desperately.

I thought it was necessary. We could be a team, you and I. And your beloved Tyra. We could find a way to work together. To be at peace. Ask her. I offered her a way for us to live in peace with the vampires…

Anton's heart broke. He met his father's desperate stare. He leaned close and whispered into his father's ear. "You will understand if I doubt your sincerity." The same words that the Master himself had said to Anton the night father had almost killed son. Anton's eyes squeezed shut as he tightened his grasp, and he held his breath until long after his father's body no longer moved.

Then he let the tears flow freely.

"I'm sorry," he whispered.

And he was. Whether he should have been or not, he was.

Alexia closed her eyes. Her head lolled against a wall, as horror-movie images flickered behind her closed eyelids in rapid-fire succession: The wizard thudding against the hood of the car. Lee stabbing one in the police cruiser. Her stepfather's friend, the one with the red hair, who… she pried her eyes open.

Don't go there.

Her gaze roved around the empty barn. She checked her cell phone. What she needed was a damned drink. But it was way too early to go anywhere, and she refused to spiral downward to the point of drinking alone in her bedroom.

Refused.

So… what to do? She bounced her feet and chewed her lip. Problem was, the whole rest of her little corner of the world had bigger problems right now. Tyra was missing. Again. Lee and Siddoh and a few of the other fighters had massive sunburns from fighting too close to dawn. Anton was out finding Tyra, so everyone was waiting with bated breath to hear how that turned out.

In an estate filled with hundreds of vampires, she was completely alone.

She tapped her feet some more and then stretched her left ankle over her right knee. An old tear to that left hamstring had left the muscles in that leg perpetually tight, and it took a lot of stretching and yoga to keep the tension from seizing her entire body.

Okay, so she could admit that maybe it wasn't only old tension from the injury that caused her pain.

Her gaze lit on one of her tattoos. It was a newer one, a snake that coiled around her calf muscle, courtesy of their friend Lucas, who had come to the estate a couple of weeks ago at Isabel's behest.

"Lucas. Perfect." Lexi clapped her hands a little at the joy of her revelation, even though nobody was around to agree with her.

She wrenched open the floor hatch and barreled down the stairs. Lucas's place was a fair hike through the maze of tunnels but she jogged it easily, without the tree branches and bracing cold of her usual morning run. His door was easy to find; even his tunnel entrance was decorated with very individualized graffiti. Lucas was simply unable to be just like anyone else. She could respect that.

Alexia knocked. When he didn't answer, she banged louder, until the door finally opened and Lucas poked his long, curly-haired head out of the door. "What the hell are you doing banging on doors at this hour, lady?"

Alexia smirked. "Like you were asleep."

He shrugged and pushed the door open wider to let

her in. Lucas was the only someone she knew who slept less than she did. Then again, he wasn't human. He could get away with it.

He was watching the Speed Channel and sipping red wine, which was pretty much what Lucas did all the time if he wasn't working. And as nice as it was for Isabel to have given Lucas a steady job and a place to live, Alexia worried that without the constant bustle of the tourist crowd, Lucas might languish a little in a place like this one.

"You know," she said. "Washington, DC, is within spitting distance from here. You could open up a shop or even get a spot at the tattoo parlor in downtown Ash Falls."

He pushed his hair out of the way as he flopped into a beanbag chair to watch television. "I could." He glanced quickly in her direction before focusing back on the autocross race already in progress. "And you could go back to living with real people, babe. Why haven't you done that?"

Alexia reached up to twist a piece of her hair and had to stop herself. It was such a stupid, nervous, little-girl habit, but so automatic she didn't even catch herself sometimes. She jammed her hands in her pockets. "Fine. I won't examine your motives if you don't examine mine."

He laughed and rolled off the beanbag, walking on his knees until he was nearly between her legs. His arms snaked around her waist, and he looked up at her. He had amazing, fiery, mesmerizing eyes. Too bad she wasn't into *him* like that. "You here to let me drink your blood, mama?"

She quirked an eyebrow. "Do you really need my blood?" His hair smelled divine. Coco-nutty.

He smiled and licked his lower lip. "No."

She smiled back. She hadn't figured so. "Then no."

"So why are you here?"

She chewed her lip again. It was starting to get sore, which was always a sign that things had been going badly. As if she needed a sign in this case. "I need…" She sighed. "I'm not sure, exactly."

He rocked back and stood. "Better not get ink if you haven't thought it out. Besides…" He gestured vaguely up and down at her. "You're so tiny, and you're running out of real estate on that canvas of yours. Wanna choose wisely."

"I know." She walked to the front door of his small house, the one that led outside, and looked in a full-length mirror that he'd tacked onto the back of it. She tried not to look too closely. Never once had she been happy with what she'd seen when she looked in the mirror, and today was no exception. Especially not after nabbing a large man with the front of an SUV like he was overgrown roadkill.

That was probably how she ought to be thinking of him.

She fingered her ears, which already had piercings going up about halfway. Her navel was already done.

Lucas came to stand behind her, his tall frame dwarfed hers in the mirror, and she focused on his face, which was handsome in a perpetually boyish way, rather than her own. "I could give you an industrial, maybe. Something on your face. Nose stud? Eyebrow? He rubbed her shoulders in a far too friendly manner, and she caught his hand when long fingers started an exaggerated creep toward her chest.

"Cut it out, you. Let's leave those alone."

He harrumphed at her but smiled again. "What, then?"

She stuck out her tongue. "What do you think?"

He shrugged. "Tongue? Sure, why not? Easy one."

She smiled. "Great." It would take her mind off things for a little while, anyway. But then she closed her eyes and saw that wizard bouncing off the hood of the Land Rover again. She thought of something she needed far more than a tongue stud. "Actually, no. I think I wanna do a tattoo after all. This is a tattoo kind of problem."

"You're sure?"

She turned to a stack of binders on the kitchen counter. "I'm sure. Where's your book of Chinese characters?"

"Right on top there." He pointed to a stool in his kitchen while he set about pulling things out of drawers. Most folks kept knives and spatulas in their kitchen; Lucas kept tattoo and piercing equipment. Gloves, ink, etc. There was an autoclave on the counter. "Have a seat on that stool, and I'll be with you in a sec."

Chapter 26

ANTON CROUCHED ON THE STONE FLOOR BY TYRA'S body and rested his forehead against hers. Honest to goodness, his heart was leaden and nearly unmoving. He had no idea what to do.

She was alive, definitely. They had that going for them. Freezing cold to the touch, though. Whatever his father had done had left her tight and tense like she was in pain. She was shaking uncontrollably. He didn't know how to make it stop.

He'd already tried blood. Fucking mess that had been. Nothing like pulling your nearly catatonic not-really girlfriend's tongue out of her mouth to lick the cut on your wrist so you don't bleed to death all over her. Unbelievably romantic. He'd tried his healing power. His current plan of crying all over her face wasn't doing a lot of good, either.

"Is Miss Tyra dead?"

Anton jumped.

The little girl was sitting up and staring at him with eyes that were far too wise for a girl of her age, which couldn't have been more than seven or eight. Then again, he couldn't even imagine what she had seen or experienced tonight, but growing up as Anton had, he could hazard a guess. And he wouldn't wish that on the worst schoolyard bully, much less this sweet-looking child.

He glanced back at Tyra and placed a hand on her

chest. It was rising and falling visibly. The *thump, thump* of her heart against his hand provided a very necessary reassurance. "No, she's not dead."

The girl blinked. "I think my mommy is dead."

What did he say to that? "We don't know that for sure."

She looked over at his father's body. "Is he dead?"

There wasn't a strong enough word for the hatred he had over this girl asking him about death over and over. But he met her too-knowing, brown-eyed gaze and answered honestly. "Yes."

She reached forward and placed her small hand on top of his. Somehow, that was the key that opened the floodgates. Moisture poured over Anton's face and splashed on his collarbone and chest. He didn't bother trying to stop it. Doing so would have taken more energy than he had just then. "We have to get Miss Tyra up."

The girl was smart indeed. Anton had been so mired in his loss, in the pain of having had to kill his own father and of being unable to get Tyra to rouse, that he had failed to consider that they were still sitting in the heart of the lion's den. "You're right. We have to go. Can you get up, sweetheart?"

"Selena."

He smiled slightly. "Selena. Do you think you can walk on your own?"

"I think so."

Good.

Selena moved slowly but seemed agile enough under her own motor. Anton gathered Tyra against him, murmuring senseless reassurances that probably didn't matter. He'd get her back to the estate, and the vampire doctors would fix her up. Everything would be just fine.

Somehow.

He glanced again at the body on the floor. *His father was dead*. The man lying there seemed so small. So unlike the monster that Anton remembered.

The hollow hurt inside him didn't make sense. The important thing was that Tyra was safe now. Without his father to keep the wizards organized, Anton suspected—no, he was certain—there would not be a strong enough leader to take over. It would be easy for the vampires to round up the remaining wizards and clean house.

The nightmare would be over.

"Okay, Selena, let's get out of here."

A sharp clap of boot steps echoed in the room. His brother, Petros, entered from a door on the far end of the space that had not been visible before. Petros. *Shit*.

"Well done, brother."

Anton cursed. He should have known they were getting out too easily. He paused, ready to drop Tyra if he had to so that he could fight again. "Selena, get behind me, please."

Petros held up a hand. "No, don't change your plans on my account. I was just leaving myself." He gestured grandly around the room. "About time for a changing of the guard, don't you think?" Petros kicked at their dead father's body like it was an old sofa he wanted to discard.

About time for a *what*? "You wanted our father to die?"

Petros nearly beamed. "Of course. Didn't you?" At Anton's stunned expression, Petros scoffed. "Oh, come on, brother. This whole operation has limped along badly for centuries. Frankly I can't believe the vampires hadn't killed off every wizard alive long before you and I were ever sired. It was time for a change. New blood. New ways." Petros smiled wider, revealing a set of very real-looking fangs.

Anton shook his head. "Fangs? You can't think you're going to fool anyone that way."

Petros laughed. "It's already worked, and it's not the only upgrade I've made." He held up a finger. "You should be thanking me, Brother. I was the one who saw to it you stayed alive out in those woods when the Master wanted to kill you, you know. If it were not for me, you wouldn't be holding your beloved Tyra in your arms just now. Well, I'd better be off. Lots to do," Petros said brightly. "Oh. A little gift for you, first." A piece of metal flashed and flipped through the air. It landed softly on the ground midway between the two of them. One of those computer flash drive things.

Anton cursed himself for the moment of stunned inattention. He scrabbled for his nearly forgotten weapon, but Petros was gone too quickly. Some sort of black hole had opened in the middle of the room and Petros just… stepped into it, like the guy was getting onto an elevator. Anton hadn't seen that before.

He sagged, taking Tyra's weight against his chest. The stone inside his chest got bigger and heavier. Petros was taking over where his father had left off. With plans to… to what, upgrade the wizard establishment, somehow?

With fangs?

Selena placed a small hand on Anton's arm. What a sad statement that this little girl was keeping him grounded. "Let's get out of here."

Tyra never would have thought she'd see the day when she was in the sun and still freezing cold. Her teeth were chattering like crazy, though, and her jaw was wired so tightly she could barely pry it open. "Anton."

He stopped so fast she thought he might drop her. "Tyra. God. Are you okay?"

"No." Not even a little bit. "But I think I can walk," she managed.

Whatever Master Asshole had done to her, she'd managed to shake it off a little out under the bright morning rays, but movement was a struggle. Still, it felt important to get out of the woods on her own two feet.

Her heart broke that she'd failed to dispatch Anton's father in time to save Anton from doing that. Holy hell, had she even known he had a brother? The conversation between the two men had been chilling. All this time they'd hoped that killing the Master would destroy the clan.

His brother had promised to take the wizards and— what, overhaul the organization? Make it better, stronger, faster? As it was, the vampire society was beating the wizard society back but barely, like a constant game of Whac-A-Mole. How would they all stay safe in the face of an even greater evil?

This was only the beginning.

She abhorred the helplessness of limping along and letting him hold her up. Anton cradled her as carefully as he could, but they had to move fast over terrain that was rocky, covered with branches, and slippery with pine needles. Fatigue or maybe concern caused him to grip her bicep with iron fingers, as if he didn't dare let her slip. It would have been endearing if it hadn't been so painful. She'd have bruises, for certain.

Anton was talking to Selena now, and Tyra could read the concern in his tone loud and clear. No way could she flex her powers then so she couldn't tap into his emotions. Listening to the undertones in his voice and the language of his body told her just as much right then, maybe even things she wouldn't have found out by trying to use her powers.

"Are you hanging in there? We have to go fast, Selena."

Tyra had to admit that the firm but gentle manner Anton used with the young girl made her go a little squishy.

She forced her mouth to work again. "Your brother... was he bluffing?"

"We can only hope." Pain lanced down her arm when his fingers gripped even tighter.

"You don't think so."

"No."

It was difficult to breathe, and the sun was hot. She didn't burn as fast in the daytime as full-blooded vampires did, but the heat was still mighty stifling. It didn't calm her agitation while she was helped as gently as she was sure Anton could manage into the front seat of a vehicle and belted. He paused for a moment with his forehead pressed against hers.

Little did he know that there was a war going on inside her. He was trying to care for her, but she had never needed or wanted that. While she could move, doing so drove a thousand needles and knives into her bones. That she had so reveled in that momentary gift of the Master's power sickened her. She hated herself.

Hated the Master. Hated Anton a little for what he had done and who he was. And maybe she hated that she was starting to care for him.

Anton helped Selena into the car. When he was seated and belted himself, he placed his hand on Tyra's knee and looked at her with deep concern. "I'm so sorry, Ty. I can tell it hurts. I don't know what else to do. If my blood didn't work and neither did my healing power, what else can I try?"

She wished she knew. "Just get me home."

Chapter 27

WHEN THE DOCTOR CHECKED SOMEONE OVER AND THEN called another doctor, and then the two of them conferred quietly in a corner for a long time before finally suggesting that they might need to call in a specialist at sundown… there was definitely a Big Problem.

As if Anton hadn't known that already.

Somehow, everyone else knowing that made it a thousand times more horrible. They finally seemed to trust him on some level because he'd been left alone with Tyra in her bedroom. She'd asked them all to leave, and he couldn't blame her.

So he lay next to her on the bed, unsure of what to say and fully clothed because when he'd started to take his ripped, bloody clothes off to get comfortable, he felt a little pervy about it. Besides, they hadn't talked much about the fact that they'd made love and he wasn't sure where they stood on that score. Now, when she was in pain from whatever his father had done, sure as hell wasn't the time.

So Anton prayed.

His father would have been ashamed.

Well, fuck him.

"I'm so sorry, Tyra."

She pulled herself up to sitting. The grimace on her face told him that the movement was painful, but she did it anyway. "Stop. You didn't do this."

Hadn't he? He rested his head on her shoulder. He would never forgive himself if she was stuck with this debilitating pain forever.

"I can't believe I knocked my father out of the way only for Petros to take over." His lips brushed against her lips when he spoke.

"You couldn't have anticipated that."

Perhaps not, but he should have. Heaven only knew what Petros had planned.

He lifted his head and ran a hand over Tyra's cheek. The bridge of her perfect nose. Gently, he kissed her lips. The corner of her mouth lifted slightly and he thought his chest would explode. She shifted to lean against the curved headboard of her bed, and one of her boots bumped his knee.

"That can't be comfortable. Let me get those off you." He jumped off the bed. Truthfully, he was overjoyed that she had let him kiss her. He couldn't bear to hurt her. She seemed fragile right now. It was hard to think of Tyra that way.

Her hand landed on his. "Anton, you don't have to."

"Please. Let me do this. Let me take care of you." He unlaced and pulled each heavy piece of footwear off as gently as he could and dropped them quietly to the floor. "Just gonna take your socks off now, Ty."

Her feet were icy to the touch, despite the thick wool coverings she'd had on. He rubbed her feet between his hands, alternating briskly and gently. His body got warm, the heat flowing out through his fingers.

His power.

He'd thought that he could only channel the heat through anger. What if that wasn't the case? It stood to reason; he could channel his healing power when he wasn't angry. But the heat was still very new.

Anton breathed into it, focusing his intentions, his desire, and his love for her into warming those feet. Into making her as comfortable as he could.

He massaged and stroked. Kneaded the balls of her feet and that spot on the back of her ankle that he found always ached on his own legs after a long day of standing, and he even rubbed her calves a little. He hadn't been able to convince her with his words so perhaps saying it with his hands would do the trick.

That he truly did love her.

That he was sure of it now, even if he hadn't been before. And that if she let him, he would take care of her always. Keep her safe at times like this when she couldn't do it for herself. Keep her warm. That much, he could do. He placed a tiny kiss on the top of her right foot before moving on to the left.

"Anton," she breathed. "Whatever you're doing, keep doing it. I can feel my foot again."

—∾∾—

It was a little like when she'd sat on her own foot for way too long. Only… more. A lot more. A mere flex of Tyra's foot had gripped her with a painful spasm and a thousand tiny pins and needles. So much physical effort for results that seemed so little.

Or would have, had it not been for Anton's grateful gasp.

She worked to move her fingers and her entire arm seized. Enough that she would have grabbed the bed and moaned in a manner unbecoming, were she not concerned about Anton's response.

"Tyra? Oh my God, it really is working. Please tell me you're okay."

His face was damp. How lovely that he was the sort of man who wasn't afraid to cry. Since she was the sort of female who hated her own feelings tremendously, maybe they could balance each other out somehow.

Who knew?

He kissed her lips gently. His eyes... oh heaven, those gray eyes of his were dark and clear at the same time. "I knew you would be fine." He laughed a little, at himself it seemed. "Okay, I didn't. I hoped you would." He rubbed gentle circles over her face and arms, slow, easy loops that breathed warmth she didn't know she'd been missing into her body.

"This seemed to do it. When I started rubbing your feet this way." He shook his head, and a sad smile ghosted across his face. "I don't know why it never occurred to me to try that before. Even when I knew I could heal. They don't have to be used to destroy, these powers. Why didn't that occur to me?"

Tyra opened her mouth to speak, but he placed a hand over hers. "I'm sorry. I'm just rambling." He pressed his palms against his eyes. "I should have gone with you to the shelter. I could have stopped this from happening."

"Don't be," she managed.

Anton took a deep breath. "I just can't seem to get a handle on it. Everything..." His hands dropped to his side, and he stared into space like he didn't know what to say.

"Exactly," she said slowly. "Everything. You had to kill your father. That alone entitles you to be overwhelmed."

He gathered her hands between his and rubbed

warmth into them. The pins and needles were less intense now. He leaned down and rubbed his stubbly cheek against the back of her hand. "I don't even want to think about what would have happened if he had managed to get that saw into you."

She combed her fingers over his unshaven stubble. There was a little bit of gray and brown hair interspersed with the black. "So don't think about it."

Against all odds, he smiled at her. Such a gorgeous smile. More charming than his father's. Anton was so much more than his father. They both were so much more than their fathers.

He touched her arms again, rubbing those delicious circles again. "May I?"

She relaxed into the bed. Maybe she could get used to this sort of pampering. "You certainly may."

Under Anton's touch the needles became more bearable. Duller. The pain gave way to pleasure. He was gentlemanly enough to bypass the clothed sections of her body, skipping down to her feet and calves again, though he did work as high up her leg as her fatigues would allow him to.

He didn't push for more. Instead, he pulled her pant legs back down and moved behind her on the bed to rub her neck and shoulders. It was comforting to lean back and allow herself to be cradled in his arms. She'd never trusted anyone before to hold her like this.

She *did* trust him, didn't she?

Anton had watched over her and continued to do so. She could pull out all of her supernatural lie-detector tests and her doubts. Truthfully, there were many doubts. A man who had grown up as Anton had. Was he really capable of good? Well, he hadn't shown her anything but. Somewhere along the way, she had to stop fighting.

She had doubts about herself, too. About her father and whether he'd done what the wizard leader claimed. As for herself, she hadn't been swayed by the Master's arguments and appeals and insistences that she belonged on his side, had she?

Not even for a second.

Tyra was jolted out of her thoughts. "Selena. I just remembered. Is she okay? What about her mother?"

Anton hugged his arms around her from behind. "Thad called over to the shelter. Things are in chaos over there. Selena's mother is alive. That's the good news. The bad is that she'll be in the hospital for a while. Thad and Isabel have Selena for right now."

Anton gave another little squeeze and continued kneading, more gently now. More holding than massaging, really. His stubble scraped against her cheek, and before she realized it, Tyra had turned her head.

The kiss was a kind of awkward stumbling, the way it seemed almost everything had been between them. Their noses dueled and they couldn't pick a side, and then finally Tyra rose onto her knees and knelt between Anton's parted thighs so that they could really sink into it.

They were just getting to the good stuff, his firm lips against her slightly chapped ones and their tongues sliding together, when the cell phone on Tyra's nightstand rang.

Chapter 28

ANTON CURSED AND ADJUSTED HIMSELF AS HE GRABBED the phone from the nightstand. Fucking Thad. He was the king of thousands of vampires. When was that guy going to learn not to micromanage?

"Yeah?"

Mood broken, Tyra was already up and out of the bed.

"I'm sorry, Anton. Are you too busy to talk to me? Should I kick your ass back out of my estate and let you fend for yourself among the humans and all those wizards you've betrayed? It's just now mid-afternoon, probably shouldn't have to fend off too many of them until nightfall."

Anton bared his teeth at the phone. "Gosh, I apologize, Thad. It's been something of a trying day." He ought to have put a little effort into covering the sarcasm out of respect to the king, but he didn't give a shit.

He'd just killed his father. He'd gotten Tyra out of… whatever was wrong with her. Everyone and everything else could fuck off for a while. A long while.

After a long pause Thad finally said, "Yes, it has." That was it.

Huh.

A shadow fell outside Tyra's window. She was hugging herself on the back patio, squinting at what was left of the sun as it dipped below the horizon. What the hell was she doing out there?

"Anyway," Thad continued after the silence, "I called to see if there's been any change with Ty."

"Actually," Anton cleared his throat. Tyra looked so incredibly alone out there. He wanted to get to her. "She's been able to move her legs a little more," he lied. "I think she might be getting her strength back. I'll keep you posted. If there's no change, I'll have you send the doctors back over."

Thad's murmur of gratitude caused a guilty pang in Anton's chest. He wasn't going to win points by telling half-truths to the king. But Ty wasn't ready to see all those guys yet. If he were being honest with himself, Anton wasn't ready to let her be seen.

"Thad, I have to, uh, go use the bathroom."

Thad cleared his throat. "Sure thing. Listen, I think I'll have someone by to check on her in a couple of hours anyway. Can't hurt."

"Sure." That was plenty of time. Anton hung up the phone, indulging in another second or two of voyeurism before heading to the living room and out the back door.

He stepped up behind her. His hands hovered, but he didn't touch her. Tyra didn't belong to him; the logical part of his brain knew that well enough. Still, standing right there behind her was the only place he ever wanted to be.

"That was Thad on the phone?" Her soft, brown curls blew in the gentle winter breeze.

"It was. He's been checking in quite a bit. I bought you a couple of hours before the curious eyes and the doctors return." He placed a tentative hand on her shoulder. The connection that had been so strong between them inside her bedroom was more tenuous out here in the waning light. "I thought maybe you might want some time."

She turned and kissed him. Hot damn, she kissed him hard, too.

That made him ten kinds of stupid when he pulled away and said, "You're feeling all right? I don't want you to strain yourself or anything."

She kissed him again, so he stopped asking questions. He could admit to being frightened. A lot of scary shit had gone down, and he didn't know what they were getting into here.

If he were honorable, he would leave her to her world.

But right now, he was rock hard in his fatigues. Both his dick and the confident hands gripping his ass were insisting that he shut the hell up, so he did. The adrenaline, the loss of control, the fear, and everything that had come before, all of it channeled into a soul-rending urgency that he couldn't have controlled if his life had depended on it.

Already his body was heating and tingling. Some strange combination of his healing and heating powers. He said a quick prayer that he wouldn't do any harm to Tyra while he was making love to her.

They wound up rolling together on the flagstone, clothing coming off piece by piece. A loose paver jabbed into his back the first time they rolled together and then against his ass the second time.

He couldn't begin to care.

When he finally got her naked and underneath him, Tyra was magnificent. Spread out and ready for him, her golden skin glowing in the waning afternoon sun. Her breasts begged for attention as they rose and fell with each breath so he bent to the task, swirling a tongue around each nipple and biting gently. He did it again, harder, when her moans and gasps indicated that she liked it.

Both of their bodies glowed faintly. The heat from their powers. It wasn't only anger that brought it out, after all. He caressed her everywhere, taking his time, letting his fingers wander. The pinks and golds from the setting sun and the ethereal radiance from her skin… he could never have imagined anything so beautiful. He rubbed circles like before but sensuously, peppering kisses in their wake.

After another long look to drink her in, he covered his body with hers and slid inside.

She gasped. "Oh my God, Anton."

He buried himself deep in her core. "God, you feel amazing." He wanted her so much that his arms shook. Wanted to channel everything into raw and wild fucking. But at the same time he wanted to make love and spend forever worshipping her body the way she truly deserved.

He pulled out slowly and pushed home again the same way. It wasn't clear yet what the future held, and damned if he would waste it on base rutting. Her chocolate gaze met his as he pushed slow and deep, desperate to keep a slow burn going, to drag out every gasp from her lips and every widening of her eyes. He placed one hand behind her head to protect it from the hard stone, and even the silky threads of hair slipping through his fingers got him closer to getting off, if such a thing were possible.

Their tongues tasted each other slowly and he switched to shallow thrusts, which she protested by wrapping her legs around his waist and forcing him deeper. He must have hit some sort of magic angle this time, because she cried out with an "Oh, oh, yes," and her sex squeezed around his cock hard enough that Anton thought he might pass out.

Nails raked over his back. Oh, he liked that. He *reeeally* liked that. "Tyra…"

Long, strong fingers kneaded his ass, and with another squeeze of those amazing muscles around his cock, Anton was totally done for. He exploded with a spark that came from nowhere and seemed to last an eternity. He clamped his teeth together and grunted hard, desperate to keep the volume down. Heaven forbid he wake a sleeping vampire and have somebody wonder what was going on out there.

Maybe sometime soon they could make love in a place, in a way where he could shout as loud as he wanted. He sure hoped so.

His soul spilled into her, along with his orgasm and every drop of his energy and his love. He did his best to collapse gently without smashing her against the flagstone, while he wondered if he hadn't permanently given away his heart.

Who the fuck was he kidding? He'd done that a long time ago.

—◊◊◊—

They really ought to move, if for no other reason than the rock biting into Tyra's ass. But it was rather quiet out there. Their bodies fused together kept away most of the chill, and she was so at peace she didn't give a damn about the rest.

"You've really never done that before, huh?" she murmured.

He lifted his head and smiled shyly. "I'll take that as a compliment." At any other time but one like this, it was easy to forget how inexperienced he was.

She ran a finger through his short, dark hair. It was a little bit salt and peppery, dark like his eyes with tiny bright flecks. It gave him a wise, distinguished look. "It was."

"I'm sorry that I…" He gestured vaguely. "I couldn't help myself."

She couldn't help but laugh at that. "Hey, what female doesn't love being wanted so much that a guy can't help himself, huh?" She cradled his stubbly jaw and pulled him to her for a kiss. "You don't have anything to worry about."

The light was fading from the sky. Soon, the moon would be out. Waning, if she wasn't mistaken. It had been awhile since she'd needed to pay attention. She hadn't been in a serious relationship, hadn't had any kind of steady mate.

Her fingers traced over the muscles on his goose-bumpy arm. "You make me feel special."

"I'm glad."

When his lips brushed hers, she asked, "Do you think there's any chance this could work out?"

Raking a hand through his hair, he sat up on his knees. When he did, he pulled out of her body, leaving her empty in more ways than one. "I don't know. I'd like to think so. I want it to, but…" His lips pressed together so tightly that they turned white. "My living here with you may not even be an option. I mean, once everyone finds out who I am? What I am? You, they'll probably forgive. You're still one of them. Nothing can change the fact that you're part vampire. But nothing can change the fact that I'm my father's son, either."

He shrugged his shoulders sadly. "And you can't tell me you would want to leave here only to be with me. Family means too much to you. I've been around you long enough to know that. You probably want someone you can have a family with, and I can't give that to you. I won't bring more wizards into the world."

He grabbed her hands and rubbed brisk circles, not the slow, luxurious ones like before. "Come on, let's get you inside. I don't want you to get cold again." He glanced up at the sky. "Besides, the sun is going down, and I don't want your brother to show up here with the doctor and find us like this. He's been on the fence about killing me enough times as it is."

They both made a good show of smiling at the joke, but Anton's smile didn't reach his eyes, and Tyra suspected hers didn't, either.

She opted for a shower when they got back inside, while Anton dressed and called Thad to let him know that Tyra was up and around. Funny how making love in thirty-degree weather on a cold patio hadn't been uncomfortable, but now as the hot water sluiced over her body, she couldn't get warm enough.

It was hard to make sense of everything. Of what Anton had said outside. The gist seemed to be a very tragic "sorry babe, I have feelings for you, too, but because of our shitty luck with the gene pool we can never be together."

Well, that was pretty much the worst kiss-off she'd

ever gotten. And where did that leave her? Able to date only vampires in the hopes that she could override the wizard genes? Able to date only humans in the hope that she could *water down* the wizard genes? Dating something that took C batteries for eternity?

Oddly, she'd always had the tragic idea that maybe she was destined to be alone for the long haul, but now the reality left her wanting to bite her own wrists open.

She slapped off the water and wrapped a fuzzy towel around herself. Anton's low rumble carried to her from another room, but she didn't know who he was talking to and she didn't bother trying to stretch her hearing so that she could find out. Maybe Anton was talking to Thad, or maybe he was calling his evil brother and making plans for the next family barbecue: main course, slow-roasted vampire with coleslaw on the side.

She sagged against the bathroom door, reluctant to leave the tiny room. Her stomach was full of knots, and her brain held nothing but static.

Chapter 29

IF THERE WAS ANY HOPE OF A FUTURE WITH TYRA, Anton needed to prove himself—really prove himself—to these vampires. For reasons he understood all too well, the doubt ran long and deep. Killing his father had furthered his own cause of vengeance as much as theirs, if they wanted to see it that way. There was also the disheartening fact that killing the Master had done a questionable amount of good, given that Petros was still on the loose. Anton would set about tying up that loose end as soon as he found out what was on the drive Petros had thrown at him.

His head drooped unceremoniously toward his chest while he waited in what Thad had said was his house manager's office. It turned out the data on the drive was corrupted, but the queen's human friend was good with computers. He tried not to eye the clean, white, unmarked blotter on the cherry desk like it was a pillow while he waited for Alexia to pull up the files.

She eyeballed him sideways. "You okay?"

Anton shook his head. "I'm fine. Thanks for asking."

He slapped what was meant to be a fraternal pat on Alexia's back. She flinched and muttered a quiet "ow" but didn't say much else. The edges of some kind of plastic bandage poked from above her tank top. Some kind of fresh injury or… there seemed to be a lot of ink on the girl's body. A new tattoo in the hours since he'd last seen her? Or had the bandages been there before and he hadn't noticed.

It seemed a good chance to kill two birds with one stone. He could practice control of his healing power while helping with whatever was hurting her back. While Alexia squinted at the screen, shoulders hunched horribly in concentration, Anton used the barest pressure to rest his fingertips against her shirt.

His fingers warmed and his eyes drifted shut of their own accord, and he was wholly unprepared for what he saw next: fences. High, ringed in barbed wire, and monochromatic like something from a depressing Nazi-era movie he'd seen once when he was very young. The only life was a small, skinny child standing inside the rings of fence after fence after fence.

Anton found himself pounding on the outermost barrier and finding the fences made of steel and not the wood they appeared to be fashioned from. He needed to get her out, his gut told him so, but he couldn't see a way in. She seemed so alone and frightened, and he couldn't heal her when she was so far away.

Pain exploded across Anton's jaw, and no sooner had he begun to commune with a cabbage-rose-covered area rug than a large boot connected with the soft part of his belly. He still didn't know what in the hell was going on. Part of his brain was stuck on helping that girl. Massive hands shoved underneath his arms, and he was pinned to the wall by a large, angry vampire. Anton thought he remembered this one's name was Lee?

"What the fuck did you do to her?"

Truthfully, Anton wasn't sure. "I didn't do anything." He gazed across the room. Alexia remained seated at the desk, eyes wide. Siddoh clapped a protective hand on her shoulder. Something—some recognition—passed from her to Anton. That girl was there inside her eyes, and Alexia seemed to know that Anton had seen something important. And it frightened her. Maybe Anton had unwittingly gotten too close to something she tried to keep hidden. He could understand that, in a way. "I didn't mean to," he finished lamely. That much was true. Whatever he'd done, he certainly hadn't meant it.

"Her back. She was hurt, and I was trying to help heal it. I don't know what happened." Anton looked from Lee, who still held him with an iron grip, to Siddoh and to Alexia again. Then to Thad and Isabel and some female with long, dark hair who had entered the room, and a shorter male who was dressed in regular clothes rather than battle gear but seemed no less imposing under the circumstances. What the hell had happened? He shifted back to Alexia. "If I hurt you, I apologize. I was trying to help."

She shook her head and made a weak show of a smile. "I'm fine." She looked around at everyone, as if she'd suddenly realized how many eyes were on her in the room. Her pale skin blushed a deep red. "Honestly, guys, I'm sorry. I guess I'm still not used to the vampire voodoo. Or whatever voodoo that was. That's all, yeah? Sorry to get everyone worked up. Lee, let him go."

She shooed Siddoh away and made a show of going back to the files Anton had given her, but clearly she was still out of sorts. Shaky. And it was equally clear from the jut of her chin and the set of her shoulders that she wasn't saying another word on the subject. What had happened to her? What had Anton unwittingly done to her?

Was Anton's healing power capable of sussing out much more than garden-variety cuts and scrapes? Whatever he'd seen in there was the kind of hurt that ran long and deep. And it wasn't physical. Anton knew all about that shit.

Lee let him go and stepped back reluctantly, taking a final look at Alexia before he left the room. Slowly everyone emptied out except Isabel, who sat by Alexia's side with a bag of knitting, and Thad, who stood in front of Anton and simply… stared.

Anton wasn't sure he really needed Thad to speak; they were both likely thinking the same thing. Anton thought of Tyra, who was probably out of the shower by now and getting dressed and wondering where he had gone.

He moved off to the side with Thad, whose face still held an icy glare. "I get it. There will always be mistrust here. Someone will always think Tyra's sleeping with the enemy, no matter what I do to prove otherwise."

Thad's head dropped backward onto his shoulders. "I really am sorry about that. I appreciate what you've done for us, but you can understand where the fear is coming from."

"I know." He tapped his hand against the wall. "She's gonna be furious if I take off without saying anything."

Thad nodded again. "She will be. But I think maybe it's better to avoid confrontation."

Anton inclined his head toward Alexia and lowered his voice to a whisper. "It was my healing power.

There's something deep inside of her, some sort of emotional hurt, I think. I really didn't intend to frighten her."

Thad placed a hand on Anton's shoulder. "I appreciate your concern. I'll talk to Isabel."

"Good." Anton gestured toward Alexia again. "What she found on the drive might be an old address for my mother. I wanted to check it out anyway. It's a long shot, but you never know."

"I'll have Ivy, my house manager, get you a car," Thad said.

"Thank you." Anton straightened his clothes as he stepped away from the wall. It wasn't his true motivation for leaving so easily, but he wouldn't say so to Thad. Not to anyone. That remaining loose end with his brother needed to be handled, and given what had just happened with Alexia, it was probably better that he handle it alone. This was the perfect opportunity to go.

Tyra was going to hate him for taking off like this, and it killed him to leave without saying good-bye. But if he said good-bye, she would try to stop him. Or come along. He couldn't risk her safety again, and he couldn't just sit back and let Petros get away without knowing he'd tried everything there was to try.

Thad was right; it was better this way. Better for Tyra to hate him. Chances were, by morning he'd be dead.

Alexia ran to grab Siddoh by the arm as he was ambling toward the hall stairwell that led to the underground tunnels. "Hey, are you off tonight?"

Her heart squeezed a little when it looked like his shoulders sagged. They were friends. She *wanted* to buy that he liked hanging out with her. The insecure teenager inside of her, though, was always afraid that her friends were tired of her shit and ready to dump her ass for something better. Convinced she was too obnoxious and too much of a pain to be worth their time. Like now.

But she needed to lean on someone solid right now, and she was hoping that Siddoh was still willing to be that someone.

He turned and raked a hand through his hair. "Yeah, I'm off tonight. You wanna go out, I assume?"

They both glanced up as Lee's boots echoed at the far end of the hall. He looked their way and kept going. She couldn't have read his expression from where they stood even if it had changed, which it probably hadn't. And it would be stupid, wishful thinking that the fact that she was still holding on to Siddoh's wrist might have made Lee jealous.

Isabel was right. It was time to grow up and let that shit go.

Siddoh's eyes narrowed and his stare slid her way. "Don't you think maybe you need to dial back on the partying a little?"

"I party far less here than I used to, you know." She stuck out her tongue and put her hands on her hips. It was kind of a juvenile move, but screw that. She wasn't out to impress Siddoh anyway.

He cupped her chin. "I'm worried about you, you know. Don't suppose you want to tell me what really happened back there with Anton and you almost passing out on your keyboard?"

She smiled her best smile. "Maybe after you get a

martini or two into me, I'll open up a little." They both knew that was a crock.

He grumbled and rolled his eyes to the ceiling, and when he blew air hard enough that his scraggly brown hair flounced around on his forehead, she knew she had him. "Swear to God, Lex, if you get us kicked out, I'm done."

"I'll be good. I promise." His look was dubious, so she held up a hand with her little finger extended. "Pinkie swear."

Siddoh shook his head and looped his arm around her neck. "What are you, twelve?"

"Sometimes, yeah." It really did seem that way sometimes, didn't it?

"All right, look." He stuffed his hands into his pockets. "I gotta shower and rest a little, balance out from nearly getting flash-fried at the shelter this morning. I never did get a good nap after feeding. Been crazy around here. So let me do that, check in at the training center… think you can handle waiting around for a few hours?"

She was careful not to let her face fall. Honestly, she wasn't quite sure that she could. Generally she loved being single. She enjoyed her independence. But times like this? She would have loved having someone to cling to, koala style. And she could lean on Siddoh for a lot, but she couldn't turn to him that way. It wouldn't be fair to either of them.

She turned to cover her disappointment. "Sounds good. Come grab me when you're ready?"

Alexia skipped back to her room. Anything to cover the fear, the dread of what she didn't want to feel. And sure enough, it found her as soon as she closed the door and lay on the bed.

She had no clue what that wizard guy had done to her, but it had been suffocating. The second his hand had touched her back, a sensation had come over her like she was in a free fall. And Alexia had always been afraid of heights, so it wasn't a feeling she relished. Too bad she wasn't a bungee-jumping adrenaline junkie.

If only.

It had been like being tossed off a cliff head first and rushing through black nothingness. No bottom. No slowing down. Nothing but faster and faster and *faster*.

She put her hands over her eyes, and it all started again. She wanted to pull her hands away to make it stop, but her body was frozen.

"Lex?" The bang on the door snapped her out of it. Siddoh.

She stumbled to the door, almost staggering, as if she were already drunk. "Hey, that was fast. I thought you said it would be a few hours."

He pulled out his phone. "It's after ten. You okay?"

Suddenly her throat hurt and her eyes burned. It couldn't be that late. She'd done nothing more than lie on the bed. "Uh. Yeah. Let me just…" She glanced around her room, which was as disheveled as she must have been with its rumpled bed and piles of clothes. She held up a hand. "Two minutes, huh?"

He frowned but backed against the far wall of the hallway. She closed the door and sucked down a few gulps of air before scrabbling frantically to throw on clean clothes and dunk her head into the sink. For a moment she stared at the blinking readout on her alarm clock, like maybe it and Siddoh were both fucking with her. She'd lost more than four hours.

What the hell had happened?

Chapter 30

TYRA'S LEG BOUNCED IMPATIENTLY ON HER SOFA while she waited for the doctor to declare her healthy enough to leave the estate. A commotion outside the door drew her attention.

"I want Miss Tyra." The front door opened and Selena entered first, leading Thad who looked more dour-faced than she'd ever seen him. It had certainly been a long time since Thad had allowed anyone to drag him anywhere like that. Probably not even Isabel. It was almost enough to make her smile.

Almost.

"I'm over here, sweetie." She patted the tan micro-suede and motioned Selena over. "Why don't you sit next to me while the doctor finishes checking me out?"

Thad gave Tyra a surprisingly apologetic look. "She woke up and she wanted you."

"It's fine." She looked at Selena and managed a smile.

She swept aside the girl's hair and glanced down at the strawberry birthmark. She tucked the girl against her side even as she narrowed her eyes at Thad. She tried to keep her voice neutral when she asked, "Where's Anton?"

Thad leaned against the wall. "He wanted to check into some things that Lex found on a thumb drive. I don't know exactly."

"Did he say when he'd be back?" She probably knew

the answer to this one already, but it would be nice to get a definite response.

Thad licked his lips and stared at her for a moment. "I'm not sure."

She sighed and closed her eyes. "You're not sure when, or you're not sure if?"

"If."

Tyra opened and closed a fist. Not so much out of anger, but because even though she'd anticipated the news, her heart had taken a pause from pumping the blood around her body and now her hands were a little numb.

"Ty, you know it's for the best."

She scowled at Thad, past the penlight that Brayden was waving in her eyes. "Do I? You know, I'm getting a little tired of everyone else trying to decide what's best for me." The realization that she'd been the last to get the memo about her wizard heritage was still not only infuriating but embarrassing.

Thad looked pointedly from Tyra to the girl nestled quietly by her side and then back again. "You've always had a rebellious streak, Ty, but you've always had the greater good in mind. So think about that."

She flopped back on the sofa. What had she been hoping for? They wouldn't be able to live here, not without constant problems. And she did want to stay with her kind.

Besides, could she ever really have a guarantee that he wouldn't turn on her or something? Having him living in their midst... perhaps even *she* wouldn't be comfortable with that. And if she couldn't trust him with her own kind, then they definitely had nothing.

Because she had arrived at a decision. She was vampire. No half anything. Being part human she could live with, but being part wizard? She would not acknowledge that. Sure as hell she would not bow down to it.

Selena looked up right then. "Was Anton the man who rescued us from that place?"

Tyra brushed some stray hairs from the girl's face. "Yeah, sweetie."

"I liked him."

A tiny, invisible hammer tapped Tyra's heart and made it crack wide open. "I liked him too." She closed her eyes and let that truth resonate through her body.

She did. She liked him. Loved him. Honestly, she wasn't sure who she'd been trying to convince with all that other bullshit.

On the surface, Ash Falls had all the trappings of a pretty, safe, sleepy little area. But Anton knew, because he'd grown up knowing, that a hell of a lot of dark and ugly lurked in the nooks and crannies. When he and Petros had been boys, they'd learned the small out-of-the-way places to go where they could stay off their father's radar screen.

The Ash Falls Old Towne Hall sat on the edge of the historic district. The place must have once doubled as a church, based on the cemetery next door. It had one of those stamped metal signs next to it, but Anton had never stopped to read it. He didn't now on his way in. The lock was already busted, and he squinted at the creak of the door as it eased open. White paint chips flaked and fell at his feet. "Place needs some serious

TLC," he whispered to nobody at all. This had been their favorite place to come as boys.

They'd had an older brother who'd been mysteriously killed when Anton was around the age of twelve. Petros had been older... eighteen? That had been the defining fork in the road for the two brothers. They'd never talked about it, but there was little question their father had been to blame. What had solidified Anton's resolve to someday break free had turned Petros hard and cold.

It was dark, but Anton could see clearly. How long would the effect of Tyra's blood last in his body? The main level was mostly empty, except for some stacked folding chairs covered in a layer of dust. He kept his ears open as he crept carefully to the set of steps at the back of the room.

He heard the whispers when he reached the doorway to the basement. Only a few men occupied the room. Five, not including Petros, who stood over the one seated in a chair chanting like he was in a trance.

"...open... gateway... power..."

What was he doing? Anton couldn't hear much at all. The double doors that led into the basement had long since fallen off their hinges, but there was a noisy furnace in the room, and inexplicably it still ran. Petros's doing, perhaps. The man in the chair stood and circled around close to the doorway where Anton was spying as another took his place in the seat. Anton shivered as the man passed. He was clearly a wizard; the evil of his aura was tenuous, but it was there.

Petros's hands moved around the next man. Anton inched closer to the edge of the doorway. More chanting.

It was a ceremony of some sort; that much was clear, but it was unlike anything Anton had ever seen the Master do. This was… holy shit. A bright ring of light formed around the man in the seat, suddenly turning fiery red and absorbing into the man's aura. This was some sort of magic transfer. Anton didn't know quite what Petros was doing or how, but that much of it was clear.

Damned if Petros hadn't found a way to transfer wizard magic. The fangs, and now this. All part of his brother's plans to ramp up the wizard establishment. Fuck, the possibilities were endless and horrifying. How much faster would he be able to create wizards if he didn't have to physically breed them first? "Jesus, just open up a prison and you've got a fresh supply of minions."

For all he knew, Petros had already thought of that.

Whatever this was, Anton had to put a stop to it. He felt for the gun at his back. When he'd left, Thad's guard had given it to him, along with a cell phone. Perhaps it had been clear that he wasn't simply planning to look for an old address on a computer file.

He'd taken aim when his brother's raised voice came through the doorway, clearly this time: "That would be unwise, Brother."

Anton froze. The gun stayed trained on his brother, aimed at the widest part of his torso. Anton had a clear shot now that Petros had stepped back from the man in the chair. The newbie wizards, or whatever they were, stood up, wary, and ready to fight, but Petros held up his hand to stay them. Clearly, he already commanded better allegiance than their father had. Not surprising.

"You can't have thought I was going to just let this go, Petros."

Petros grinned. "I suppose not. It would be nice to call a truce the way we could have when we were boys. I agree not to come after your precious Tyra anymore, and you agree to leave me alone. You ride off into the sunset—or the moonlight, I suppose—and we leave each other to our lives."

Anton pulled the hammer down.

"No? Well, I should warn you that I did see the chance that this sort of thing might happen. How about this? There's a protective barrier about the perimeter of this room. You fire that weapon, and it's going to hurt you more than it hurts me."

Cold air stung Anton's nostrils, and his teeth bit into his lips hard enough that he tasted blood. Of course, Petros had planned for this. The question of what exactly would happen was the thing to figure out.

Then he absorbed a vital piece of information. A closer look at the doorway revealed a gentle, reddish glow. He'd seen this before. At Petros's first kill, he'd been so proud of the power he'd gained that he'd shown off to Anton what he could do. There was a chance here that Anton could use that knowledge to his advantage. He returned Petros's smile.

"Hard not to stick with what's tried and true, eh, Petros?"

The look on his brother's face was blank. He didn't remember, and that was fine. Anton fired twice. Fast as he could. Then he hit the deck. The barrier exploded.

He covered his face and prayed, as the flames washed over him, that maybe the second bullet had hit its mark. Then he focused on using his own power to heat his body. Instinct told him to fight fire with fire.

There was a clamor and a bang. Windows exploding. Chairs toppling. Wizards escaping the building. As soon as the fire stopped licking his back, Anton jumped up. He needed to get out. His brother and his buddies were gone, except for one poor bastard left behind who'd taken the bullets intended for Petros. *Fuck*.

"Sorry, man," Anton muttered. It was tough to feel too bad for the dead newbie. Chances were good that he would have wound up slaying untold numbers of vampires, had he been given the opportunity.

The flames were already climbing the walls when Anton made it to fresh air. He braced his hands on his knees and sucked wind, groping in his fatigues for the cell phone Lee had given him. The vampires needed to know what Petros was up to. If nothing else, they needed to brace themselves. His thumb hovered, ready to call Tyra but afraid she might be too angry to listen.

Instead, Anton called the vampire he'd come to think of as an unlikely sort of friend. "Xander," he said into the phone. "I've got some important information for you, buddy."

Chapter 31

XANDER STOOD IN THERESA'S FOYER. "YOU'RE REALLY sure this is a good idea?"

She laid a hand on his shoulder, smoothing it over the front of his jacket. Tam used to do the same thing before he went out for the night. Maybe it was something mates just did. Xander couldn't be sure. Not that he was going out to fight exactly, although that remained to be seen. And not that Theresa was his mate. This whole thing was confusing.

"You're doing the right thing," she said.

"Hope so."

They all but tripped over each other in their good-byes. She walked him out to the front stoop where they both stood and stared for a while, not sure what to say to each other. And Xander, for his part, couldn't put his finger on why. And then the baby cried from the bassinet in the living room, and he could admit, if only to himself, that he was relieved he didn't have to figure it out.

It was a speedy trek across the estate grounds to borrow one of the community vehicles. He'd never asked Theresa's age, but it was clear that she was from an old bloodline as much from the strength of her blood as from her bearing and her style.

Tam had been modern. Independent. Which he'd loved and respected, until the night that going out alone had gotten her killed.

All the air left his lungs as he slid behind the wheel of one of the estate's Land Rovers and programmed in the address Xander had given him. And now, God only knew why, he was going to retrieve the enemy and bring him home, in a manner of speaking.

"Stupid doing-the-right-thing bullshit," he muttered to himself. The hills and valleys of Ash Falls were soon behind him, and the glittery lights of Washington, DC, lay ahead. At this time of night, he wondered if he would find anything at all.

Xander double-parked illegally outside a row of townhouses. A parking ticket was the least of his issues. Thank the moon and stars, Anton was seated on a bench swing on the porch of one of the townhouses, staring at… well, not much of anything as far as Xander could tell.

"They're going to be selling this place soon," Anton said.

Talk about your non sequiturs. The comment was the only indication that Anton knew Xander was there. "So, find anything interesting?"

"It's under foreclosure now. Someone who was maybe my biological mother used to live here," Anton murmured. The man ran a hand over his head and face. "She died last year."

Shit. Talk about too little, too late. "I'm sorry to hear that."

Anton shook his head. "It was stupid. I'm not sure what I thought I might find here. Should have known Petros wouldn't really give me anything useful. It was a head fuck like everything else. Like father, like son."

Xander shrugged. "Sometimes it's hard to be at peace

until you have all the history. You had to try. Sorry it didn't work out."

Anton faced Xander for the first time since he'd settled on the bench. How had he, of all vampires, been tapped to be this guy's new friend? Sure as hell, this whole thing had the tight, itchy sensation that it was heading that way, and Xander wasn't so sure he liked it.

Wasn't sure he hated it, either.

"Thanks."

Xander had to laugh at that. "Yeah, I can't take credit. Theresa, my… uh, the female I've been helping to take care of. She said it to me earlier. Made sense." He gave Anton a fake punch in the arm. "But you know you got stuck with the genetic short straw, and you're gonna have to play the hand you were dealt with whatever information you do or don't have about your past. I don't think that means you have to disappear into the night like some sort of Old West gunslinger."

Anton quirked an eyebrow at him, and Xander shrugged. "What? I like those human Old West movies. That and anything with Gene Hackman in it. Anyway…" He punched Anton a little harder this time.

"Ow."

"Pansy. Anyway, you haven't had the pleasure of meeting Agnessa, have you?" Anton's blank stare said it all. You sure as hell *knew* when you met Agnessa. So Xander continued. "Back in the day, she and Lee, Thad's second in command, were a couple. Thing is, Agnessa is part vampire, part succubus. More the latter, from what anyone can tell. The last in existence as far as anyone knows. Know much about those?"

Anton blinked.

"Didn't figure. Well, the short version is that they need sex to survive more than they need blood, if you get my drift. So Agnessa had a little problem staying faithful. And everyone knows. Everyone." He leaned in to Anton like they were whispering in a movie theater. "Rumor is that Lee put up with it for a long time, until a couple of decades ago when he caught Nessa in bed with Thad."

Anton jerked. "Thad, as in the king."

"A long time ago, when it was still his father's rule."

Anton shook his head. "That's… why are you telling me this?"

Xander chuckled. "Thing about Nessa is that I don't think she can even really live anywhere except the estate. She wouldn't blend in with the humans. When you meet her, you'll understand. And there aren't any more of her mother's kind around."

He noted a slight nod of interest from Anton. Whether the dude knew it or not, Xander had him on the hook. Powers of persuasion, he had 'em.

"Anyway nobody likes her because everyone knows how she broke Lee's heart and how she did it by shagging the prince. But she still lives at the estate and manages to hold her head up proudly, even though folks scatter like startled cockroaches when she walks into a room. Sure, not many of the residents like her or trust her, but we all manage to coexist peacefully enough."

"I'm betting she was never responsible for anyone's mate getting killed."

Xander pressed his lips together. "I believe you when you say that you weren't directly involved unless you were forced. If I can buy it, others will come to believe that as well. And Nessa ended relationships. Not by way of death, but she ended them. In a way you two have something in common. She can't help her genetics any more than you can."

Anton leaned forward. The porch swing creaked in protest. They'd be lucky if the thing didn't collapse under both of them. "What about Tyra?"

Xander stood. "I hear Tyra's pretty pissed at you for taking off, buddy."

Anton didn't move. "Maybe she's too pissed."

Xander held out a hand. "Come on, that's bullshit. With females, anger's never really about anger. Now look, I'm sticking my neck out here. Don't make me sorry. Come back and help us use that insider knowledge of yours to kick more wizard ass, huh?"

Anton's feet shuffled on the slate tiles of the porch. His face twisted up like he'd bitten into something sour. "I'm not so sure that I can do it, Xander. Even knowing they're evil, even knowing it's the right thing to do. I want to help you guys fight but I really do hate to kill. I don't think I could do it night after night like you do."

"Huh." Xander planted his boots and pushed back on the swing a little. "I have to admit I hadn't thought about that." A frigid blast of wind prompted him to pull his zipper up farther, and he remembered the warmth of Theresa's bed. "It's kill or be killed. You know that as well as I do. It also gets easier. Know what, though? I remember being told you helped heal me out in the woods when that wizard blast hit me."

Anton's toe scuffed at a spot on the porch. "I can heal, sure. So what? You think anyone's gonna want to be reminded of how I got that power?"

"So maybe there are other options for helping with the fight. You can help us with your knowledge. Maybe over time you'll think of little things that aren't coming to you now. And maybe instead of going out to fight, you can help us by healing the guys who come in wounded. Some nights the docs are spread awfully thin. Might be a way to spread goodwill by using the powers you've claimed for something positive."

"Maybe."

"Won't know unless we try, man."

Cold air gripped Xander's fingers. He waited for what seemed like an endless number of minutes while the gears whirred almost visibly in Anton's head. He was about to give up and back away when one gloved palm landed in his.

———*w*———

Anton had barely put his foot on the bottom step of the mansion's brightly lit front entrance when the blood in his veins surged hot and livid. He knew as certainly as he knew his own name that he would look up in a few seconds to see Tyra standing in the open doorway.

He wasn't disappointed.

Wow. He knew she'd be angry, but this fury speeding through his system was beyond comprehension.

Somehow, as if even if the weather was angry on her behalf, the wind picked up and her dark brown curls danced around her face. She was framed so beautifully by the long, white columns on the mansion's long front porch that he was tempted to run up the long set of stone stairs and pull her into his arms, even though she was mad at him.

A smattering of snow had started to fall, and it hovered and worshipped nearby. None of it was brave enough to come in for a landing. Her skin probably had a surface temperature of more than a hundred degrees right now.

Elegant, brass-handled double doors opened, and Siddoh and Alexia passed by on their way somewhere. A gruffly muttered warning from Siddoh to "stand clear" made a smattering of onlookers vanish from the porch as if the vampire had waved his own magic wand.

All the while Tyra stared at Anton, hair swirling and eyes flashing. Waiting. Anton could see the momentum gathering around her almost like a visible force. Any second now the yelling was going start, and damned if he knew what to say. He'd mulled it over the entire trip back from DC. Not that he'd had much time to think, the way that crazy fucker Xander drove.

Another surge in Anton's blood and Tyra stormed down the stairs. She stood toe to toe with him, staring at him with dark, bottomless, terrifying eyes for an endless stretch of moments. And then she smacked him on the arm. Hard.

"Ow." He rubbed the sore spot. "Okay, fine, I deserved that. I really think, though, that we should go inside and talk—Sonofa—"

She'd taken a few steps back. He'd assumed erroneously that was so she could follow his suggestion to head inside where they could talk things out like something resembling normal adults. No, she'd backed up so she could plant her feet for a good roundhouse kick to his head. He narrowly dodged, but the cold ground was slippery with the dusting of newly fallen snow, and he landed on his ass. How could he have forgotten how long those legs of hers were?

And was he weird for thinking it was kind of hot that his woman was trying to beat the shit out of him?

His woman? His… for now he'd stick with "woman."

Something about the way she was advancing on him with her squared shoulders and her fists of fury told Anton that she wouldn't exactly embrace the title of "his" openly. Wow, he'd screwed the pooch big time on that one, hadn't he?

"Tyra. Shit." He rolled backward just as a boot-covered foot lashed out with his testicles' names written all over it.

She slipped but didn't fall. "Why the hell did you even bother coming back here, Anton? I was getting used to the idea of you being gone."

He staggered to his feet and she stormed forward. Her hands were open now, and for the first time he noticed her fingernails. Well-manicured and trimmed, but long enough to do damage the way she had them extended like they were claws. "I was only gone for a few hours."

"But you weren't going to come back, were you?" He grabbed her wrists to stop her from coming forward, which only encouraged her to get her knee working on engaging his balls again. *Brilliant, Anton.* "Were you?"

He sighed. "Tyra, can't we go inside and discuss—"

"No." Her staccato shout was loud enough that Anton was surprised it didn't draw the crowd back outside. But there was no time to consider that because along with the shout came a hard shove, and somehow he lost his footing or something. It was enough for her to gain a moment of advantage, and true to her nature, she took her opening.

"Shit, Tyra." A fireball landed near enough to singe his bootlaces, and Anton took the very manly action of running away as fast as he could manage. Not that he could outrun her. He was faster than a garden-variety human, but vampires were faster still.

They were too close to the main house, though, and to cars and other residences. If she was going to start hurling projectiles, he wanted her to do it someplace safe. So he headed for the nearest tree line with dirt peppering his ankles as fireballs chased his retreat. Dammit, had she gone over the edge straight to plain old crazy?

Anton ducked behind a tree when he hit the woods and waited until he had the benefit of dry leaves and snapping branches to gauge her approach. "What the hell are you doing, Tyra, trying to blow up your brother's property?"

When the flaming orbs seemed to have taken a pause, he stepped from behind the tree to face her. Sweat from the fight and from the exertion of using her power caused her hair to cling to her face and her shirt to cling to her body.

"How could you just… *leave*, like that?"

"I was trying to do what was best for you." He gestured at the property beyond them. "What was best for everyone here."

She scoffed. "Well, that's excellent, Anton, and you've lived here for how long?"

He frowned. "What do you mean?"

She stepped closer. One long finger jabbed hard at a sore spot on his left pectoral. Both of their bodies vibrated in sync, as much from the cold as from anger. "I mean, you don't get to be the one to make decisions about what is best for me and my kind, Anton." Her eyes flashed in the moonlight. "Is it the whole 'live fast, leave a pretty corpse' thing you're really after? Seems to me you've been on one suicide mission after another. Maybe you're just gonna keep running into stupid situations until you crash and burn."

Chapter 32

SEEING ANTON ON THE FRONT STEP HAD STIRRED anger so primeval inside Tyra that she'd been half tempted to tear him limb from limb. Part of her was grateful he was back in one piece. Part of her hated him for leaving. Apparently that was the part of her in charge. At least, it *had* been.

They'd made it all the way to the woods before her anger cooled. What it left behind was a tangled mix of embarrassment, shame, hope, and fear. She had handled so many things so badly, and maybe she should have gone ahead and let him leave. Certainly, attacking him when he returned had been ungrateful. So many things *hurt* though, from the inside out. She didn't want him to leave again. She didn't want him to *die*, for crying out loud. God, when she'd heard he went looking for his brother by himself… Her vision blurred.

In an effort to brush away a snowflake on her cheek, she accidentally started the waterworks.

"Tyra, dammit. I'm sorry."

"No, Anton, you were probably right to go. We can't—" Oh God, it was so unbelievably warm in his arms. And so comforting. Had she really forgotten that quickly what it was like? She closed her eyes, and big, fat tears came rolling down her cheeks.

"I'm sorry, Tyra."

She tried putting Angry Tyra back at the helm and

landed the world's lamest punch against his shoulder. "You don't get to do that. You don't get to decide—"

And then he kissed her, and without any permission from her whatsoever, all the ice around her heart melted and she fell right into him. "I'm really sorry, Tyra," he murmured against her lips. "This is…" More kissing. His fingers were warm, despite the cold, as his hand crept under her shirt. That power of his was quite a double-edged sword. Nice to have at times like these, but knowing how he'd acquired it tasted bitter.

"Neither of us can undo our pasts and where we've come from. I don't know how we'll navigate through things with your kind, but I'd like to try. I can help you fight. I can help your brother with what I know. Maybe one day your kind here will come to trust me."

He kissed the corner of her mouth and whispered in her ear. "I'm as afraid of everything as you are. I can feel it in my veins, you know. But maybe we can lean on each other for that."

Maybe they could.

Somehow they'd walked a few paces together until her back was against a tree whose branches had broken off in a storm. His erection pressed against her hip through the layers of both their clothing. His hand slid up the length of her inner thigh, caressing and pressing at the juncture of her thighs. "Oh, jeez. Anton. Seriously." Before she completely took leave of her senses, they really did need to talk more. Males and their hormones.

With all the resistance she could muster, she gripped his shoulder and pushed him backward. "Anton."

He blinked. Already, his eyes were a little glazed. Just like a man—all about sex. "Look, you're really sure about staying? Because I don't think I can take it if you leave again."

"I really don't want to leave you again." He tightened his grip around her waist and pulled her in for another kiss.

She punched against his chest. "Anton."

"Ow."

"I mean it."

"So do I."

"Sir, do you have a moment?" Xander caught the king coming out of the room where he usually received subjects.

"Xander, you've known me for a century. Don't call me 'sir.'"

Xander nodded. Thad seemed… it was hard for Xander to get a read on him these days. Xander wasn't much older than Thad and could easily remember having grown up and trained side by side. They'd laughed and celebrated together. Now Thad was serious and strung tight, but still someone Xander knew and could talk to… or so it seemed. But was he?

Somehow, now that he'd opened his big mouth, Xander was thinking perhaps he should have waited until he ran into Lee or Siddoh or perhaps even his buddy Flay to discuss this. But Thad had been the one to put him on guard duty.

"I wanted to find out about the possibility of returning to active duty."

Thad creased his forehead and crossed his arms over his chest. "You're willing to feed?"

"Yes." The back of Xander's neck got hot. *No need*

to get squirmy, Xander. Be matter of fact about it and move on.

Thad's chin dropped to his chest for a moment. "What's Theresa say?"

Xander found himself stuck in a silent stutter. Shaking off the temporary paralysis so he could answer was a harder fight than it ought to have been. "She seems to be doing rather well. The baby is healthy. She's getting around without trouble, and her spirits are remarkable. She's handling Eamon's passing far better than I handled Tam's."

"But have you discussed it with her, pulling out of guard duty? We all know it's not exactly her physical safety I'm concerned with."

Xander swallowed. "Not exactly. I haven't discussed it with her."

Thad rubbed his temple a little. "Talk to her before you decide anything. You've had months to get used to being without a mate. She's just easing into it and dealing with a new baby besides. I don't like the idea of leaving her on her own yet."

The king's response both relieved and agitated Xander. He bounced on his heels for a moment. An argument perched on the tip of his tongue, but Thad stood before him with his chest and chin jutting forward.

The king knew. He knew Xander wanted to argue and was challenging him to do it.

"Is there some kind of problem, Xander?"

Xander blinked and studied the diamond-patterned carpet runner. Well, that would probably depend on one's definition of the word. And frankly, Xander couldn't even put his finger on what had him so agitated.

Maybe that he was an interloper on sacred ground every time he took Theresa's vein, and his heart broke when he thought of Tam while he did. It broke even more when he realized that he hadn't thought of Tam at all.

That brief moment of connection when he'd been on his way out to look for Anton had been wrong on so many levels. Nothing tangible, but something had passed between him and Theresa, or at least something had entered his field of awareness. It was clear that he had gone someplace in his head that he ought never to go again.

But he could barely define it for himself so he sure as hell couldn't say it aloud and, least of all, give it to the king as a reason to stop guarding a newly widowed mother. Sheesh, he was a selfish dickhead.

"Xander?"

Not a stupid enough one to keep hassling the king over this, though. He shook his head. "Yeah. No. Sorry, Thad. It's not a problem. Anxious to get back out to active duty, you know?"

Well, that was part of the truth, anyway.

Thad's heavy hand landed on Xander's shoulder, and he started. He'd been staring at the dust molecules again and hadn't realized it.

"I know it's been hard missing the fight these past months." Thad laughed. "Believe me. I've only been out of the field a few weeks, and already it's got me going stir-crazy. So I get it. At the same time, I want to make sure Theresa's in a good place first. I don't want to leave her hanging, and our next generation is even more important now than it ever was.

"We don't know what we're facing down the road

with these wizards, but there's a good chance that boy will grow up to be a fighter. You know it takes a village, and all that."

Xander nodded. "Right. Understood." He took a step back, not really sure what to say next, and nearly leapt for joy when Isabel appeared in the hall with a young girl. "She's asking for Tyra again. Do we know where she is?"

Xander took that as his chance to escape. A snippet of cheesy porn music complete with bow-chicka-wow-wows played in his head. Unless Anton was a bigger idiot than Xander had him pegged for, he could guess exactly where Tyra was. And hell, if Anton was that much of an idiot, the dude was on his own in the next go-round. Xander had a limit on the number of times he would stick his neck out for a former enemy of their race looking to turn it all around, and before tonight he would have said that limit was zero.

He grunted, and a puff of air clouded in front of his face as he sped across the grounds. Never say never.

When he arrived back at Theresa's, both mother and baby were asleep on the sofa. The wee one was curled into a crooked question mark shape on Theresa's stomach, chewing its fist as it slept. Theresa's light brown curls fell across her face in pleasant disarray. It was a refreshing change to see her at a time when her guard was down.

The leather of Xander's boots creaked faintly when he stepped closer. He stopped in the center of the living room. There was a chair near the door in the entryway, and he went to sit there instead to keep watch while they slept. He remained there, wide-awake and determined not to get comfortable.

Chapter 33

"YOU THREE ARE ALL ON MY SHIT LIST." THAD PACED Tyra's living room with his hands clasped behind his back. Smoke actually seemed to be coming from his ears.

Tyra struggled to remain still where she stood. For once, it was clear that getting in her brother's face wasn't the answer.

Anton, who was perched next to her on a bar stool in her breakfast nook, reached to take her hand. "He has a right to be angry," he whispered. "We're all under stress here. Let him vent."

"Goddamn right I've got a right to be angry." Thad pointed a finger at Anton and then at Tyra. "Look, no offense, man, but we agreed, Ty, that it would be best to let him go." He whirled on Xander. "And you. You said you wanted to go talk to him. I didn't hear anything about you hauling his carcass back to the estate, and I don't think lying by omission is the kind of shit you want to pull with me when you're trying to get your ass put back on active duty."

Xander's jaw clenched, but he stayed silent. Probably wise.

Anton slid off the stool and took a step forward. "Thad, if you want me to leave, I will."

"What?" Tyra jerked. He'd promised her that he would stay. "Anton."

Anton held up a hand. "*And* I've also promised Ty

that I won't leave her again. So you see, that would leave me in the somewhat difficult position of having to go back on my word, but I've got to respect your laws in this little world, and I will."

Thad and Anton moved toward each other in the center of the room, two stags about to engage in a horn lock. Meanwhile, Xander and Tyra made eye contact from across the room. They'd fought together but had never really been friends, yet suddenly in this unlikely scenario they were on the same page, and that page had a whole lot of annoyance written on it. Each in their own way had managed to put aside baggage and worries and past hurt to come to terms with bringing Anton back here to the estate, and Anton and Thad were still having a pissing match over it.

She rubbed her eyes. So much had happened, and she was bone weary. She wanted to be angry at someone, but she was even almost too tired for that. "Thad."

Someone knocked hard on the front door. When she opened it, she recognized the man as the father of Thad's house manager, Ivy. He didn't come to the house much but she'd seen him on her rare visits to the Elder Council meetings. His name escaped her at the moment. Gus… Gunderson. No, it was a color, maybe, like… Gray. Black?

It was then that the cluster of other vampires caught her attention, all residents of the estate and all wearing such grimly determined faces that she wondered why they weren't carrying torches and pitchforks. Ugh. Why hadn't she seen this coming?

She hadn't wanted to.

"Let us talk to the wizard," the elder said.

She narrowed her stare at the elder and then panned over the rest of the crowd. It was a mix. Mostly elders and some civilians who lived on the premises, but she was relieved to note that not many of her teammates were in the group. There were, however, females and children. For the children, it was paramount that this be resolved peacefully.

"Uh, yeah, I don't think so. See, you guys have this whole angry-mob thing going, and he's done nothing wrong."

All this did was get them agitated and restless and jostling each other. Clearly, her negotiation tactics needed work. Her pulse quickened. The front door opened and her heart pounded even more. Fear that Anton might decide to throw himself to the wolves dueled with concern that Thad might come out here and put himself in danger in front of his angry subjects.

Hot shame washed over her as she moved to guard the door from whoever was coming out of it. From the moment she'd woken up in that shelter, she'd handled all of this so damned badly. "Xander."

He smiled broadly, and his fangs flashed in the moonlight. His body language was at ease, and she was at once comforted and confused. What did he know that she didn't?

He raised a hand, even as he ushered Tyra behind him with one arm, which made her blood simmer. He didn't have to protect her, after all.

"Good morning, everyone. Evening, Elder Grayson."

Grayson, that was it. Tyra resisted the urge to thunk her forehead in front of the crowd of restlessly shifting bodies.

Xander cleared his throat. "Listen, I get that everyone's a little upset over Tyra here sleeping with the enemy and all that." He jerked a thumb in Tyra's direction.

Her eyes widened. Oh, he did *not* say that.

But he had, and bless his traitorous little heart, he was still talking. "But I want everyone here to understand something. I was the one responsible for bringing the wizard back to the estate, so don't anyone blame Tyra here for that."

More murmuring and restless shifting from the peanut gallery. A baby cried near the back. A baby. Someone had actually brought a baby. Jeez. Elder Grayson stepped forward. "What the hell is this about?"

Xander leaned his shoulders against the cold of Tyra's beige vinyl siding and cracked his knuckles. He gazed up at the sparsely populated sky and the three-quarter moon and hoped that Tam, wherever she was, would be proud of him for this. He'd like to think so.

He scanned the crowd populated with young ones and females who had no business getting swept up or even standing by as witness to what would surely go down if they let Anton come out of Tyra's house. Certainly, no good could come of letting this get out of hand. He hadn't brought Anton back for that.

Next to him, Tyra leaned back against the door, and despite the distance between their bodies, heat radiated off her. He would bet any amount of money that her body was strung tight, and he wouldn't blame her. She didn't know what he had planned, and even Xander himself didn't know how his message would be received.

He lowered his eyes and assumed a somber expression. It wasn't hard, thinking of Tam. "Most of you know I lost my mate a few months ago."

The crowd stilled considerably, uttering a few murmurs of agreement or understanding. Some eyes got wider. Folks were listening. Good.

"We had a fight." Tears pressed behind his eyes, and he let them flow because this was not a time to be stoic. This was a time to get anger to shift, and if it shifted to sad, then all the better. "And when I returned from patrol, she'd left a gift and a note saying that she'd bring back my favorite food. But she never came home. Even with all of us out there on patrol, the wizards still manage to grab a vampire or two some nights and one night it was my Tam."

He ignored the snot drip that landed on his boot. "So nobody gets it more than I do, what it means to have a wizard living inside our estate, you know?"

From the creased foreheads and wide eyes on the vampires crowded around Tyra's stoop, it wasn't clear that they did know. The inferno radiating out of Tyra dialed down a notch but he didn't dare look in her direction. Somehow, that was the key to keeping his composure.

He jerked a thumb toward the door. "That guy in there, he was there when Tam was…" He swallowed past the hard lump in his throat. "When they claimed her power. He was kind enough to share with me that she wasn't conscious when they did it. She didn't… hopefully feel any pain." Tension radiated out of Tyra, but Xander needed to keep going before he lost his shit. "He's a good man who was born in a bad place. He helped us kill their leader, and he has knowledge that can help us defeat these bastards once and for all. Isn't that what we really want?"

Everyone seemed too confused to respond. *Jeez,*

everyone, superior species, much? "Come on, eye on the prize, folks."

Tyra stepped forward. "Guys. Anton was born in the wrong place at the wrong time. He wants to help us defeat the wizards. Wouldn't you like to see us put an end to the fighting?"

Didn't he just say all that? This time, thank fuck, murmurs of assent rose from the crowd. Next to Xander, Tyra blew an audible sigh of relief. Only Elder Grayson remained stern and unmoved. Xander met the elder male's gaze directly.

"If that wizard starts trouble, I'll be the first to make him pay for it. You have my word. But we only shoot ourselves in the foot if we take him down before he's helped us defeat the wizards. And isn't that our true goal? Besides, we're not any better than the wizards if we're out here forming lynch mobs without cause."

The rest of the group murmured more heartily this time. Xander straightened and peered up at the sky. "Good. Now I suggest everyone get their children back to their homes. Dawn is approaching, and none of us can defeat the enemy if we're burnt to a crisp."

Slowly the murmurs became grumbles, and everyone turned and trekked back to their homes. Elder Grayson was the last. His long, silvery hair waved in the morning breeze as he studied Xander with a look reminiscent of a small-time crook whose dastardly plans had been thwarted. That reaction didn't make an awful lot of sense, but Xander made a note to mention it to Thad, just in case.

Xander started when a warm hand wrapped around his and, before he could process, arms as well. Then

Tyra's forehead landed on his shoulder and her mass of curly hair was blowing into his face. She hugged him hard—the kind of hug his grandmother used to give when he was a child. In response, he used to say, "I can't breathe when you do that." But this time he didn't say a thing. Didn't do anything but hold on.

"I don't know exactly why you did that, but thank you."

He nodded against the top of her head. "It was the right thing to do. And like I said, I want revenge. For Tam's death. For your father. For all the ones we've lost." The very thought charged him with energy and motivation he hadn't known in months.

He'd make it up to Tam for not saving her.

Chapter 34

WET BLANKET THAT HE WAS, SIDDOH HAD CUT ALEXIA off after only two martinis. She managed to pull him onto the dance floor, sort of, for "We Found Love" before they left. If they'd been lovers, it was the kind of song they could have done a little sway and grind to. And after a couple of drinks and desperately needing to drown out all the odious shit in her head, it had been a little tempting.

He was an impressive-looking vampire. Why the hell didn't he get her motor revving? Not like he didn't fit the bad-boy category the way Lee did. In some ways he was worse even—more of a rule-breaker. It was a wonder Thad didn't throw him in the brig or… whatever happened when the soldiers got in trouble around here. Siddoh sure seemed to get into plenty of disagreements with Thad and Lee.

The house was quiet when they got inside. This close to morning, a lot of the household was probably getting ready for bed. She was tempted to tell Siddoh that she needed him to hang out and talk, but she couldn't do that. Once in a while, she needed to be able to handle things on her own.

When she got to her door, though, she paused and squirmed a little, like the time she and Isabel had watched *The Ring* right before going to bed. It hadn't seemed that scary, and then she'd found herself completely unable and unwilling to go to bed for the next twenty-four hours. Okay, days. Or to watch anything recorded on a VHS tape, lest she accidentally cause an angry spirit to crawl out of her television the way it had happened in the movie. Hey, if vampires could exist, anything was possible.

"Need to pick a sleep schedule, Lex." She wound up giving her room a pass entirely and heading down to the kitchen. She was waiting for the sleek Krups kettle she coveted to boil water for tea when the unmistakable double-tap of high heels came into the kitchen behind her.

Only one vampire in the place came to mind who would be wearing shoes like that at this hour.

"There's a little adage about how a watched pot doesn't boil, I believe."

Alexia didn't turn around. What was she doing here? "No, it boils eventually. Whoever made up that adage was an impatient asshole." She bit the inside of her cheek before anything even bitchier came out.

Agnessa laughed one of those not-a-care-in-the-world laughs. Did she know the things everyone said about her, or did she just not care? She had to know, right? Alexia would have given almost anything to be able to hold herself with the kind of confidence Agnessa had.

"May I make a suggestion?"

"Uh." Suggestion about what? "Sure."

A box of tea Lexi hadn't realized she was holding was pulled from her hand. Agnessa crossed to the pantry and returned with another box.

"Sleepytime?"

Agnessa smiled, showing a definite pair of fangs. The

rumor Alexia had heard was that Agnessa needed other body fluids than blood to stay alive. Why, then, did she have fangs? Curious. "You'll have a terrible time getting to sleep with green tea."

That was actually kind of the point. "Thanks."

Agnessa slid a ten-pound jar of organic raw honey across the counter. "This wasn't here until a week or two ago, and neither was the tea selection. I guess both of them must be yours."

"That would be a clever guess." Alexia smiled slightly. According to Isabel, Agnessa was Thad's royal spiritual advisor-oracle-priestess-seer-whatever-person. One would think she could do better than guess.

"Is it all right if I join you?" Agnessa surprised her by pulling down a second mug. It had a caption that read "Smile, it makes people wonder what you've been up to." Agnessa's lips were almost as red as the cartoon ones on the mug.

Alexia poured hot water into her favorite *X-Files* mug that insisted "The truth is out there" and handed the kettle over. "Knock yourself out."

Agnessa pointed down to the floor. "I adore your boots."

"Thanks." She tried to picture Agnessa, in those pricey stilettos she always wore, tromping around in Lexi's cherry-red Doc Martens.

Agnessa threw her head back and laughed. "I know what you're thinking. I couldn't pull off the look. But they're so cute on you."

"Imagine how you'd make everyone's head explode if you started wearing boots and cargo pants," Alexia murmured. Immediately her hand flew over her mouth. She hadn't meant to say that out loud.

But Agnessa laughed harder. "I would, wouldn't I?"

Lexi stirred a dollop of honey into her tea and offered one to Agnessa as well. She hated to think it, but Agnessa actually seemed pretty cool. This was Lee's ex she was standing here talking to. And Lord knew, *everyone* knew the rumors. Isabel had discovered a whole new brand of jealousy when Thad had told her about why Lee and Agnessa weren't together anymore. Alexia didn't really want to like her.

Wasn't as if she had a ton of friends, though.

"I've never had it this way," Agnessa said when she sipped the tea. "It's delicious."

Damn. Alexia was still blowing on hers. Vampires and their pain thresholds. "Honey's my big weakness. I rationalize it, though, because even though it's sugar, it's good for you. Lots of antioxidants and stuff," Alexia said.

Agnessa's heels click, click, clicked over to the sink to drop her spoon in. "Smart and good fashion sense."

Lexi didn't take compliments well. Getting one from the estate's resident whatever-she-was? Lexi hiked a shoulder up to her ear. "I'm pretty average, actually. Unless you're talking height. I'm definitely below average on that count."

Agnessa flipped her glossy platinum hair over her shoulder. A diamond choker that probably cost more than every vehicle Lexi had ever owned adorned Agnessa's throat. Thad's spiritual advisor would definitely fall into the high-maintenance category. Or what Alexia would refer to as the "likes expensive stuff" category. Lexi's theory, really, was that almost everyone fell into that category. Some people just didn't wear it in public the way that Agnessa did.

"Don't sell yourself short. You went dancing?"

Lexi gulped her tea, and it was still way too hot. Shit. Damn. *Ow*. "Siddoh and I went out for a little while."

"It's good that you're doing that. It can be isolating here when you're the only one of your kind. Believe me, I know."

Yes, she probably would, wouldn't she?

"And it would be hard for you to leave, too."

Alexia almost choked on her tea. Did Agnessa know she'd been considering that? "I guess it would."

"You can't simply pluck out a memory when a human has lived among vampires for so long. You lived with Isabel for years before you came here, didn't you?"

"Two years. And she tried back then, but it didn't work." Fuck, she was crying. When the hell had that happened? Holy shit, she hated to cry more than almost anything, and here she was doing it for the second time in as many nights.

Agnessa click-clacked over to the pantry with the Sleepytime. She kept her back to Alexia while she arranged boxes of tea. "I hate when things are out of order, don't you?"

Lexi pressed herself against the counter. Clearly, Agnessa hadn't seen her bedroom. Only a couple of weeks in this place, and they hadn't let her bring anything from their apartment in Orlando. She'd still managed to make a mess of her new room. She managed to make a mess everywhere she went.

"I'm going to put the black, green, and white on one end, and the herbal on the other so you can find it all easily."

Alexia scratched her arm. "Great. Thanks." It would be out of order again in a couple of days, tops. Not that she could bring herself to say that aloud.

"It's a soul-mate kind of thing, you know?"

Alexia's head jiggled. No wonder everyone said this chick was weird. "I'm sorry, I don't have any idea what you're talking about."

Agnessa slid a tin of Tazo's Joy tea into place and pushed the pantry door shut. "You and Isabel must have connected on a deep level when you met. Sisterly or like soul mates or whatever you want to call it." A flip-floppy hand gesture made the light catch on another sparkly bracelet. Were those all real diamonds? Who needed that much bling? "The soul-deep connection makes a memory harder to erase. Get it?"

"I… guess?" Agnessa clicked close again, and Lexi popped a spoonful of raw honey in her mouth to avoid having to say more on the subject. She still didn't really have a clue, but the direction of the conversation had passed uncomfortable and was heading down the road toward Squicksville.

Each of the albino vampire's long, scarlet-tipped fingers touched each of Alexia's fingertips, and a tangible ball of *something* formed between their two hands. "Every two beings that come into contact, they exchange energy. I'm sharing mine with you right now. You feel that?"

Alexia's mouth fell slack. Talk about wacky. The überdisturbing part was that Alexia couldn't have pulled her hand away if Lee himself came in and held a gun to her head. And in this place, who knew if he might? But hell. Whatever this shit was, the invisible press against her fingers was as real as anything. "Yeah. I don't know what it is, but I definitely feel it."

"I told you," Agnessa said brightly. "Energy." She pulled their hands further apart, and the ball in Alexia's hand grew. "Hang on to that. You might need it later." At last she stepped away. Alexia could have sworn the ball stayed. "So you see, when you get your hooks into someone energetically, it requires abilities on another plane to remove the associated memories. Spiritual surgery, if you will."

Creepier and creepier. Alexia curled her fingers around her mug. The peculiar ball went away. Halle-fricking-lujah. *Spiritual surgery?* She'd run out of the room if she weren't so afraid of making sudden movements. "O… kay."

Agnessa turned on one narrow heel. "Think hard. It wouldn't be reversible. Maybe wait until after the baby comes."

What a crazy wench. Alexia blinked and dumped the Sleepytime tea in the sink. After all that weirdness, no way was she going to be able to relax.

Tyra had left Xander on the porch. He had said he'd see himself home, though she wondered if he might not stand out there looking at the sky until the last remaining dark.

She found Thad and Anton on opposite ends of her living room having a staring contest like two silent, wary cats.

Thad spoke without moving. "Everything okay out there?"

"I think so. I *hope* so." She looked out the window through the partly open blind. The crowd had dispersed, everyone scattering back toward their homes. "Xander seemed to convince them all to leave." She turned to Anton. "Not sure what you did to get him in your corner, but good job on that."

Anton's only response was to nod grimly. That left her curious. What *had* he done?

She turned back to Thad. "So what's the word, Brother?"

Thad cleared his throat. "I have serious concerns, and I am holding you personally responsible. I'm also pulling you off active duty for a while because you're going to need to get a handle on things. And you two," he gestured between Anton and Tyra, "need to figure out what the hell you're doing."

Tyra almost—almost—jumped up and threw her arms around Thad. He wasn't going to make Anton leave. They would figure out how to deal with the rest one way or the other.

"Thad, thank you."

"Don't thank me." Thad leveled a stony glare at her, and she put on her best serious-sad face. It wasn't like she didn't take the road ahead sincerely. They had a lot to work out, and she got that. But… God, she hadn't realized it—*truly* realized it—until she saw that Anton had come back. She couldn't handle him leaving again.

Anything else she could fight against, but not that.

She took a deep breath. "I know you're mad. I'm sorry."

"Don't say that, either. I am so beyond angry right now. That doesn't even cut it." His fists opened and closed. "For fuck's sake, Tyra, if you weren't my sister, you probably would be strung up in an interrogation shed right now. Do you know that? You have bungled this whole thing so unforgivably, and no offense, pal," he pointed at Anton and then back at Tyra, "but hundreds of us live here on this compound, and we're all fucking lucky that he turned out to *actually* be one of the good guys because you put us all at risk with this *Rambo* shit you tried to pull."

Tyra scowled. "I don't think *Rambo* is really an accurate comparison, Thad."

Anton's hand landed on her shoulder. "Let him talk."

Thad snapped his fingers loudly and pointed at Anton. "Smart. Man. Ty, shut the fuck up and let me talk. Whatever human movie reference you happen to find appropriate. My point is that it was fucking stupid. It's still fucking stupid. First fucking thing when the sun goes down I want this asshole sitting down with me and my generals, and I want him helping us to work up a profile on that brother of his."

She moved to advance on Thad, but it was Anton, oddly enough, whose hand held her back. "He killed one of our greatest enemies, Thad. Doesn't that speak for itself?"

"Some might not see it that way," Anton murmured.

"No," Thad said quietly. "Some won't. Anton's going to need to watch his back, and you're going to need to help him. And if it comes down to it, if there's a situation of civil unrest brewing inside this estate, then you're going to have a decision to make."

Acid churned in Tyra's stomach and her head throbbed angrily. "Okay," she said.

He left after that, and Anton's arms came around her. "It may come down to that, you know. I don't want it to.

I'll do my best not to make waves, but I can't promise anything. We need to discuss a plan B."

Her stomach lurched and her vision swam. "I can't think about that right now. I know we need to, but I'm so overwhelmed."

He gathered her into his arms and sank with her onto the sofa. Somehow, she'd managed not to really think about it until that very moment, but what if Anton wasn't truly safe there? She didn't want to believe that vampires in their own midst would kill without cause.

It was possible, though, wasn't it? Anything was. Maybe believing that they could make things work between them—that they could find peace here together—only made her a fool.

Chapter 35

ANTON HELD ON TO TYRA UNTIL HIS MUSCLES ACHED and long past that. Until the dawn cast the room in a warm glow, and then the sun streamed in full force and Tyra's skin started to radiate a little more than seemed strictly healthy. Her body was exhausted and limp against him, but her eyes were sharp and angry. She was doing the math and coming around to the same answers he had.

Maybe admitting that they wanted to be together wasn't enough.

"We should close the blinds," he said.

"I've been alive for more than a century, Anton. I know how much sunlight I can handle."

He stiffened and pulled away. They were both exhausted and frustrated, and Anton, for one, was freaking starving. Maybe vampires could get away with not eating very often, but he sure couldn't. And frankly, he'd gotten spoiled having a hot dinner every day in that homeless shelter. "You got any food in here?"

That seemed to upset her apple cart. "God, of course. I can't believe I didn't think to offer you food." She followed him into the kitchen area. "What are you in the mood for?" She got busy grabbing pots and pans in the way she seemed to do everything else. Cool and efficient, with a cauldron of God-only-knew-what bubbling below the surface.

Anton shrugged. "Anything. I don't actually remember

when I last ate. Hell, I'd go for that fucking beef-and-cabbage shit at the shelter. I'm so hungry I'd even go for some of the slop I used to get growing up."

He was flooded by memories of his father. Not only the food, which was no big deal, really. It was usually some kind of mediocre crap, though occasionally if his father was very pleased, it was something hot and tasty, because it didn't take much to perk those idiots up and keep them in line.

But somehow, remembering the food brought all of it back. For a moment his vision went dark and he gripped the edge of Tyra's stove for balance. It had a slick, shiny surface, but then Tyra was there, and she was warm and solid against him. It didn't cease to amaze him how she could be no bigger than he was in size but could still hold his body in her arms as if he was that little girl sleeping in her guest room. He found he didn't mind it as much as maybe he ought to.

Sort of like before, when he'd realized it kind of rang his bell a little to be with a woman strong enough to fuck him up. Having that same woman hold and comfort him was extremely gratifying as well.

"Anton." Her hand brushed across his cheek.

"Don't do that," he murmured. "I'm probably filthy."

"Do you think I care about that? Here." She pulled him to the floor and they sat together on a small, shaggy area rug in front of the stove. She reached into a nearby cabinet that seemed to turn in a circle like some little embedded carousel and pulled out a box of Kudos bars. "This okay for now?"

He ripped one open and took a bite. "Mmm. Is it okay if I eat the whole box?"

She laughed. God, what a beautiful laugh. And he had brought so much darkness into her world. Who would have thought you could bring darkness into a vampire's life? He shook his head a little. This needed to be about more. Not about survival and defeating wizards so that she and her kind could be safe. It had to be about living. And laughter. He needed to find a way to help her do more of that. Those thirty seconds of laughter alone had erased twenty years from her face.

Her face got a little more serious, but she smiled and snatched a granola bar from the box. "I was thinking. There's a vampire community in DC we could look into. Georgetown. Very hip area. City. The family owns some townhouses over there, I think. Maybe if we weren't here on the estate, things wouldn't be so tense."

Ah, damn. He put a hand on her knee. "Tyra, you need to be with your family. You're going to want to fight."

She bit her lip. "I still could. We patrol those areas. It's not as active. Most of the vampires are here in Ash Falls so most of the wizards are too, but it doesn't mean we don't still have problems in the District. And when we do, they're worse because it's more densely populated with humans."

His gut clenched. "You'd hate that, wouldn't you?"

She shrugged. "Less action? Maybe. But…" She shrugged her shoulders. "It's something to think about. I don't like the idea that any of us are unsafe here on the estate." She pressed her lips together and bounced the balls of her feet a little. A nervous tic, the feet. "I'm worried most about Thad, actually. He didn't say it, so I don't know if he hasn't thought it or he just didn't want to call it out, but what if someone living here at the estate feels strongly enough that he was wrong to let you stay and tries to harm him for it?"

Anton's heart hammered. He hadn't thought of that. Shit, even he knew these guys would be screwed without their leader. Thad had been part of the point in taking out his father.

Anton closed his eyes for a second and let everything tumble in his head. Tyra seemed content to let him chew on his thoughts, and God bless her for it. What were they going to do? He didn't want to make Tyra give up the home that she loved, but they couldn't be looking over their shoulders on the estate all the time, either.

Finally, he opened his eyes. If Thad was willing to go along with it, he had an idea that might work. "Okay, here's what I think we need to do."

The tunnel door leading into Xander's old home was rusty from disuse, and it groaned in protest when he pushed it open. Except for the vaguely musty air that came from the home having been closed for so many months, it lay very much in wait for its owners to return. He almost opened his mouth to apologize for neglecting it.

After Tam's death, he hadn't been able to return, and then he'd been surfing the couch at Theresa's house. The bed in the bedroom was still unmade. He wandered through the small dwelling, oddly afraid to disturb anything in what he had once thought of as his own little castle. Now he was a stranger in his own home.

Even as he insisted to himself that he didn't want to look at the note she'd left for him that night, he was almost magnetically drawn to it. It lay askew near the leg of the dining room table on the beige carpet where he'd dropped it, taped to a CD case. Some human singer he'd never heard of: Matt Alber.

He opened the card as he had before. It took effort not to brace himself for the impact of the cold terror that swept through him as he read her apology.

> *Xander, I'm so sorry we've been fighting so much lately, my love. I found this song and thought of us—track 5—please listen, I think you'll get it. I love you. I'm in this forever, and I'm still holding on until the end. Went out to get lingonberry crepes from IHOP. We can have a snack and talk when you come back from patrol. And we can fix this. I know we can. We always do.*

And that night he'd dropped the whole thing right there and run for the door, even though he'd known it was too late. Her death had shot through his veins like lightning, and he would need only to close his eyes to live it all over again. It was one of the reasons he didn't sleep as much these days. Even vampires had to sleep with their eyes closed.

He turned the CD over now and scanned the track list. "End of the World," he read aloud. It seemed appropriate. For Xander that night, it nearly had been.

He dropped the disk into the CD player on the bookshelf. Its clock blinked 12:00, because at some point the power had gone out and nobody had been around to take care of things. A beautiful piano melody and a melodic voice filled the room. He sat on the couch and hugged a pillow to his chest. Pottery Barn, because Tam had loved that place and pretty much everything in their home had been ordered from there.

Her constant Internet shopping had been one of their sources of ongoing bickering. Not that they couldn't afford it so much as that he hated the clutter and saw it as wasteful. Now he would gladly go back in time and let her have as many faux fur throws as she wanted from that damned store, if only he could.

The voice on the CD was lamenting about squeezing out every moment before the end, and suddenly the dam burst. Xander buried his face in the pillow and sobbed quietly. Had they? Fuck, had they? There had been a lot of passion, but he and Tam had fought like cats and dogs. He had loved her but he had spent so much time angry, too. And now it seemed like it had all been such a waste. What if he hadn't tried hard enough?

How had they gone from being so in love at the beginning to being so furious all the time? And once mated, vampires rarely split up, which given their long lifespan… well at the time, it had started to seem suffocating to him. And now…

The song ended, and Xander crossed the room, punching the "Track Repeat" button. He stood in the dining room and made a slow circle.

The song played again, and he did understand what Tam had wanted him to hear that night. She would have continued to fight for them. Though there was never going to be any way to know, he'd like to believe that he would have hung on, too. He shook his head and ignored the tears that rolled down his face. In many ways, she had been far stronger than he had.

But now?

He walked to the CD player again and punched the "Stop" button, grabbed a slightly dusty tissue from a dispenser on the living room end table, and blew his nose. The house, all two thousand square feet of it, suddenly closed in on him like it wanted to expel him from the premises. He started for the tunnel door to head back to Theresa's.

He paused to take one final look from the basement door. There was nothing he wanted to take. The thing about sentimental mementos was that sometimes they only caused more pain. He had enough of that to last him a lifetime. He'd ask if someone could handle clearing it out for him, and surely someone else could use the place.

The door closed with a creak and a thud behind him. "Bye, Tam." His quiet whisper echoed in the dimly lit corridor.

So where did this leave him? Hopefully, Theresa wouldn't need him much longer. Guess this made him another homeless schlub hanging out in the barracks again. He ambled slowly back toward Theresa's. Maybe he could get off guard duty soon. Being there didn't feel right anymore, either.

Chapter 36

TYRA SWUNG THE HEAVY DUFFEL OVER HER SHOULDER and motioned to the small figure next to her. "Come on, keep your head down and stay close to me."

The girl nodded and pulled the strings tight on her hoodie.

Anton stepped up to the door. "Do me a favor and let me go first."

Tyra sighed. "Anton, we talked about this."

His cheeks hollowed like maybe he was biting the insides of them. "Exactly. If anyone tries to do a smash-and-grab tonight, they are going to be angling for me and I want to give them an easy target." He pointed to the other duffel, still lying by her feet. "Now come on, we already laid all this out. Don't go trying to change the game plan now. Hand me the bag."

She hefted the bag of rocks. "Here. You sure this will be enough to take with us?"

"This'll be plenty." He grunted and slid the strap over his shoulder. "We don't want to weigh ourselves down with too much." He glanced behind them into the living room. Xander had readily come back to help, as had Zarek, another of the soldiers. "You guys good to go?"

They nodded an affirmative, and Anton pulled open the door. The night air was calm, no storms or snow predicted, and aside from a few random sounds in the distance of life happening on the estate, everything seemed to be business as usual. Anton moved slowly, ears surely pricked as hers were for any signs to the contrary.

Tyra's car, a graphite Outlander, sat in the driveway looking like home base for a game of tag. In theory, all they needed was to get to it and get inside, and they could ride out of there. The plan was to check out one of the clan townhouses in the city to see if it would meet their needs… Tyra sighed. She'd just started down the stairs, a paler, smaller hand clasped in hers, when the quiet "pop" of a silenced shot came from the shadows of a neighboring house—the new tattoo artist's—and Anton staggered backward. A second shot hit her upper arm and her vision colored with the same dark shade that had quickly bloomed over the shoulder of his white Redskins sweatshirt.

Tyra squeezed the hand she was holding. "Get inside. Now. Xander!" She ran toward the shots. They could go ahead and try to shoot her; it would be hard to do once she'd ripped their arms off. A tangle of thorns grabbed at her clothing. Of course it would be a thorny bush.

Fangs sank into her forearm but she managed to get her hands in a mass of hair, enough to stun the vampire by hitting the back of his head against the brick of the house behind him. They both tumbled to the ground and rolled through a stinging, nasty, prickly mess before she managed to get a knee between the legs and—yep, definitely a male. Not that such a move didn't hurt females plenty too, but that was definitely a male response.

"Fuck."

Moonlight glinted on a shiny object nearby. The gun. *Get the motherflipping gun, Ty.* Apparently great minds thought similarly, because her opponent wriggled and shimmied, flipping in an effort to go after the weapon at the same time. A long ponytail caught under her knee.

Tyra pressed her lips together and lunged forward, using the hair as a kind of leash. Knee planted in the small of the older male's back, she pulled up enough on the ponytail that the moonlight illuminated the face of Elder Grayson.

Behind her there was shuffling and talking. Someone—Xander, sounded like—was talking on his phone. Probably reporting in to Thad. Why the hell weren't they helping out here?

"What the hell are you doing, sir?"

Elder Grayson's lips peeled back angrily from his lips. His fangs glinted in the moonlight. "You have brought a scourge into this place, and you are going to regret it. Mark my words."

She stared into the murky hate in his eyes. "Why are you so unwilling to accept that he wants to bring peace for our kind? That maybe he can actually help do that?"

Elder Grayson's face carried the expression of someone who had just smelled something disgusting. "You should not exist in this world, either of you. Our races were not meant to mix. Only trouble can come from it. Our king is going to bring this race to his knees if he continues this way."

Dread settled in Tyra's gut. What was this? She'd never heard any vampire speak this way. They were, after all, freaks of nature in their own right. Or enhancements. However one chose to look at it. Vampires were as much a minority race as wizards, perhaps more so, the only difference being that the wizards were unwilling to live and let live. As the humans would be, if the vampires did not keep their existence hidden.

But really… to say that they were abominations? That sounded like some kind of Sunday-morning human televangelist special, not the kind of enlightened thinking she'd come to expect from her kind. Sure, Elder Grayson was one of their oldest but…

She shook her head. Xander hung up his phone, and Zarek stood by holding a pair of titanium cuffs. Off to the side, Alexia had pulled off her hoodie and was helping Anton bandage his arm. He was alert and talking, and the other bullet had hit the vest he was wearing, thank God. Nothing life threatening. She didn't have to kill anyone after all. She maintained her kneeling position on Elder Grayson. Disrespectful, sure, but she didn't dare let him up.

Tyra frowned at Zarek. "Thanks for the help, you guys."

The two males shrugged and smirked, murmuring lame excuses on the order of "You had it all under control" and "We didn't want to interrupt."

Uh-huh.

Zarek stepped forward. "I'll take it from here. Xander told Thad we'd be bringing Elder Grayson up to the house to talk to him."

She nodded and sighed, suddenly completely wiped out. As soon as Zarek had his hands on the old male, she ran to Anton and butted her forehead against his.

"I'll, uh, leave you two alone," Alexia whispered. "Go back to the main house and check on Selena."

"Thanks, Lex," Tyra said. "Do me a favor and call one of the docs, will you?"

Anton shook his head against hers. "I don't need a doctor. I'm fine."

Tyra didn't watch or listen for a response from the small human, though. She closed her eyes and rested against Anton for a moment, waiting for her heart to stop racing.

—∿—

Ivy must have been a far stronger female than she looked. Then again, hell probably had no fury like a female whose father had just been frog-marched down the hallway in handcuffs. To her credit, she hadn't yelled or screamed, but a steady stream of tears flowed down her face like a faucet that hadn't been turned off all the way.

Thad gave a nod of thanks to Siddoh, whose biceps strained with the effort of holding her back.

Thad looked around the receiving room. It was an inviting room, mostly filled with comfortable furniture and a very large flat-screen television. They used it for small receptions sometimes. His father had used it to receive subjects, and very recently Isabel had done the same thing. Turned out his female was better at giving the folks face time than he was, and boy did he love her for that.

His anxiety was ratchetted high enough without having to settle property disputes and arranged mating problems or whose dog got who else's dog pregnant. No, thank you.

Thad sat in a large, maroon velvet chair, the closest thing that passed for a throne in the place, wishing he could sink into the floor. No part of this role was easy. But this? He hadn't expected to be staring down a member of his own Elder Council for trying to kill a member of the royal family.

Siddoh and Ivy remained at the rear of the room while Elder Grayson was brought forward, and Thad stared the elder vampire down until it seemed the elder vampire ought to have withered to dust right there on the immaculately combed carpet. Finally, Ivy gave up the fight and relaxed in Siddoh's arms, but Siddoh seemed smart enough to keep hold of her. Good.

Thad rubbed his eyes. Nobody in the room had any idea how cold he felt inside. How fast his heart was pounding. How he had no clue what to say. How exhausted he was. Was this what the next nine hundred years were going to be like?

He cleared his throat. "Elder Grayson, I don't think I have to tell you how much it angers me that you and I are facing each other like this. And even more so that you've put me in such an awkward position. You've been a member of the Council in good standing, and Ivy has been a good servant to this household. She meant a lot to my father and she means a lot to me. And only her presence here has kept me from having you sent straight to one of the interrogation sheds to spend the day in contemplation of your actions." Elder Grayson seemed to have no response for this so Thad continued. "This is an extreme betrayal—"

"Betrayal." This was barked by Elder Grayson, who suddenly seemed to have woken from his stupor.

Ivy started tugging to get free of Siddoh's grasp again. Not as hard this time but definitely tugging. Bingo. Smart guy, that Siddoh. Just when you thought he was screwing around all the time. Siddoh spoke into her ear, and Ivy stopped her struggles. She relaxed against him, nodding quietly.

Elder Grayson was still cuffed and held by Xander and Zarek, who Grayson paid little attention to. He was busy staring Thad down like his eyes alone might have the power to turn the king to stone.

Thad swallowed. *Like Isabel says. Fake it till you make it.* "Elder Grayson. You shot at my sister and her mate on protected vampire property. What the hell would you like me to call it? I'm damned tempted to call it treason."

Elder Grayson strained a little at his bonds and at the two males holding him. "Your father would be ashamed, Thaddeus. You've lost sight of what is important to this race, allowing a danger like that into our midst."

Thad didn't allow a single muscle to twitch in his face. The reality? He wasn't sure on any level that he'd handled things properly with Anton. He thought he had. He *hoped* he had. But no way on planet earth would he give outward indication of his doubts. "I think you need to take a long, hard look in the mirror before making such statements. You endangered the lives of our kind in your own right this evening. And in a far more insidious way." He looked up to Xander and Zarek. "I want him in holding until tomorrow."

Siddoh's eyebrows jumped, which was probably the closest he would come to questioning Thad's actions. Siddoh's observation was astute; the punishment wasn't much, given the circumstances. Thad had needed to take swift action of *some* kind, but he wasn't certain yet what course of action was best. He didn't know of anything like this happening before in their history.

Realistically, the vampires had never been known to shelter a member of an enemy race. Never had one of their own attacked a member of the royal family from inside. On the surface, it could be argued that Elder Grayson's motives were to uphold the greater good, but... Thad tapped his finger against his upper lip. When he factored the male's actions from the Elders' Council meeting? Something was rotten in Ash Falls.

Siddoh leaned down to Ivy as her father was led past. "Come on, sweetheart, why don't we go to the kitchen for some tea?" Ivy brushed the tears from her face and nodded. Lee had stepped in for a bit and locked his intense aqua-colored eyes on Thad for a beat before he nodded slightly and filed out behind the prisoner.

Thad waited until the room was empty before he allowed his head to drop backward onto his shoulders. The Council meeting. The attack on Tyra. Was Elder Grayson acting alone or was this a larger conspiracy? The stamped stucco looking back held no answers for him.

That stare from Lee. He'd known Thad's suspicions. Shared them. Thad trusted his best friend and guard with his life. A threat from their own kind was far more dangerous than a wizard in their midst ever could be. Together, he and Lee would find a way to get answers.

Chapter 37

THEY BARELY MADE IT BACK INSIDE THE DOOR.

Tyra had bared her fangs and punched two holes in her wrist, and a hum had gone from Anton's head to his cock and back again as soon as the tang of copper and strawberries had exploded on his tongue. Then she'd torn off his clothes—to check if he was okay, she'd said, but by then Anton's frayed nerves and unspent adrenaline and what few functioning brain cells he had were firmly engaged in other activities entirely. All that energy and blood had rushed straight to his swollen cock.

"Anton." No sooner had she licked closed the punctures on her arm and he'd licked away the traces of blood than he'd begun to kiss her lips and fucking devour her whole. He needed to breathe her in because maybe having her inside him was the only way he could be sure that she would be safe.

Oh, man. She'd been amazing out there. Watching her fight like that. He'd been so proud of her.

"Anton." Her hand pushed at his chest, and he pulled back, panting.

"Seriously?"

She lay on the floor, chest heaving and swollen lips parted, suspended in motion. Her head sort of wobbled back and forth with a look of dazed disbelief on her flushed face. "Are you sure you're really okay? You got shot a little while ago, you know."

He surged forward and attacked her lips again. Her breasts were warm and firm and fit perfectly in each of his palms. He took only a moment to appreciate the fact before they rolled together and he set her astride him in the dark foyer. Even though he still wore pants, the thick ridge of his erection jerked and sought to get closer to her. He could barely make out her smile. "See how okay I am?"

Her palm caressed his face and trailed gently over his chest and stomach. It was amazing how such a gentle touch could soothe and arouse so completely at the same time. He groaned and lifted his hips a scant amount to grind against her and was gratified when she laughed a little.

"You can't blame me for worrying. You've been through a lot. We both have."

But even as she voiced what passed for a reservation, her finger went to the fly of his fatigues and slipped the buttons free. He groaned. "Oh, definitely." He exhaled heavily. "You're right. We have." He swallowed hard when she tugged the last of the buttons on his fly free. "You were—gaah…" Warm fingers and cool air caressed his erection when it popped free of his briefs. He struggled to finish his thought while he still had blood flow in his northern hemisphere. "You were fucking amazing out there. Watching you—dammit, Tyra."

Wet heat engulfed his cock and he couldn't believe he was doing it, but he gripped her shoulders and tugged her up the length of his body.

She eyed him dubiously. "You did not just stop me from blowing you."

He clunked his head against the floor. *No, because that would have been stupid.* "Let me say this, Tyra."

Down below, his cock was hot, hard, and painfully angry. *Down, boy*.

She sighed and laid a head on his shoulder. "I'm sorry, guess I don't always handle…" She gestured between the two of them. "This part of it very well."

He smiled. "Tyra, I get it. You met, in a manner of speaking, my father. I take 'emotionally unavailable' to a whole new level. We're both going to have to put a little effort into this, okay?"

She nodded and closed her eyes. "Be patient with me."

He kissed her jaw. "I have to tell you that it was terrifying out there. And thrilling at the same time. The same as before, fighting alongside you. It hit me that you're probably never going to need my help. Is that okay with you?"

Her eyes opened wide. "Sure. It's okay with me. I don't really know anything different. Is it okay with you?"

He exhaled. He admired her so much. Of course it was okay. It seemed to defy logic. It seemed that his caveman guy brain should want a tiny woman that he could club and throw over his shoulder. *Should, should, should*. Screw "should." He nudged her chin so that he could kiss her properly. "I love the way you are. I wouldn't want to change any of it." He shrugged a little. "I admit I worry about keeping you safe, protecting you… I'm going to do everything I can. I'm going to work with Thad. We'll figure it out."

She kissed him again. "You love me?"

He frowned. "Of course. Haven't I said that from the beginning?"

She sighed and rolled her eyes. "But that was different. That was…" She studied him. "I mean, it is different now, right? This isn't the same as the crush you had on me from afar, is it?"

His cock deflated, and he wanted to beat his head against a brick wall. Clearly, he hadn't been doing anything right if she still questioned what he felt for her. How could she possibly, after what they'd been through?

—◆—

For the first time since Anton had carried her out of that bizarre portal, she allowed herself to be open to his emotions. His pain moved through her veins like shards of icy glass that bumped along and into each other, and she wanted to curl around herself and close off to all of it.

This was why it was so hard to really be with someone. It had been easy with Siddoh. No real commitment, no real feelings to muddy up the works, not until the end. And no one she could worry would leave her alone like her mother had… her mother, who according to her father had loved her so much.

She sighed and pressed herself against Anton's body and stared into his dark eyes. "I can see it now, you know?"

He frowned. He clearly didn't see it.

She smiled at him. "I was thinking about my mom. I always wondered how she could have left me with my father and not looked back. It hadn't occurred to me before that maybe she knew something about this whole wizard business, and that maybe she did what she did for my safety." She rubbed a cheek against Anton's rough stubble. "It seems like sort of a stupid no-brainer now, but I was too busy being angry with her to think of that before now. I kept wondering how she could give me up. How she could give my father up. It still hurts, but I guess I get it now."

He exhaled softly. "I'm glad that you do," he murmured. His hand came up to touch her hair. She kissed his palm as it ghosted past her face and then kissed his lips lightly. He wasn't a vampire, and she realized that, until this moment, she had not truly given him the credit he was due for how strong he'd been to go through all of this for her.

He lay there on the floor, nude and glorious and wearing the open hurt of what he still believed was her rejection of him. And he was man enough to show every bit of it to her. Most vampire males would have offered a flip response and left the room by now. He had fought for her in every way imaginable.

He had killed his father for her. For all of them.

She wasn't sure she could ever have done something like that. That took… she wasn't even sure what that took. And for him to want to live here with her, knowing the kind of hate and mistrust that would surround him? For him to turn against his own kind? Maybe he loved her and maybe he didn't agree with their ways, but to betray everything he'd ever known still took an unimaginable strength.

"I'm sorry," she blurted out.

He licked his lips and cocked his head sideways. "For what?"

She frowned. "I know I said the wrong thing earlier. I questioned your feelings. I shouldn't have."

He shook his head. An arm snaked around her body and pulled her on top of him. Immediately a spark sizzled between them at the renewed intimacy of all their pleasure points touching at once.

A large, comforting hand came to either side of her head. "Honey…"

Something unexpected and hard to define swelled inside Tyra. She'd been called that before, but never by someone from whom it meant something. And she hadn't realized it didn't mean much before, or that it meant so much from him, until he said it.

She bit her lower lip. "Yes, Anton?"

His gray gaze bored into hers. "You were raised as the second-fiddle older half sister to the king of all of vampire-kind."

She rolled her eyes. Jeez, it sounded kind of sad when he put it that way.

He smiled wryly. "It's not a bad thing, but it's the truth." He huffed out a breath of air. "Your father loved you, at least. But I get how that wasn't enough. At least you had that, though. Someone loved you. Your father. Your brother. Probably your mother too, if she left you here to be cared for. My father—" He cut off and pressed his lips together, and his face got a little red.

The tide of his emotion nearly made her cry, it so was throat-cloggingly powerful. "My father didn't love me. Or like me. He enjoyed me like a pet or something, and even then, I wasn't so much fun when I didn't perform the way he wanted."

"Anton, I'm so sorry."

"No." He shook his head. "No, that's not my point. My point is that between the two of us, we've got a whole fleet of issues and baggage and reasons why we don't really know how to handle normal and healthy. That concerns me quite a bit."

He was right. As Tyra's heart began to sink, though, something she couldn't put her finger on helped buoy it back up. "But I'd like to try," he said.

Maybe that something was hope. Whatever it was, it poured out from inside her like someone had turned the sun on inside her chest.

She grabbed him and kissed him as hard as she could. Relief swamped her senses, drowning out everything else. She slammed shut the channel on his emotions, deciding to rely on communication for a change. It was a skill they both needed to work on.

Anton's arms came around her back, and a large hand settled firmly on her ass. The friction of their bodies had him hard again, and they were both panting and needy in no time.

It had been a hell of a night, and connecting physically was something they could stand to work on, too.

Chapter 38

ANTON GROANED AND SHIFTED, SEATING HIMSELF IN Tyra's tight heat.

If he lived to be a hundred, he would never get tired of being inside her. Wow. Would he be able to live that long? His heart flipped in his chest. He'd never thought to ask, and oh God, he wouldn't ask now because....

Her hands planted on his chest and his hands gripped her hips. He reveled in the roll and pitch of her hips, the bunch of her stomach muscles, and the gentle sway of her breasts. Her face was full of blissed-out pleasure, her lips parted and her eyes wide, and he experienced a wonder unlike any other: he had put that pleasure on her face. Him.

Holy cow.

He gripped her hips tighter. His fingers dug in, and the slight pang of guilt over handling her a little too roughly was chased away by her gasp of pleasure and the hard slam of her body against his. Realizing he loved it when she rode him hard, he encouraged it, bringing her down harder with each stroke, murmuring filthy things like "yeah, fuck me," that he never imagined himself saying. He was too caught up in it all to be embarrassed, even though later he probably would be.

She leaned low and threaded her fingers through his; he managed to catch a nipple in his mouth briefly and loved the hard, wrinkly skin against his teeth, the low moan from her throat. The hard squeeze of her sex and the faster, faster, harder slide that told him she was almost there.

And thank glory hallelujah because he'd been riding the edge, and it was only through sheer force of will he'd never known he possessed that he hadn't let go already.

But then her thighs squeezed against him hard, her breasts slid, sweaty and perfect against his skin, and the wintery scent of her hair passed under his nose as she buried her face in the crook of his shoulder.

The pinch and burn of her bite and the suckle at his vein set off a chain reaction he couldn't have stopped for any threat or money. He bucked and shouted beneath her, and she simply squeezed harder and held on, moaning and riding him through it all. Somewhere in the middle she licked at him and threw back her head, moaning and panting through a release of her own. A trickle of blood ran down the corner of her mouth, and he swiped it away with his thumb, strangely eager to taste himself.

He didn't note anything particularly special about the flavor as he touched his tongue to the stuff, not like the sweet strawberry flavor of hers, but if she loved it, that was all that mattered. And she seemed to.

They floated together from their cloud of bliss back down to the carpet, and he wondered at his good fortune. He'd been dealt a lot of crap, no arguments there, but Tyra was... everything. He could never have imagined loving her like this. Even when he had watched her and longed to protect her.

He hoped he could show her that, eventually.

No.

He *would* show her that, eventually.

Whatever it took, however long their lives were together, he would devote that time to protecting her as best he could and to proving his love.

She reached to the back of the sofa and pulled a blanket on top of them.

"You know," he said quietly, "your bedroom isn't that far."

"I know. I don't feel ready to move yet."

He understood.

"I love you too," she murmured against his chest.

Anton closed his eyes and hugged her against him.

"I'm sorry that I questioned you before."

He lifted his head. "We're going to have to set ground rules about you eavesdropping on my feelings."

Her smile was sleepy. If they didn't move soon, they were going to wake up on the floor later and be very sorry for it. "I wasn't. I know I didn't respond the right way before."

His eyebrows drew together. He wasn't quite sure he believed her; something about the expression on her face was slightly guilty.

She rolled her eyes. "Okay. Earlier I was, and I could tell that I hurt you, and I'm sorry." She bit her lips a little. "I told you I'm not very good at this."

He kissed the top of her head. "It's okay. We'll have plenty of time to get good. I hope."

Her head tipped up, and her brown eyes were smiling and warm. "We will. You know if you drink my blood, it'll…" For some reason, this made her blush a deep crimson. Damn, it was adorable to see her flustered that way. "There's no way to know, exactly. I don't think any vampire in history has mated for life with a wizard. But we do know that drinking vampire blood extends wizard life spans."

He had to ask. "I don't know why this is making you blush, exactly."

She shook her head. "I guess it's silly, but you know you only cease to age as long as we…" She laughed and put her hands over her face. "It's so stupid. I never thought about spending the rest of my life with someone before, and here we are… we met in a homeless shelter. Anton, you were supposed to kill me. Or kidnap me."

His gut clenched. "Don't fucking remind me."

"Well, you have to admit, it's pretty out there. I've been more or less single for over a century, Anton. I still feel a little funny thinking of myself as anyone's mate, much less yours. Much less telling anyone. I'm sorry. Is that silly?"

"Yes." His expression was deadpan, but he was tempted to roll his eyes. "Tyra, I'm pretty sure everyone else is already referring to us as that."

Her eyes widened. "They are?"

A laugh burst out of Anton. It rolled on and on until she was staring at him as if he'd grown a second head on his shoulders, which only made him snort harder.

Tyra hovered above him, her expression dubious, like maybe she wasn't certain whether she wanted to laugh with him or haul off and hit him with her kung-fu action power. Maybe it would turn out to be both. He'd kind of already established he was okay with that.

She went with option C and pinched him.

"Hey!"

"I'm glad I make you laugh." She tried to keep her

face deadpan, but deep in those brown eyes was a sparkle of amusement.

He *was* glad. "There hasn't been a lot to laugh about."
His fingers tangled in her hair. "I want to laugh with you
for a long time."

She smiled and kissed him. Now *that* he could
do forever.

———

The baby had woken while the doctor was in with
Theresa. It yowled and rooted at its little fist, squirming
desperately in its Moses basket while trying to find a
mother who was nowhere in sight. Something Theresa
had said to Xander tugged at his heart—something
about how newborns had never had to feel hunger in the
womb, and so after they were born, hunger could seem
an awful lot like pain. And with this information scroll-
ing like a news ticker tape in his head, he lifted the child
awkwardly with heavy, clumsy arms. His heart pounded
like a kettledrum.

This little, squirmy thing was so light and delicate.
Xander was surprised anew at how very tiny and fragile
the baby was every time he dared to pick it up. He didn't
do it often. Usually only if Theresa asked him to.

He glanced left and right guiltily, like he might suddenly be called out for doing something he ought not
to be. He inhaled deeply. The little one's hair smelled
sweet, like something unidentifiable but altogether
baby-like. Some sort of automatic muscle memory had
him cupping the little bundle with hands that always
seemed too large and pulling it close against his chest,
which quieted the crying immediately. The little mouth

gaped and rooted like a fish, though, and Xander offered his pinkie for it to suckle on. That seemed to do the trick for a moment. It sighed and snuffled, and its little eyes fluttered shut again.

"I'm sorry. That's all I've got to offer you," he said quietly. "Your mother will be back soon." He glanced toward Theresa's bedroom door as if to prove a point, not that little Eamon cared.

It was amazing how once the baby was back to sleep, all the tension drained from Xander's body. He hadn't realized how quickly such a tiny thing's crying had cranked him up until he'd managed to make it stop.

A smile spread over his face even as tiny, puffy little lips flutter-sucked on his pinkie in sleep. Pretty amazing. He had a master's from the University of Maryland's online degree program and he'd killed hundreds of wizards, but he'd never felt more accomplished than right now, calming this feral little infant.

How odd.

"…and make sure you continue to get plenty of rest." Voices approached the door of Theresa's bedroom.

Xander slipped his finger from the baby's mouth and quietly returned him to the bassinet. The doc opened the door and Theresa stepped out, her face bunched and confused. She glanced into the blanket-lined Moses basket where the baby lay sleeping. "Is everything okay? I thought I heard him cry."

Xander shrugged, and it was a larger effort than it ought to have been. His arms and shoulders were made of lead again. "He woke up for a minute. I got him back to sleep. He's going to be really hungry next time, though."

The doctor had his back turned and was busy

gathering a coat and a bag of doctor-type things, and Theresa shot Xander a smile of gratitude that was so bright, it almost hurt him to look at it. He didn't want to see that from her. Didn't want her to feel it for him. He glanced at the sleeping baby.

"I was wondering, how are you doing? Physically? With the baby and everything?"

Her eyebrows jumped. The doctor handed her some papers and murmured some instructions, and Xander made a point of staring into space and filling his head with white noise while they talked.

When the front door had clicked closed, she sat in the overstuffed leather chair opposite his. "What do you mean?"

He exhaled. "I mean, I would like to get back to active duty, but I don't want to do that until you feel able to handle things on your own, and it hasn't been very long since…" Since Eamon died. "…the baby was born, and I don't want to leave you hanging if you still feel that you need help here."

She rested her face on a single finger. It made her eyebrow appear to be perpetually raised, as if in a question. "I'm sure it's been hard, being away from the action all this time. I want you to know how helpful it's been, having your company. Thank you. But you know, I can get someone else here to keep me company. I don't need to waste one of the king's fighters to keep some stupid woman and her baby company."

Xander's chest hurt all of a sudden. "You aren't stupid." He growled a little more forcefully than was strictly necessary. "Sorry, it's been a trying couple of days. But you aren't stupid. Nor is the baby."

She shrugged. "Maybe not stupid. You know what I mean, though. I don't need you here, Xander. Get back to your duties. Your life. Carry on." She smiled at him. "Thank you for allowing us to lean on you these past few weeks."

His tongue was as thick and heavy as his arms had been before. "You're welcome."

The baby stirred and whimpered again, and she rose to reach for it. The act lit a fire under Xander's ass, and he almost knocked the remote control off the end table in his rush to stand.

"Let me go make you some tea. Chamomile?"

She nodded and smiled, apparently grateful for the offer. It had become his way of gracefully leaving the room when she nursed the baby. It was a beautiful and natural thing, and Theresa was always extremely tasteful about it. But truthfully, it made him squirm. It drove home in a way that nothing else did that parenthood was something he and Tam had never had for themselves. And now, never would.

Chapter 39

TYRA AND ANTON MOVED THEMSELVES TO THE COMFORT of her bed. Not to make love so much as to talk. There were an awful lot of what-ifs to deal with.

An awful lot.

Personally, she was content to mull them quietly while she laid her head on his chest and his heart thumped against her ear.

"I don't think that I can ever be a good father."

Apparently Anton was not so content.

Tyra sat up next to him. "You already told me you didn't want children."

His face twisted into a grimace. "I kept feeling this…" He made a fluttering gesture with his fingers. "This awful feeling deep in my gut, you know? And I don't know what it is. So much has happened that I didn't know if it was something that had already been or our future, and I think you want it more than you're saying. My father only cared for me so far as it was necessary to keep me alive and tortured me when it suited him. He turned me into someone horrible, Tyra. I can't be responsible for bringing up another innocent life."

She wasn't sure whether she wanted to smack him or put her arms around him, but she went for the latter. His body was rigid in her grasp for many seconds before he finally melted and eased against her. His breath whooshed out of his body like it was leaving a balloon.

"Anton, the fact that you worry about it proves that you would be a good father."

He squeezed his eyes shut tightly and sat up next to her. "Tyra, you don't know what it was like. And what about the fact that we're both part wizard? We could never hope to have children of our own."

"No." She rested her head on his shoulder. "I don't know what it was like. I can imagine, I think. I hope someday you'll be able to tell me." Her fingers played over the dark, coarse hair on his chest. "We don't need to worry about the rest of it for now. You're right…" Something knifelike stabbed into her chest. "I didn't realize how much it would upset me, knowing I couldn't bring life into the world. But maybe it just means there's another path for you and me, and that's okay, too. The important thing is that we're together, right?"

He stared at a blank space on her bedroom wall, eyes unseeing, for an interminable passage of time. How could she have believed that he was anything but good? He'd been a scared child forced into a life he hadn't wanted. It hadn't been his fault, and she ached to make it better for him if she possibly could.

"I was barely a teenager the first time, you know? They taunted me and pushed me, and my father said that I would be punished as a traitor if I didn't. I didn't know what that meant. I didn't know if it meant torture, or if they'd kill me, or—"

She put a finger to his lips. "Baby, when I said maybe someday you should tell me about it, I didn't mean right now. I meant someday when you're ready."

An impatient hand shoved her finger from his face. "No, I want to do it now. You haven't trusted me, and

I know you hated me when you realized I had taken part in that ritual. Maybe a part of you still does." His face contorted into an angry mask and his lips pressed together. In the dim light of her bedroom it was tough to see, but his skin hinted at a reddish glow. They were going to have to work on him controlling that power of his. Or his anger. Maybe both.

"Anton, I don't hate you."

"You don't?" His lips pressed together. "You didn't hate me when you realized I'd helped to kill vampires? Don't you still? Even a little? Knowing I cut them open, took their hearts out, and—"

"Stop." The word echoed around the room before she even knew it was leaving her mouth. "Anton, we don't need to do this. I said I love you. I said I forgave you."

"But did you really?" Suddenly he was out of bed, naked and pacing and glowing a little, like a weird oversized night light. He'd never be able to hide his anger from her if he didn't get that power under control. "Because if you love me, you have to accept all of me, even that part of me. I did what I had to do to survive, and I don't know that you've truly accepted and forgiven it, and if you haven't…"

He stopped and ran a hand through his hair, sighing deeply. His color, thankfully, faded to normal when he did that. "How can we build a future when we already have so much stacked against us, including that one very basic flaw? How can you say you love me when you are still so angry with me over such a big thing?"

The speedy *thumpa-thumpa* of her heart made it clear that Anton's words resonated, but she grasped desperately at one last-ditch attempt to protest. She even trotted out a little nervous laughter in an attempt to lighten the mood. Heaven please, anything to lighten the mood. "Anton, I get angry at Thad all the time. Sometimes I even hate him. He's my brother, and I still love him. I love you too."

"He didn't kill anyone important to you, Tyra." He advanced on her now and she held her ground, though she would admit only to herself that her feet seemed inclined to back up a few paces. She wasn't intimidated, but this side of him was... ugly. Love wasn't always pretty, though, was it?

Her heart hammered harder, and suddenly everything in her brain was like smoke. "You didn't kill anyone I knew personally."

He laughed sharply. "Oh, come on, Tyra."

Okay, that was terrible. She sighed. "All right. You're right." She inhaled deeply and held the breath for a good while before she released it. "I admit it. I'm angry still. I love you..." She shook her head, and suddenly it started to throb, like what she was about to say was too difficult for it to comprehend.

"I do love you. I want us to have a future. But I still hate that you participated in that disgusting ritual. I hate that you killed those vampires. I hate that you have any powers. I hate that now I have your powers because it will be a daily eternal reminder of what you did. And I hate knowing that as long as we are together, I will be a pariah among my own kind because everyone will know who you are and what you've done. And what I am.

"But..." She put her hands on her hips. "I love that you protected me. That you stood up to your father for me. To Siddoh. To Thad. Watched over me. Killed for me. You went after your brother…" Her eyes burned. "Nobody has ever made me feel so valued or worth fighting for. It's a hard thing to reconcile."

Her heart echoed almost audibly in the intense silence that followed. He stared at her, and though an entire queen-sized bed separated them, she didn't need her powers of empathy to read the hurt that was pouring out of him. Knowing it and hearing it from her were surely two very different things.

He walked out to the living room where their clothes still lay discarded in the foyer. He pulled his on quietly, without a word.

"Anton, you asked me to be honest."

Nothing.

"Anton."

He walked around to the sofa and sat in the dark living room. Still no word.

"Anton." She pulled a chenille throw around herself and sat tentatively on the far end of the sofa. Hours ago—minutes ago—they had finally seemed to bridge the distance between them, and suddenly there were miles between them on this sofa. How on earth had this happened? "Anton, would you talk to me please?"

He sat in silence, tapping his finger on the arm of the sofa, the only sound coming from the appliances in the kitchen and the clock on the wall. Finally, he blew out a long sigh. "Thank you for being honest."

―⁓―

Anton turned to face Tyra. Her beauty took his breath away. Maybe it always would. He moved closer, unable to keep his fingers away from the satiny smoothness of her arms and shoulders. She sagged against him. "I vomited after," he said. "I'm sorry, I know that's disgusting, but the whole ritual was disgusting. And yes, they laughed at me for that, too. I didn't think it took because I threw up…" He shrugged a little. "I guess that was this heat thing. It's why I never knew I had it until I fought with Thad in that interrogation building. I got so angry, and that's when it came out."

Even the memory of it twisted his gut. She didn't speak, so he continued. "And I used every means I could to avoid taking part after that. Until I knew a vampire had come in who could heal. And I knew…" He paused for a second. It shamed him thoroughly, what he had done. He'd done it with a purpose. He'd done it to survive and perhaps someday to escape, but still he hated himself for what he had done.

"I knew he was going to die regardless. I'd tried to think of ways of helping them escape for years but couldn't come up with one. The exit portal was always well guarded. I picked him because I thought maybe someday if I tried to escape myself, I would need it. In case I was injured trying to leave."

Her hand was cool and smooth against his face. "Anton." She understood. At least a little. The tone of her voice was different somehow, and he knew that she did. Tears slid silently down her face.

"I'm so sorry, Tyra. I truly am."

"I know," she whispered. She brought her face close, and their lips brushed gently. "I'm sorry too. That you had to do that. And so that you know, I'm not trying to read you or anything. I'm only trying to be here for you, okay?"

He nodded. "Thank you."

It was like his body weighed less. He pulled her against himself and squeezed hard. Grateful again that she was such a strong, sturdy female. Right then, he was grateful. Period. "I hope you can forgive me someday."

She nodded against his chest. "I can. Maybe in a way I already have. It isn't that I blame you. I hate what you did. But I know you didn't have malicious intent. I do hate it, though." She pulled back from him and searched his face, looking for understanding of her own.

"I know," he said. A fresh set of tears threatened and he blinked them away. The sleeve of his flannel served as a chamois for his face, and he took a deep breath. "I hate myself plenty for what I did. I hate that I did it. Hell, I don't feel too great that I killed three wizards in the woods when I was trying to get Xander back to the estate, and that was for a far better cause."

She laughed dryly. "Now wizards I've never minded killing."

He got a little cold and panicked. "I want to help you, but I'm not sure I want to keep fighting this way against the wizards. I really don't want to kill them. You must think I'm a major pussy, huh?"

She laughed again but then immediately slapped a hand over her mouth. "Oh my God, no. I'm sorry, I didn't laugh because that was funny. Nothing could be further from the truth. What you've lived through—to do what you've done to survive, even though you hated to—I'm amazed by that. I've never minded killing my enemies. You hated to kill but you did it to protect one of my fellow vampires. That's very brave."

He cleared his throat. "Thank you." He ran a hand

through her hair. Her curls were loose and soft, and slipped deliciously through his fingers. He would never tire of the feeling if he lived to be a thousand. "Tyra, I meant it. I need to know you can forgive me. We cannot build a life in this place without a strong foundation. There will be a lot of strong winds trying to blow us down. If you can't promise me now that we're solid, this uncertainty between us will fester and tear us apart. If you need time, then I can leave here and can give you—"

Her hand shot out and grasped his wrist. It might never cease to amaze him, the strength of that grip.

He thought he might explode. In the good way.

She blew out a breath that lasted roughly forever, and through it all, his pulse pounded in his ears while he waited for her to speak. Finally, she crossed her arms over herself like she was giving herself a hug and scooted close to him. Her skin was reassuring and warm and solid. She was a home he'd never truly known he was missing until he'd laid eyes on her.

"Anton, I can't imagine what you had to go through. It was tough, growing up without a mother. Seeing Thad with his…" She got quiet, and for a moment her gaze was far away, in the past somewhere. "But I lived here on this estate, and when I got old enough, I trained to kill wizards as a way of channeling my anger and my loneliness. And I found ways to help humans, because my father had told me that my mom was poor and a little bit mentally ill. That it wasn't that he didn't want to be with her, but that she hadn't wanted him and wouldn't allow him to help her. That she'd left me here because she'd at least known that she couldn't take care of me herself."

She shook her head and slid a palm along his jaw. He loved when she did that, maybe because it had come to mean something—a loving gesture. A thing she did when she was comforting. When she was claiming him as hers.

"I can't begin to imagine being forced to live the way you did, and as angry as I am at what you did, I'm as angry at what was done to you. If I could, I'd bring back your father to kill him again myself."

Anton fell against her, drawing the silk of her skin again his too-tough hide. "Careful what you wish for, Tyra. He's a mean enough bastard. He might actually be able to do it." And though it wasn't logical, Anton fought hard for a fistful of seconds to tamp down the surge of panic that clawed at his throat from the inside, because damn… he'd been sure, but with his father… fuck knew, anything was possible.

And then there was Petros. *Oh God*.

But he pulled her to him, and when the throw around her body came loose, he allowed all of the fear to fall away, if only for a little while. Surely, they could spare a little while longer…

Epilogue

IT WAS BITTERLY COLD. TYRA JAMMED HER GLOVED hands into her pockets, grumbling inaudibly from behind her pasted smile. She was happy. Truly. But she wasn't as impervious to the cold as the garden-variety full-blooded vampire, and it had been a good five minutes since she'd been able to feel her toes.

Still, what Isabel wanted, Isabel got. And Isabel had wanted an outdoor handfasting. On Valentine's Day. In Virginia. In thirty-degree weather. Brrr.

Her heart went out to Alexia and Selena and her mother, who all stood huddled on the opposite side of the small circle of guests, wrapped in so many layers of down that they were barely recognizable as moving objects, looking more like miniature versions of the Michelin man.

Tyra'd had a long talk with the girl's mother. Having to break the news that the girl was gonna need to start a steady diet of blood in her teen years to avoid dying an early death had been not only painful, but just plain hard to get across.

Thad and Isabel stood at the head of the circle, hands bound by a long, multicolored cord. With her gently swelling belly, Isabel was so radiant in the glow of the moon and the joy of the evening that nothing short of a localized nuclear strike could have wiped the look off her face.

Agnessa, Thad's spiritual adviser, presided. "And may you remain ever faithful, may the bounty of the universe smile upon you, and may these friends and loved ones always be your guides and your strength until the end of your time on this earth."

Tyra couldn't help but glance around. Rich words, coming from Agnessa. They were probably all thinking it, but everyone else kept a straight face. Even Lee, who stood at the perimeter keeping guard even though they were on the mansion's front lawn.

Two flasks of wines were produced, one white, one red, and poured into a single glass. Agnessa held the goblet as if it contained the secrets to the universe. Hell, for all Tyra knew, it did. She passed it to Thad and then Isabel, who each took a sip. Thad's was much heartier than Isabel's, and the queen's whisper of "There's a dead bug in the glass" sent a laugh through the circle and seemed to chase away whatever odd current of tension had been hanging around.

Agnessa held the wine goblet aloft. "The drinking of the combined wine signifies the joining together of two bodies and the blood from those bodies. Once mixed, the blood of two partners can never be separated again."

Across the way, Alexia stumbled suddenly. Probably those clunky boots the girl had on.

The goblet was passed again in front of Thad and Isabel with a flourish before being handed off to a helper on the side. "What God and the universe have joined together tonight, let no being rend asunder." Agnessa bowed her head toward the happy couple, and for only a second, there may have been an actual flicker of sadness on the Oracle's face. "May I officially present to you all

Thaddeus Yavn Morgan and his mate, Isabel Anthony Morgan." She straightened and smiled at Thad. If Tyra had spotted sadness, it was now gone. "You may kiss your mate."

Thad was way ahead of Agnessa, having already slipped free of the colored rope to take Isabel's face in his hands, and Isabel had stepped forward to do the same. Suddenly the warmth that radiated from their love spread out all around, and even Tyra wasn't cold anymore.

Or maybe that was because Anton had come from behind to wrap his arms around her. She leaned against his firmness and sighed. It took a little getting used to, but leaning on him was easier now, and she found she quite liked it when she allowed herself to.

Chapped lips brushed against her ear. "I would like to do this with you," he murmured.

She blinked. Why it surprised her, she couldn't say for sure. They had talked many times this past month about forever. He had moved into her home, but she hadn't thought about making it so... permanent. "You would?"

His chin rested on the top of her head. "Wouldn't you?"

She inhaled and the winter air stung her nose. Well-wishers had formed a knot around Thad and Isabel, and Siddoh and Lee had moved in close for extra protection. Over the couple's heads, Siddoh caught Tyra's eye and smiled, bowing his head slightly. She and Anton didn't need his blessing, but it was nice to know that he was giving it, all the same.

Isabel's joy was immense and tangible even from so many feet away, which was amazing, given the story Tyra had heard about Isabel turning and running away when Thad had first found her.

Perhaps if Isabel could be this happy, Tyra could allow herself to be as well. She nodded against Anton's throat. "I think maybe I would someday."

He pulled her closer, strong arms tightening around hers. "Something to think about, right? Maybe someday there's even a chance we could have more. A family."

She was afraid to hope.

They'd agreed she would stay closed off to his emotions, but she couldn't help looking. Okay, maybe it was an accidentally on purpose kind of a slip. For a split second, she allowed the channel to open, and Anton's disappointment came through loud and clear. "Hey." She put a palm to his face. His skin was cold, and she relished the thought of warming him up as soon as it was polite for them to disappear.

His gray eyes were shuttered, and for a second she could see his disappointment. They had agreed to wait awhile until some of the unrest about Anton living among the vampires died down before they held any kind of ceremony.

Finally, he smiled. "You promise that you're mine?"

She wound her hands around his neck and pulled his lips down to meet hers. "Are you kidding? After everything we've gone through?"

He smiled and pressed his forehead against hers. He nodded slightly. "Okay."

A breeze kicked up around them, and snow began to fall. The warmth from their bodies cocooned them and wrapped them in their own little bubble. And just like that, she knew that everything *would* be okay.

Acknowledgments

Many, many thanks to my fabulous editors, Deb Werksman and Cat Clyne. Your creative awesomeness astounds me. Thanks also to Susie Benton, Skye Agnew, Beth Pehlke (the best publicist a gal could ask for), Danielle Jackson, Lara Campbell, and everyone else at Sourcebooks who has been so amazing. Eric Ruben, you are just such an awesome agent. To all the readers, bloggers, and book clubbers who contacted me about *King of Darkness* to show your support, your enthusiasm is the reason writers write, guys. *Big Bear Hugs* to *Damon Suede*! Honey, I truly don't have enough thank-yous—you're an absolutely unbelievable friend, and this book and I are both far, far better for knowing you.

Poppy Dennison, your support and commentary have been so great. Thanks, babe. To Christopher Koehler, I've never had so much fun being miserable with anybody. Carol Buswell, thanks for reaching out to give me a lift, and for giving me a fine artist's perspective on characterization. Mark and Catie Hubbard, thank you for your friendship and support since the beginning of this series. Kristina Kopnisky, thanks for keepin' it real. Many thanks also to Kevin Giang and to my street team, the "Staab Mob!"

I must also say a big squeezy-hug thanks to Tes Hilaire, Kerri Nelson, Robin Covington, Laura Kaye, Sloan Parker, Angelo Three (*much* appreciation for the fighting tips!), and all the other fellow authors who have helped and shown support along the way. Mikki Bruns, thank you for helping out when I was in a jam with deadlines. Mom and Dad, Grandma, and "Nana" Susan, all my love to all you guys from the bottom of my heart. *Most of all to my Tom—I appreciate you so much. I couldn't do any of this without you and your infinite patience and understanding. Your support means the world, baby.*

About the Author

Elisabeth Staab lives with her pets and kids in Northern Virginia with her hero and soul mate, Tom. She has been a telemarketer, a web page editor, a software developer, a reader for the blind, a technical trainer, a coffee shop barista, a teacher, a tutor, a homemaker, a government project manager, a graphic designer, a bookseller, and a professional eBayer. Finally, she's realized that her true passion is writing, which is what her high-school guidance counselor originally suggested.

Elisabeth believes that all kinds of safe, sane, and consensual love should be celebrated—but she loves the fantasy-filled realm of paranormal romance the most.

Discover a new LOVE

Are You In Love With Love Stories?

Here's an online romance readers club that's just for YOU!

Where you can:

- **Meet** great *authors*
- **Party** with new *friends*
- **Get** new *books* before everyone else
- **Discover** great *new reads*

All at incredibly BIG savings!

**Join the party at
DiscoveraNewLove.com!**

♥ ♥ ♥ ♥ ♥ ♥ ♥ ♥

King of Darkness

by Elisabeth Staab

—⁓—

Eternal commitment is not on her agenda...

Scorned by the vampire community for her lack of power,
Isabel Anthony lives a carefree existence masquerading as
human—although, drifting through the debauched human
nightlife, she prefers the patrons' blood to other indulgences.
But when she meets the sexy, arrogant king of the vampires,
this party-girl's life turns dark and dangerous.

But time's running out for the King of Vampires

Dead-set on finding the prophesied mate who will unlock his
fiery powers, Thad Morgan must find his queen before their
race is destroyed. Their enemies are gaining ground, and Thad
needs his powers to unite his subjects. But when his search
leads him to the defiant Isabel, he wonders if fate has gotten
it seriously wrong...

—⁓—

For more Elisabeth Staab books, visit:

www.sourcebooks.com

Deliver Me from Darkness

by Tes Hilaire

Angel to vampire is a long way to fall.

A stranger in the night…

He had once been a warrior of the Light, one of the revered Paladin. A protector. But now he lives in darkness, and the shadows are his sanctuary. Every day is a struggle to overcome the bloodlust. Especially the day Karissa shows up on his doorstep.

Comes knocking on the door

She is light and bright and everything beautiful—despite her scratches and torn clothes. Every creature of the night is after her. So is every male Paladin. Because Karissa is the last female of their kind. But she is *his*. Roland may not have a soul, but he can't deny his heart.

For more Tes Hilaire, visit:

www.sourcebooks.com